FOLIAGE

AN INTERNATIONAL BANKING SPY THRILLER

A LOUISE MOSCOW NOVEL
BOOK I

LORRAINE EVANOFF

FOLIAGE
AN INTERNATIONAL BANKING SPY THRILLER

Third Printing – May 2020
Library of Congress Control Number: 2015914796

To join my mailing list for new releases, please sign up here:
www.louisemoscownovel.com/newsletter

To my husband, Robert L. Levy.

LIZ GREEN
01308 898491

ACKNOWLEDGMENTS

My editor, Susan Giffin.

Jonathan Beaty and S.C. Gwynne, writers of *The Outlaw Bank: A Wild Ride into the Secret Heart of BCCI*, (Random House, New York).

ONE

The banker squinted at the man's dusty suit, his collar streaked brown with sweat from running down the back alleys of Lahore. He knew his way through the alleys by rote, having navigated them since childhood. He had forgone driving, lest his car be booby-trapped. He loosened his tie and wiped sweat from his forehead with a soiled handkerchief.

"What a shame you have to sell for half the value," the banker said to the man. "Such a lovely home, and it has been in your family so long."

The man's appearance, crestfallen and disheveled, contrasted with the bank's gleaming décor. "I was lucky to get what I could for it on such short notice." The man placed his briefcase on the desk and read the document.

The banker offered him a pen. "Just sign the deed of release here, and it is officially transferred."

A teller arrived and placed a case filled with bundles of cash next to the man's briefcase and began transferring the cash.

He stood, closing his briefcase hastily, and bowed politely. "Thank you."

"Good luck…" But the man was already out the door.

He prayed silently as he approached the front door of the family home he no longer owned. As he opened it, feeling the unlatched door give way, he knew he had arrived too late. The sound of his wife weeping echoed in the other end of the house, and a single gunshot rang out. He ran to the back parlor, but a man in the doorway blocked his entry. His wife lay on the temple bed, naked, bruised; a single line of blood mixed with snot dripped from her nose. *The worst had happened.* She stared blankly at the smoke rising from the gun barrel pointed down at her dead brother-in-law. The man stood motionless, gripping the briefcase full of cash, an utter failure. The gun now pointed in his direction as the killer-rapist walked toward him. The accomplice continued to restrain him with a raised finger. Young, barely twenty-five years old but wise in the ways of rape and murder, he tucked the gun into his jacket and slipped the briefcase from the man's grip. He opened the case and eyeballed the amount of cash. He removed one bundle and handed it to his victim. "Spend what you have left wisely, and don't do anything else foolish." The killer nodded to his cohort that they were leaving.

"You are from a good Pakistani family, a fellow Mohajir. There is nothing noble in what you are doing," the man whimpered.

"And yet, you are still alive."

The two thugs walked out and continued casually down the road, confident no one would pursue them. They got into a black sedan. Mirza drove and his abettor sat silently in the passenger seat.

Powerful forces were creating a paradigm shift, a sea-change all over the planet. It was 1988 and businesses of all kinds, legal and illicit, prospered unchecked. Mirza knew it wouldn't last, and when it all went down, he wouldn't go down with it. Yes, he was from a noble and prominent Pakistani family. The problem was the definition of honorable changed depending on the situation. And in his situation, it was honorable to stay on the side of the powerful, the side pulling the strings, the side of destiny. And he controlled his own destiny.

Mirza pulled the car over at the Lahore International Airport. "Did you bring your passport as I requested?"

"Yes…"

"Take this and get out. Never come back." He handed the briefcase full of cash to his accomplice.

"Are you trying to get me killed?!"

"I'm saving your pathetic life. Disappear. Take nothing but your passport and this. Get the first flight out of here. I will cover for you long enough for you to get a new identity and make a new life somewhere else."

"What about you?"

"I have a plan. Just take care of yourself."

"How do I know you will cover for me?"

"Little brother, I am the only family you have left. This is your only option."

"God bless you, brother."

He was gone.

T W O

The pristine 1956 Bentley Continental pulled up to the crowd forming outside the fifteenth-century chateau. The flashing camera strobes from the paparazzi lent a slow-motion effect to his movements as he got out and handed the keys to the valet. Not a celebrity but renowned in his own right, Jean-Philippe de Villeneuve drew a smattering of applause and a few requests for his autograph from the gatherers. He waved them off reverently and disappeared through the towering hedges flanking the estate.

Security gave a passing glance at Jean-Philippe's credentials as he entered the ballroom. Starlets and other beautiful people pulsated to the dance music of Roxette and Madonna or chatted and posed self-consciously. The crowd was peppered with a few A-list celebs: De Niro, Stallone, Whoopie.

Jean-Philippe came to a door guarded by a hulking official-looking type. Again, his credentials prevailed, and he was let in to where the *real* players played. The increased level of power was palpable. Low lighting, elegant décor, free flowing champagne, *foie gras d'oie*, caviar, and muted rhythms created an atmosphere of a more discrete revelry. For Jean-Philippe, this was just another party during the 1989 Cannes International Film Festival. Production companies, distributors, and trade magazines throw lavish galas every year on private yachts and at exclusive five-star hotel beaches and terraces along La Croisette. In this case, it was a rented chateau in Mougins, a small village in the hills above Cannes.

Jean-Philippe found a corner, leaned against the wall, and began pushing buttons on his Motorola MicroTAC mobile phone, which had been outfitted with a secret camera. The host of the party, Agha Hasan Abedi, seemed to appear out of nowhere, accompanied by his second-in-command, Alauddin Shaikh. They shook hands.

"Jean-Philippe, my friend, no phones, please, and of course no cameras," Shaikh said in a slight Bengali accent. Jean-Philippe nodded an apologetic *understood.* "If there's anything I can do for you, just name it." Whatever he named, Abedi and Shaikh could deliver, and Jean-Philippe knew it. The party was hosted by Abedi's company, the Bank of Credit and Commerce International, which had financed a couple of French film productions for the sole purpose of having a legitimate presence at such film festivals.

Jean-Philippe looked around. "What more could I want?"

Shaikh indicated the women in the room. "We hired all of these beautiful models for our honored guests. We hope you will consider banking with us soon. Enjoy yourself, my friend." He slipped away.

Jean-Philippe had noticed about a dozen women mingling around, all with supermodel potential had they the right drive, mentality, and representation. But they were here for the easy money, and they were well paid. Jean-Philippe wasn't here for a woman, though. He observed two official-looking men conferring. He recognized one of them to be the attorney of General Manuel Noriega. No one's presence here would surprise him, considering the extremely high level of security he had assessed. In addition to the bouncers checking invitations, he had identified several international undercover agents. They would be unnoticeable to anyone else, but Jean-Philippe was adept at recognizing secret service. He assumed Noriega and other high-ranking officials were in some private room while his attorney scouted for models to bring to him. Agha Hasan Abedi disappeared into one of those private rooms, while Alauddin Shaikh interrupted the conversation to shift the men's attention to several barely clothed models.

At that moment, another model even more stunning than the others entered the party. As she cat-walked across the room to greet two of her friends, the strap of her sheathe dress fell, revealing a bouncing breast. Without missing a beat, she flipped the shoulder strap back into place with the casualness of replacing a wisp of stray hair behind her ear. The two men ended their discussion, shook hands, and moved on to the business of offering the models libations and other medicinal pleasures.

The *photo op* he had been waiting for just transpired: the two men shaking hands. Photos of them with the models were just a bonus. He snapped more photos silently and sipped champagne.

THREE

Cleaned up, Mirza looked like a Pakistani James Bond. Indian men were growing popular with French-speaking women, thanks to a pop song in France about a young woman discovering the sexual prowess of a Hindu man. Though Mirza was Muslim, born in Pakistan, his dark eyes, long lashes, and fine facial features made him look Hindu. He stood out in the high-stakes room at Casino de Monte-Carlo, and the women inched closer to his table.

"Faites vos jeux!" the dealer repeated as Mirza placed his $5,000 chip on black. "Les jeux sont faits! Rien ne va plus!"

The roulette wheel sputtered, and the little black ball skipped and jumped, clinging to the fast-moving edge. Centrifugal force kicked it up once more, then centripetal force won out and it settled on black.

Mirza took his winnings and rose from his chair. He held it out for a beautiful woman who had been standing behind him. He nodded for her to sit. "Good timing."

"Thank you. Nice tuxedo." She sat placing her chip on black.

"De rigueur in Monte Carlo."

"Are you in town for the Cannes Film Festival?"

"Do I look like I'm from Bollywood?"

"Well, yes, I thought you might be famous."

"Actually, I am from Pakistan. But it is a common mistake."

"Don't they make movies in Pakistan?"

"I suppose they do. But we are better known for banking."

"Les jeux sont faits! Rien ne va plus!" The roulette ball danced and tripped, hurtling itself against change of direction and velocity, until it rested again on black.

"Sorry, banking is not as exciting as cinema. But can I buy you a drink?"

She took her winnings and stared into his ebony eyes, not sure if she saw the good kind of excitement or bad. "Sure. I'm Shannon." He kissed her hand and led her away.

It turned out to be the good kind of excitement. In his lavish hotel suite, young hipsters drank, danced, gambled, and fooled around. It was a mix of westernized Ivy League-educated sons of sheikhs and their respective entourages.

Shannon loved being stared at when she walked into a room. Mirza led her to the bar where a server handed her a glass of champagne. Several other beautiful American girls eyed her, not as welcoming. "Will you excuse me for a moment?" She nodded okay. Mirza left her and joined one of the princes across the room.

Mirza and the prince observed her as they talked. "She is beautiful."

"You're welcome," Mirza replied.

"Do you have it?"

"Of course. The stash is in the bedroom. Just be sure to take your private plane if you bring it home."

"Bolivian?"

"The best blow in the world." They watched the American girl mingling with some male guests.

"She fends for herself well."

"More than just a pretty face. She's the daughter of a U.S. senator, well-educated but bored with being a beauty pageant contestant."

"She seems to make friends easily. Even with those other cutthroat bitches icing her out."

"She'll fit right in."

FOUR

"Bien venue a Paris," the Air France flight captain welcomed the passengers to Paris Charles de Gaulle Airport over the intercom. Louise Moscow exited the plane with the other passengers. Memories of her first trip to Paris flashed through her mind. Now she was here on business, flying first class. Why did she have to think of that stupid trip with her girlfriend Suzanne Clark from college? After their summer-abroad program on the southwest coast of France, they took a side trip to Paris. Since then, she advised people going to France to visit Paris first, then the countryside. Spending the summer in a small town before coming to Paris leaves one wholly unprepared for the City of Lights.

The summer-exchange program was in the small fishing village of Archachon. The seaside culture was relaxed and carefree. She and Suzanne were popular with the locals. making friends came easily, and by the end of the summer, Louise would walk through the streets, greeting people with a handshake or bisou like a local. The friendly wine-region culture gave her confidence, and her French greatly improved. She thought she had learned everything she needed to know about the French.

But overconfidence skewed her expectations of Paris. The French have an expression, *Paris est la plus belle poubelle du monde*, an alliterative play-on-words meaning *Paris is the most beautiful trashcan in the world*. She quickly learned just how trashy it could be. Their first night in Paris they headed to the famous café Les Deux Magots in the Latin-Quarter. After an hour of drinking in the noisy smoke-filled bistro, their conversational French degraded from competent to sloppy. Their American charm had no effect on Parisian men, who are more discerning than the folksy Archachon. The girls came off as naïve tourists seeking romantic adventure.

Since childhood, Louise had always been shy and awkward in public, whereas Suzanne was sharp and quick-witted, even when speaking French. Louise's confidence quickly dwindled, and she tripped over her words.

Suzanne scoffed, so Louise left, and Suzanne followed her. They walked the narrow cobblestone streets back to their respective lodgings. Louise was staying at the Hôtel Le Littré, offered by a family friend and renowned violin dealer, Peter Edwards, who resided in London and kept a corporate suite at the luxury hotel. She had worked for Peter during college, delivering priceless violins between New York and Chicago, giving her free travel and some extra spending money.

Suzanne, on the other hand, was staying at the student hostel. Louise had planned to invite Suzanne to share her large suite. But now she was reconsidering. She had always felt bullied by her, and her cattiness at the café was the last straw. Louise walked behind Suzanne down the *rue* lit by converted gaslights past ancient apartment buildings, tiny shops, and art galleries toward Montparnasse. They walked in silence, heels clicking on the cobblestones. They passed a recessed doorway where Louise noticed someone standing in the shadows. She looked back to see a pasty little man emerge from the doorway and follow them. She sped past Suzanne.

"Plus vite," said Louise, warning Suzanne to walk faster. She shrugged, sneering at Louise's poor French accent through a puff of cigarette smoke. Louise looked back again to confirm what she thought she had seen: the pasty little man smiling as he jiggled his genitals. She sensed no real danger but walked faster, repeating her warning, albeit in drunken French, that someone was following them, "Plus vite! On nous suit." Their Felliniesque parade continued about twenty meters further until finally Suzanne turned to see the man who was now only steps behind her.

They broke into a sprint, leaving the pervert behind. After they gained a good distance, furious, Suzanne said, "Why didn't you say it in English?" Louise shrugged. Suzanne had been less like a friend and more like a tyrant over their two-year relationship. That little scare gave them invaluable wisdom needed to survive separately the rest of their stay in Paris. And Louise learned to choose her friends more wisely in the future.

"Mademoiselle Moscow?" The chauffeur held a handwritten sign with her name. Now this was more like it. Her college days were far behind her, her French was fluent, and she was well advanced down a career path in international banking. She was back in Paris for an interview with a fast-growing international bank that had paid for her trip. She knew of the Bank of Credit and Commerce International, better known as BCCI, through finance industry buzz. Its management team had carefully selected Louise from among the hottest industry professionals working at the biggest investment banks.

She had been with J.P. Morgan, the investment bank at 23 Wall Street for five years. Founded in 1854, J.P. Morgan distinguished itself with several firsts in banking: financing the formation of the first billion-dollar corporation—U.S. Steel, fast-tracking toward investment banking services, and being the first commercial bank that the Federal Reserve permitted to underwrite a corporate debt offering, then issuing commercial paper and taking companies public in what is known as IPOs.

This corporate restructuring experience was what BCCI wanted Louise to bring to their institution. In exchange, Louise would greatly expand her business networking, live in Europe and use her foreign language skills, and get a substantial increase in pay. The bank's owner, Agha Hasan Abedi, personally invited Louise to the Paris branch to interview for the position of personal banker for high-profile international clientele.

Louise requested a suite at the Hôtel Le Littré to give her a sense of familiarity. Meeting with high-level executives was nothing new, but she wanted every advantage she could get. The driver took her to Le Littré and handed her bags to the bellboy. She tried to tip the driver, but he refused.

"Everything is taken care of," he said, giving the bellboy a nod of understanding. "Have a pleasant evening, Mademoiselle. I'll be back tomorrow morning to pick you up."

After a restful night, Louise ordered room service and ate breakfast on the terrace with a view of the ubiquitous Eiffel Tower not far in the distance. Her driver arrived and took her to the BCCI Paris branch on the Champs-Élysées. Her first three interviews with the directors of human resources, finance, and operations went smoothly. Meeting Louise was only a formality. Unbeknownst to her, they all knew that Abedi had already made his decision. Only the director of human resources asked her any questions of substance.

He scanned her curriculum vitae. "Degree in computer science from Princeton. Harvard MBA. You were made senior vice president of J.P. Morgan in just five years." He put down the CV.

Louise blushed. "You are well informed."

"Mr. Abedi chose you personally."

Investment banking had not been Louise's intended career path. Her first love was science, but, under pressure from her father, as a compromise she opted for more practical endeavors. Computer science allowed for a little of both science and business, then she earned her Harvard MBA to ensure the best possible career options.

But, growing up in Edison, New Jersey, she had been surrounded by science memorabilia of Thomas Alva Edison. Louise learned to read by age four, which opened her to a world of discovery, instead of dressing in tutus and playing with dolls. By age ten, she had read anything and everything related to science. She came to idolize Albert Einstein, pretending her father's desk was her patent office, and refusing to comb her blonde tresses until they frizzed out wildly.

"So, why would a successful young American woman want to move to Europe and work for a middle Eastern bank?" the director asked.

"I have a great affinity for the middle East and Muslim culture."

"I see from your resume you speak Arabic."

"A little. I spent some time in Morocco and made an effort to speak as much as possible."

"That is admirable." He rose, holding out his hand. "I hope to see you again soon. Salam alaykum."

"Wa alaykum as-salam." She blushed again at her rusty accent. But he appreciated the effort and graciously shook her hand in a sign of respect.

She waited in the reception area, psyching herself up for the fourth interview in as many hours. This time, she was to meet with the head of the Paris branch, Nazir Chinoy, her potential boss. She was shown to Chinoy's office, which featured stunning views overlooking the Champs-Élysées.

Chinoy had been working for BCCI since 1978 when Abedi first opened Pakistani branches in Lahore and Islamabad. Abedi recruited the young Chinoy, who was then with the Bank of America's Lahore branch, to run the Pakistani branches and "devise marketing strategies to enhance the business of the bank in Pakistan." This choice illustrated another link in the alliances Abedi was forging in America.[1] Soon, five of the Lahore Bank of America's senior officers were either on BCCI's board of directors or helped to manage Abedi's bank. For the next decade, the two banks would move billions of dollars a week through each other's international offices, and Bank of America would serve as an invaluable ally.

Chinoy was tall, slender, impeccably dressed, charming, and shifty-eyed. When Louise spoke, he focused on her as though absorbing her every word but then would turn his eyes away and change the subject, seemingly deleting the conversation from his memory. Neither she nor anyone else would ever know what he was really thinking.

Chinoy spoke with a delicate Urdu accent. "BCCI is the Third World's only multi-national bank, the first of its kind. You would be dealing with clientele of the highest levels of importance. Having impeccable training, talent, and competence are key to this position, but discretion is top priority."

"Of course."

"A woman of few words. Excellent."

"Yes."

Chinoy rose and extended his hand. "You will be hearing from us."

Louise stood and shook his hand. "Merci, au revoir."

"À tres bientôt."

Without receiving a firm job offer, Louise left Chinoy's office, feeling less confident than she had felt on arrival. She regretted not speaking more.

She returned to her suite and immediately started packing her things.

She sat in front of the mirror, placing her toiletries into her travel kit, when she caught her own reflection. A few blonde tresses had loosened from her chignon and now framed her face. She wondered how she would look bald. She thought about how a person's hair can frame the face, complementing or detracting from it, the way a picture frame can complement or detract from a work of art. Changing her coiffure was one of her few creative outlets, allowing her to become a whole different person on a whim. She removed the single large hairpin letting her hair fall and massaged her scalp, leaving her with a bouffant. She preferred this big mussed-up hair best, but few people ever saw it.

A soft swishing sound prompted her to turn and see an envelope slide under the door. She assumed it was the hotel bill. She grabbed her things and called downstairs for a car to the airport. She picked up the envelope and realized it wasn't from the hotel. She read the note. *Enclosed: Airline Tickets to Seoul South Korea. Departure tomorrow. Good luck.* Louise had made it through the fourth interview and was heading to Seoul for the fifth and final interview with Abedi. She sat back down in front of the mirror and unpacked her sundries.

FIVE

When it came to getting things done, Agha Hasan Abedi was a magician. If he needed to influence an outcome, he waved his magic wand. Right now, in his London office, some of the most powerful men in the world were working for him. Abedi's U.S. attorneys, Clark Clifford, one of the biggest powers in the Democratic Party, and his partner, Robert Altman, played a large part in his scheme.[2] The two attorneys in essence represented the front men acting on behalf of BCCI to make Abedi's blind ambition come true: to own a bank in the United States. In order to do so, Abedi had hired the most influential law firm in America: Clifford & Warnke.

For the past ten years, Clark Clifford[3] had been advancing Abedi's goal. Clifford represented Abedi's front men in the 1978 takeover of the American bank, Financial General, tipping the scales in Abedi's favor. After three years of infighting, Financial General had succeeded in forcing up the bid from an opening offer of $15 a share to $28.50. However, even if the two parties successfully settled, there was still a problem of regulatory approval. In early 1981, Clifford received a call from an old acquaintance from the Johnson administration and one of the principal stockholders in Financial General: Armand Hammer, the legendary chairman of Occidental Petroleum. Hammer said, "Why don't we declare an armistice?" A day and a half later, the Arab investors would purchase Financial General from its current shareholders for a tidy premium; many of them doubled their money.

Federal and state banking officials demanded a public hearing. They wanted it on public record. The meeting on April 23, 1981, was Clifford's masterstroke. Present were the key "investors" led by Kamal Adham, whom Clifford and Altman insisted on calling His Excellency, even though Adham was a commoner and bore no royal title of any kind. Adham told the regulators that he and his partners would be passive investors and that BCCI would exercise no control over Financial General. When Financial General tendered its shares in 1982, it officially renamed itself First American

Bankshares (FAB). The number of shareholders had grown from the original four to fourteen. They included a galaxy of the middle East's wealthy and powerful, including Sheikh Zayed bin Sultan al-Nahayan.

In spite of Clifford and Altman's assurances to regulators that BCCI would have nothing to do with the management of First American Bank, the two would act simultaneously as lead U.S. counsel for BCCI, chief counsel for FAB, and chairman and president of FAB. In 1982 they began traveling as often as once a month to London, mostly to meet alone with Abedi regarding the management of First American Bank.[4]

Between 1986 and 1990, 71 percent of incoming wire transfers to First American Bank were from BCCI Panama, which happened to be among the most corrupt BCCI branches. That was how Abedi got things done. No sum was too much.

Now Clifford and Altman were in London trying to tip the scales again. "This is more than a snag." Clifford walked to the window and looked out over the River Thames, his back to his client. "What's he doing here?"

"Don't worry about him," Abedi said, never looking at Mirza. "He is family." Mirza stoically guarded the door.

"Here is how we will go about *fixing* the Jack Blum problem." The *problem* was the lawyer, Jack Blum, whom Senator John Kerry had enlisted to head an ongoing investigation of BCCI. The head of BCCI's Latin American operations, Amjad Awan, had called head of the Seoul branch, Swaleh Naqvi, about receiving a subpoena from Senator Kerry's subcommittee, headed by Blum. Naqvi told Awan to fly to Washington to see Robert Altman, and Altman told Awan to shred his documents and leave the United States immediately. "We have enlisted several Democratic senators to kill the Kerry investigation. Concurrently, the Pakistani government is putting pressure on the U.S. State Department to curtail further hearings by Senator John Kerry."

"Excellent," said Abedi. "Our Saudi partner, Ghaith Rashad Pharaon, has also engaged Charlie Jones to help suppress further hearings." What Abedi didn't mention was that Charlie Jones of Hindsville, Georgia, had been paid a considerable amount of money to accomplish the task of enlisting two U.S. senators to do what was necessary to suppress the hearings and eliminate Jack Blum.

"We will get this taken care of," Clifford assured Abedi.

Abedi bowed as the two attorneys headed for the door. "We have full faith in your success, as always."

After the attorneys left, Abedi closed the door and turned to Mirza. "Be ready. We may need to take more extreme measures. Now I must take the plane to Seoul, and you go to Brussels as planned."

SIX

Greg Kessler looked out over the city from his penthouse suite on the twenty-seventh floor of the Hilton Brussels as he went through some papers. The massive hotel had caused a rupture with the style of Boulevard de Waterloo when it was built. At that time, the buildings along the boulevard were all in neo-rococo, neo-classical or neo-renaissance style, and its tower became one of the most widely recognized buildings on the skyline.

The phone rang. "Hello? I'll be right down."

Greg exited the elevator to the lobby. But instead of finding his client, he was approached by a Pakistani man accompanied by a two-hundred-and-twenty-pound French guy.

"My name is Mirza, and this is Andre. Mr. Abedi from BCCI sent us to negotiate with you." He handed Greg their BCCI business cards.

"You're getting out of this thing," blurted Andre. "This is our deal."

"You're out," added Mirza, "and tell your client you're out."

"But we had a deal…" Greg said.

"No more deals, ever. Consider yourself out of the arms trade," Mirza said.

Greg turned and walked away. This was not the kind of business negotiations he was used to. He went to his room and placed a call. "There has been a change of plans."

SEVEN

Louise boarded the Korean Airlines flight from Charles de Gaulle Airport to Seoul, South Korea, on her way to meet with Agha Hasan Abedi, as well as the head of the Seoul branch of BCCI, Swaleh Naqvi. Instead of having a drink after take-off, Louise had the urge to meditate.

When she was ten years old, she had become a fan of the Maharishi Mahesh Yogi, one-time guru to the Beatles. When the Maharishi came to New York City for a training conference, her mother took her to see him.

The Maharishi was training thirty teachers and opened the event to the public, the belief being that meditation has an overall effect on channeling world peace. It was then that Louise learned that the year of her birth determined her *mantra*. He instructed attendees to close their eyes and repeat the mantra for twenty minutes. As the group fell into silent meditation, the energy had a psychic effect on Louise. She went into a deeper awareness, like observing her own thoughts from the outside. The sensation evoked an image of a kind of *mask* that, while enabling her to watch her thoughts, simultaneously watched her. This ability to observe herself watching her own thoughts gave her unique objectivity to her subjectivity. She believed it was the reason she had always excelled in school and why things always seem to come easily to her. She was like her own objective observer. She began having dreams she could fly, which, some believe, signifies confidence in having the skills necessary to achieve one's dreams. She practiced TM* for twenty minutes twice a day through her high school years, but when she went to college, she dropped it because of her hectic schedule.

Now she was feeling a sense of coming full circle, and meditation would reinforce that circle. As the plane approached thirty thousand feet, she folded her legs into the lotus position. She placed her hands on her knees and closed her eyes, repeating her mantra in time with her breathing. Almost instantly, she felt something she had never experienced before. Her senses became heightened, but this time, she felt the full effect of the speed and altitude of the airplane at five hundred and fifty miles per hour and thirty-five thousand feet. She even had a sense of the sub-zero temperatures outside. The culmination of the sensations gave her the feeling she was actually riding on top of the airplane with the wind blowing through her hair. She stayed in that mode for the full twenty minutes, her head bobbing and swaying with the movement of the plane, enjoying the ride. It was freeing, powerful. Like a magic carpet ride.

After landing in Seoul, she headed straight to the interview. Louise had heard rumors about Agha Hasan Abedi having a mesmerizing aura. The whole experience so far had been pretty surreal, and that didn't end when she met Abedi. The receptionist showed her into an antechamber, which led to Abedi's office. As she walked toward his office, the door opened by itself. She entered and turned, expecting to see whoever opened the door, but the only person in the room was Abedi seated at his desk.[5] He stood to shake her hand.

"Congratulations Miss Moscow. You have been approved for service and will start as soon as you relocate to Paris."

"Thank you."

"The position requires you to work with the highest-level executives," explained Abedi. "The chain of command delegated to your Paris branch officer, Chinoy, will come directly from the top. We are assigning you to our newest and one of our most important clients, Jörg Soros."

Louise thought *be careful what you wish for.* She admired Jörg Soros, the wealthy Hungarian-American financier and philanthropist who had played a significant role in the peaceful transition from communism to capitalism in Hungary in 1984.

"It will be an honor."

"Chinoy told me you are a woman of few words."

"Chinoy told me discretion was of the utmost importance."

"Excellent." He handed her an envelope. She smiled and opened the envelope, expecting to find an employment agreement. Instead she found what looked like about $5,000 in cash. She looked at him, confused.

Abedi reassured her. "Company policy, positive reinforcement. Your discretion, even between colleagues, is sacrosanct. It is a function of our internal controls to keep communication between departments to a minimum. No transmission of information is allowed between colleagues, co-workers, or supervisors unless explicitly requested by the head of that branch. You will be reminded of this policy constantly in case you forget."

She hesitated, looking him in the eye. Although Abedi looked like just another middle Eastern businessman, his background was astonishing. Except for a hardened determination, his piercing mahogany eyes betrayed nothing of what he had seen over the years.

EIGHT

In 1947 at twenty-five years of age, Agha Hasan Abedi witnessed one of the most violent demographic upheavals in modern history: the migration of fourteen million Muslims from India to the newly created nation of East and West Pakistan, and the deaths of three million people in the violent civil war that resulted in the birth of the state. That year, Abedi joined the mass migration with all the urban Muslims from north-central India, the old heart of the Moghul Empire, traveling west to the newly created state of Pakistan. They were called *mohajirs* (refugees), and they were utterly unlike either the Muslims of present-day Pakistan, or those from the provinces of Bengal and Assam that became East Pakistan.[6]

Abedi could still recall the stench and heat from the crush of people. He and his father boarded trains packed inside and out, seated precariously on duffle bags stacked atop train cars, clinging to the side rails and window frames. Now he wore a western suit and elegant long dark hair. But back then, everyone wore kurtas and bare feet, carrying whatever meager possessions they could. The only continuity in the chaos was the direction they were headed—west—and Abedi's determination to find new footing.

Abedi came from a family of men considered to be among the inner circle of confidents working as well-established courtiers for the rajahs at the palace in Mahmudabad, India, the old heart of the Moghul Empire. Abedi was a double minority, Muslim, which made up only 20 percent of the population of north-central India, and also Shiite, which accounted for only 15 percent of Muslims.

The Shiites were known for obsessive attention to work, politics, and religion. In contrast to the more dispassionate and detached Sunni Muslims, the Shiites are passionately demonstrative and fond of putting on elaborate shows of penance and mourning. Shiites have a mystical bent as well, reflected in their devotion to martyrdom, belief in saints, and worship at the tombs of holy men. Abedi's family was intensely religious, and Abedi emulated the rajahs who were generous, impulsive, and romantic. Abedi's philanthropy and his fondness for perfume, gourmet cuisine, fine clothing, art, and the color white for its purity can all be attributed to his Shiite Muslim heritage.

The migration took him from his home in the big city of Bombay, India's financial capital, where he had settled into the world of banking. After graduating with a degree in law and English from Lucknow university, a phone call from his father's boss, the rajah himself, landed him a job at a new Islamic institution called the Habib Bank. Educated Muslim elites of north-central India were itching to expand outward and upward and were eager for power and influence. Though Abedi was still a double minority, he was luckier than most. His job in the Habib Bank moved with him to the city of Lahore, the scene of some of the most violent fighting of the civil war of 1946 and 1947.

When he finally arrived in the newly settled Pakistan, instead of looking for the familiar sight of a neem tree, he would seek the familiarity of banking. His career as a banker would begin in a semi-feudal country that had virtually no banking industry at all. Although Abedi came into a financial vacuum in 1947, he and his fellow mohajirs would quickly change that. By the late 1950s, Abedi had recruited a leading textile manufacturer and his clan of "twenty-two families" whose fortune would dominate Pakistani commerce in the decades to come. By 1959, with no capital of his own, Abedi launched a rival to his old employer, the first new bank in Pakistan since its independence. He called it United Bank Limited. United became the first bank in Pakistan to computerize its records and the first to introduce the notion of "customer service." Another policy that set Abedi apart was lending to poor farmers and small business owners. These were hardly profitable loans, but Abedi had always been keen on serving poor farmers. Reminiscent of the paternalism of the rajahs, Abedi set up charities at the bank for widows, orphans, and students from poor families.

Abedi was also among the first bankers in the Third World to realize that dollar deposits from Middle East oil exports would turn the banking world on its head and make any enterprising people rich along the way. He was the first to seek a type of deposit that had not yet acquired the name that would become a household word in the English-speaking world by the mid-1970s: *Petrodollars.*

To that end, Abedi had chosen one of the oddest places on Earth to look for a new client—Abu Dhabi,[7] a small town on the verge of unfathomable wealth due to oil discoveries in the Gulf. After a coup in 1967, Sheikh Zayed bin Sultan al-Nahyan became the emir of Abu Dhabi and eventually the leader of the United Arab Emirates. Sheikh Zayed Bin Sultan Al Nahyan's background as a tribal chieftain had more in common with the Arabia of the Middle Ages than with the Western world of the Twentieth Century. When the explorer Wilfred Thesiger first discovered Zayed in the late 1940s, he described him as a *powerfully built man of about thirty with a brown beard sitting on the bare sand next to his rifle, wearing a Bedouin smock, a dagger, and a cartridge belt.*

In 1967 Zayed was now leader of the oil rich nation and had been wondering what he was going to do with all the new oil money. It was then that Abedi made the pilgrimage to Abu Dhabi to introduce himself to the emir. After that, Abedi often traveled to the Emirates to secure his relationship with Zayad as a close friend and one of United Bank's biggest depositors.

In late 1971, when Zulfikar Ali Bhutto became the new president of Pakistan, he took over Abedi's United Bank and placed Abedi under house arrest. But Abedi was undeterred. With the contacts he had built under United Bank, he decided to build what no one had ever built before—a multinational Third World bank that would break the chokehold that the giant European colonial banks had on the developing world. The capital and deposits to fuel the bank's growth would come from the one part of the developing world that had resources, the countries of the oil-producing consortium OPEC.

Abedi had cultivated the friendship of the local representative of Bank of America in Karachi, a Dutchman named Dick Van Oenen, who had an office in Abedi's United Bank building. In the early 1970s, Bank of America was the largest bank in the world, and its ambitious chairman, A.W. "Tom" Clausen, was drooling at the prospect of opening up the Arabian Gulf. Van Oenen decided to take Abedi to the United States to pitch his idea to Clausen. Abedi effectively promised B of A management the keys to the kingdom, access to the coffers of OPEC. In exchange, Bank of America would provide $625,000 in capital and would take a 30 percent share in the new bank and a seat on the board of directors. In subsequent weeks, Abedi convinced his friend Sheikh Zayed to put up another $1.875 million. As soon as Abedi was released from house arrest, he had the capital base for his new bank.

In a ballroom at the five-star Phoenicia Hotel in pre-civil war Beirut, Abedi and a group of about a hundred of his fellow mohajirs forming the core of the bank's management team launched a company that Abedi called the Bank of Credit and Commerce International. Two years later, BCCI was formally incorporated in Luxembourg, a place where Van Oenen had told Abedi he would be free of First World regulatory interference.

The timing of BCCI's launch was nothing short of miraculous. The institution he had created in order to absorb and manipulate oil deposits stood just thirteen months away from an event that would initiate the greatest transfer of wealth from haves to have-nots in history. The Yom Kippur War in October 1973 led to an Arab oil embargo against the West, which resulted in a fourfold increase in the price of oil. Countries such as Saudi Arabia, Kuwait, and Abu Dhabi were no longer just rich. They were shamelessly rich and politically powerful. Abu Dhabi and the other kingdoms were now independent from the British. They federated into a group called the United Arab Emirates. Both the U.A.E.'s president, Sheikh Zayed bin Sultan Al-Nahayan, and its vice president, Sheikh Mohammed bin Rashid al Maktoum, considered Abedi a close adviser and friend. By the late 1970s, BCCI had effectively merged with Sheikh Zayed's Private Department, which handled and invested the Emirate's astonishing new wealth.

The year 1972 marked the beginning of an unprecedented international banking boom, driven by a magical and relatively new commodity called the *Eurodollar*, which would last twenty years and move some $600 billion from the First World to the Third World. Banks would soon be falling all over themselves to get a piece of the business Abedi had been nurturing quietly for years. He was among the first to anticipate one of the most jarring economic shifts in history: the rise of the Islamic nations of OPEC (Organization of Petroleum Exporting Countries) in the 1970s. And he was perhaps the first to see the opportunity that lay in hundreds of billions of dollars of petro-deposits, opening a BCCI office in Karachi in early 1978.

As BCCI swept into the 1980s, the bank was arguably the most successful in the world. Every two weeks, a new BCCI branch opened somewhere, with the addition of more than $1 billion in new assets each year. However, western banking authorities resolutely refused to let Abedi into the club, influencing an increasingly nervous Bank of America to sell its equity. Nonetheless, Abedi had built the world's first Third World consortium bank, one that had extraordinary access to the huge dollar surpluses being generated in the Middle East. His shareholders were a glittering who's-who in the Gulf, among them Saudi princes, rulers of Arabia, and even the former head of Saudi intelligence. Given the opportunity, Abedi had the ability simply to write a check for Chase Manhattan, Citicorp, or any bank he chose. That would certainly come to pass. It was only a question of when.[8]

NINE

Louise placed the envelope in her bag and shook Abedi's hand. "Thank you. This will help with my relocation."

"That is for you. Your relocation will all be taken care of by BCCI. Thank you for making the trip. Naqvi will answer any questions you may have."

When Louise left Abedi's office, the door closed silently by itself. She was positive it wasn't anything mechanical. She had never seen anything like it.[9]

She arrived in Naqvi's office with many questions, but none that she wanted to pose to him. Was the cash a signing bonus? Was it a bribe? Did Abedi really have the power to open and close doors with his mind?

Swaleh Naqvi stood to greet Louise. "Ah, welcome, our newest addition. We are very excited to have such a brilliant American mind join us. Abedi told you who your first client will be?"

"Yes, Mr. Soros."

"He is a very important client for us. It is fortuitous timing to have recruited you right now. You will provide the same level of service Mr. Soros expects from the great western banks. Your talent for analysis and corporate structure are just what we need in our next phase of expansion." Naqvi was very energetic and astute. She imagined he was always one step ahead of anyone in a conversation. "I too am a numbers person. I do all calculations in my head. Everything up here." He pointed to his temple. "Go ahead ask me anything."

"Well, I…"

"It's all up here." Still pointing at his head. "But we understand you prefer something in writing, so here is your paperwork." Naqvi signaled her to be seated as he sat at his desk and handed her an employment agreement.

"Please have your attorney review the agreement and we will finalize as soon as possible. Do you need a cash advance? All relocation expenses are to be paid by the Paris branch. They have already rented you an apartment, and you will have a driver at your disposal."

"No, I don't need any more cash. I'll be sure to get these documents taken care of right away."

Naqvi stood up and walked to the door. She rose to follow him. He showed her to the reception area. "Thank you for coming all this way. We will invite you back to Seoul after you are situated."

"You're welcome. I look forward to seeing you again."

"The driver will take you to your hotel or if you would like he can take you shopping on us. Don't be shy. Anything you like."

"How nice."

"Anything at all. Have a nice day."

A lovely young receptionist escorted Louise to the car. "Is he serious about the shopping?" Louise asked.

"Deadly serious. Go ahead. Enjoy yourself."

"Thank you."

The corporate culture at BCCI would definitely take some adjustment. She had never heard of these kinds of perks anywhere on Wall Street. In addition to having a lawyer review the employment agreement, she would also check into the undeclared cash hand-outs and gifts.

T E N

The green tie with white shamrocks mesmerized Mirza. The prosecutor's gray hair, wrinkled suit, potbelly, and Saint Patrick's Day tie were hardly intimidating. Yet when he spoke, Mirza trembled.

"Your client has volunteered to testify. We have assembled a grand jury to hear the testimony."

Mirza's attorney spoke to the judge. "Your Honor, my client wishes to waive his right to a grand jury hearing. He prefers to simply testify in exchange for protection."

The prosecutor objected. "These are serious accusations and we will not risk mistrial due to botched procedures."

Because of the Fifth Amendment, the federal legal system must use grand juries to bring charges, at least for certain offenses. The Fifth Amendment to the U.S. Constitution requires that charges for all federal felonies—capital and "infamous" crimes—be brought by a grand jury indictment, unless a defendant waives his or her right to be indicted by a grand jury. If a defendant waives his or her right to be indicted by a grand jury, the prosecutor can charge him or her by using an "information." The difference between a *grand jury indictment* and an *information* is that a grand jury must approve an indictment, while a prosecutor can issue an information without the grand jury.

"I'm afraid if the prosecuting attorney himself wants a grand jury, there's little we can do," said the judge.

Mirza's attorney spoke with him privately. Mirza had been a pragmatic businessman, performing all nature of work, from merciless assassination to kidnapping and other forms of intimidation. Yet the thought of coming under investigation by the United States Federal Bureau of Investigation was terrifying.

His attorney stood. "Okay, my client will testify to the grand jury."

Mirza was sworn in, gave his name, and country of residence, Pakistan.

The prosecutor began questioning. "Mr. Mirza, what is your occupation?"

"I am a secret agent with the *Black Network*."

"Please explain what the Black Network is."

"It is a secret enforcement arm of BCCI."

"BCCI?"

"The Bank of Credit and Commerce International."

"And what do you do for them?"

"Anything they need me to. Mainly intimidation."

A grand jury member asked, "And you came forward to offer important information in exchange for clemency?"

"Yes."

"What information?"

"I have heard about the John Kerry hearings. Another person at BCCI, Amjad Awan, who is head of Latin American operations, called me to tell me about receiving a subpoena from Senator Kerry's subcommittee. Awan told me that he contacted the head of Seoul operations, Swaleh Naqvi, to tell him about the subpoena. Naqvi told Awan to fly to Washington to see Robert Altman, and Altman told Awan to shred his documents and leave the United States immediately. Awan didn't do it. He wouldn't leave. Then he was afraid that he would be fired for having disobeyed Naqvi and Altman, but he didn't want to leave Florida because his children were in school there. Now I am afraid that I will be subpoenaed."

The grand jury continued questioning Mirza, and he recounted everything he had heard in the London office about BCCI's intention of *fixing Jack Blum*, the Democratic senators are trying to "kill" the hearings, and the Pakistani government putting pressure on the U.S. State Department to stop further hearings.

"How would they stop further hearings?" asked the jury foreman.

"It is being orchestrated by several people, including BCCI's U.S. attorneys Clark Clifford and Robert Altman through their contacts in the Senate. Also, the Saudi partner Ghaith Rashad Pharaon engaged Mr. Charlie Jones of Hindsville, Georgia, to help suppress further hearings. Jones was paid a lot of money. He enlisted two U.S. senators to do what was necessary to suppress the hearings and eliminate Jack Blum."

The prosecutor looked at his watch. "It's getting late and it's Saint Patrick's Day.

The foreman replied, "We will adjourn until March 20th."

ELEVEN

Arrangements for Louise's relocation to Paris were swift and efficient. As soon as she had received the call from BCCI and booked her trip to Paris for interviews, she started to prepare her family and friends for her departure. She pre-arranged vacating her New York apartment, shipping, storage, and change of address. Although J.P. Morgan management would be disappointed by her resignation, given the fast pace of the finance industry, they were set up to transition high-level staff on short notice. Her two-week notice gave her ample time to tie up loose ends and visit with friends.

The biggest challenge would be telling her parents, George and Mary Moscow. Mary had accepted Louise's independent nature at a young age because Louise always excelled at whatever she set her mind to do. However, her father had always been very protective. She decided to drive out to Westchester County and surprise them to break the news. But it was Louise who was surprised by how supportive they both were when she announced her job change.

"Congratulations, sweetie," her mom said, kissing her on the cheek.

Louise looked at her father. "Dad? What do you think?"

George Moscow was a Harvard Law School graduate, but he looked more like a button man for the mob than an intellectual. He was big, around six feet tall and over two hundred pounds, with hooded eyes and a nose that appeared to have been broken at least once. He looked street smart and tough and talked out of the side of his mouth, like a wise guy who never said anything that wasn't confidential or incriminating.[10]

"If this is what you want, I'm happy for you." Louise breathed a sigh of relief. However, she knew full well her father would investigate the company and let her know what he found out.

"Why don't you have a little going-away party here at the ranch?" Mary offered. After Louise left for college, her parents moved from Edison, New Jersey, to her father's family ranch in Westchester County, about thirty-five miles north of New York City.

"Thanks, I will!"

Three days later, on the eve of her departure, she held a small gathering of her closest friends at the house. Louise's two oldest friends, Renée and JoAnn, were coming up from Edison, and some New York friends were also invited.

After running errands, Louise arrived at her parents' ranch house, wearing sweats and her hair in a ponytail. She was surprised to see her ex-fiancé Michael in the kitchen, talking to her mom. He seemed genuinely surprised and happy to see her.

"Louise! You're looking beautiful."

"Michael, what are you doing here?"

"Didn't you invite me to your going-away party?"

"Oh…" She looked at Mary who winked. "Yes, of course." She gave Michael an awkward kiss on the cheek. "Thanks for coming."

"Congratulations on your new job."

"Thanks. Well, I'm a mess so I'm going to shower and change. See you in a minute."

Louise had barely finished getting ready when the doorbell rang. Everyone who had been invited came, and it turned into a party. Louise clanked a fork against her glass to make a toast.

"Thanks everyone for coming to see me off on my new adventure. Next time you're in Paris, be sure to look me up!"

"Cheers!" from everyone.

Renée reached into her purse and brought out a hard-covered book about half an inch thick. "Guess what I brought!"

"No! Is that our eighth-grade yearbook?" They leafed through, laughing at the outdated pictures of themselves.

JoAnn read some of the signatures on the inside cover aloud. *"Renée, you are the coolest girl in school. Stay that way!"* They laughed uncontrollably.

"And the best part of it?" laughed Louise. "You stayed that way!"

Just then, Louise's father entered, and everyone went silent. George Moscow, a New York City detective in charge of the white-collar fraud—and Louise's moral compass—was accompanied by another man. Louise immediately recognized the other man as Bob Morgan, the New York district attorney.[11]

Louise sprang to her feet. "Daddy!" She hugged him tightly.

George gave her a kiss on the cheek. "We'll leave you to your friends. Bob and I have some business."

Bob Morgan was seventy years old, a lean figure with silver hair, a high domed forehead, and a Patrician manner. He was soft-spoken, courtly, and one of the most important men in New York. There were several reasons for this, and perhaps the least of them was that he was the most renowned district attorney in the nation. Morgan was esteemed because he was an influential man of high principle raised in a tradition of public service. The New York D.A.'s straight shooting had kept him in public office for thirty years as the top federal and local prosecutor in a city that long ago had institutionalized patronage politics, kickbacks, municipal corruption, and electoral manipulation. unlike most elected officials, he didn't keep track to the nearest decimal point the margin of votes that kept him in office because it had been years since he faced serious challenge. Some of the guests knew who George and Bob were. But even those who didn't know them were struck by their presence.

"Congratulations on your new job," Bob said. To Louise's shock, Michael stood and shook George and Bob's hands.

"Enjoy your party. I'll join you a little later," George said. Then all three men went into George's office. She realized Michael hadn't come for her going-away party. He was meeting with her father. She watched them through the half-open door having a conversation. Talking with George Moscow was like consulting the Delphi oracle: you received a pronouncement, a veiled revelation of truth, and went away trying to figure out what it meant.[12] However, this time George seemed to be exchanging information with Michael and Bob. Michael noticed Louise watching them and quietly closed the door. She was tempted to burst in on them, but she controlled herself.

TWELVE

Unbeknownst to Louise, George Moscow was the lead prosecutor running an investigation into BCCI. The investigation had a chain of command that was twisted out of necessity for maximum confidentiality. It started with Senator John Kerry's subcommittee. Kerry came into the Senate during the Reagan years. He had been a war hero in Vietnam, and later one of the founders of Vietnam Veterans against the war. In 1971 he gained national attention by throwing away his medals at an antiwar rally. That act seemed doubly remarkable because he was a graduate of Yale; his mother also happened to be part of the vastly wealthy Forbes family, Boston Brahmins for over one hundred years.

Barely into his second term, Kerry made a splash with his investigation into the drug trade in Latin America and into the affairs of the Panamanian dictator Manuel Noriega.[13] John Kerry's subcommittee had been obstructed from investigating BCCI, so Kerry instructed his chief investigator, Jack Blum, to take over the investigation. Blum, a lawyer who had been a Senate investigator for the Foreign Relations Committee, was said to be "like Audubon of the Potomac. He could gaze across the power-broker restaurants where he dined, name the denizen, and describe the feeding habits and mating rites of the species that held real power in the permanent federal bureaucracy." Jack Blum was George Moscow's boss.

Morgan was already well informed about the investigation. Blum took over the investigation into BCCI, and what he uncovered was disturbing. Blum had learned of a detailed report of an informant testifying to a grand jury against BCCI during two meetings in March 1989. The informant, Mirza, was privy to top management decisions within BCCI's American operations. He also claimed to be an agent with a secret enforcement arm of BCCI. The informant also said that Charlie Jones of Hindsville, Georgia, had been "paid a considerable amount of money" to suppress further hearings. Jones had enlisted two U.S. senators "to do what was necessary to eliminate

Jack Blum." For Blum, it had become personal, so he began to pursue his own private crusade against BCCI. That's when he approached Morgan.

Blum was well aware of Morgan's reputation. There are only a relative handful of people in the United States in positions of influence who have devoted their careers to exposing government and business corruption, and fewer still who have managed to retain those positions for very long while doing so. Morgan knew Blum had been running Senator Kerry's hearings into the drug-money laundering. So, when Blum requested to meet him because he had a very important story to tell him, Morgan was prepared to listen attentively.

Blum went to Morgan's office to explain what he had learned. "This is about the biggest bank fraud in the history of the world," Blum began. "What I'm telling you is that the BCCI shareholders aren't the independent investors they were portrayed to be, and therefore BCCI secretly owns and controls one of the most important banks in Washington, DC. Their U.S. attorneys, Clark Clifford and his partner, Robert Altman, are part of some criminal scheme, fronting for this giant criminal bank. And the Justice Department has known all about it for years and isn't doing anything about it."

The Justice Department took its orders from the White House. That made Morgan the only law enforcement game in town. Blum told Morgan about the secret agent with the Black Network who had testified against BCCI before the grand jury, that the feds were blocking the investigation and the recorded testimony, and that the report was missing.

Morgan had only one question: "Is there evidence of money laundering through New York?"

"Yes," Blum told him, "and there is evidence that BCCI also owns First American Bank, which had a major office in New York."

"If New York is the banking center of the world and the money is laundered through here, there is our jurisdiction," Morgan declared. "If the United States attorney is not doing it, I'm doing it."

Morgan had realized for years that arresting small-time drug dealers in an effort to stanch the tide was futile, and that to do something effective one had to attack the financial conduits that made it all possible: the untouchable respectable banks. The Bank Secrecy Act of 1968, the first law that forced reluctant banks to open at least some of their records to law enforcement, was drafted in Morgan's offices. Now Jack Blum was investigating an international bank that was born from the drug trade, a bank that laundered drug money as part of corporate policy, and a bank that apparently remained open because its enormous cash flow had bought influence in the corridors of power in Washington, Karachi, London, Paris, and Beijing. After that meeting, Morgan made an official request for the informant's recorded testimony and the full report. He was told they didn't exist.

In order to keep the investigation discreet, Blum further twisted the chain of command, turning the case over to George Moscow's office. George was to keep Morgan in the loop confidentially. They all thought their telephones may be bugged, and somebody had been tailing the D.A.'s men. George Moscow had had to work completely undercover so as not to be shut down. If anyone could keep his cover, it was George. He had learned from the best. His father had been the chief political correspondent for *The New York Times*, and George was trained from birth not to blow a cover. Not even his own daughter Louise knew about this investigation, and it was unlikely BCCI even knew of him, which is precisely why Blum assigned him to the investigation. Morgan listened intently as George filled him in on the latest.

Louise was still watching the door to the office and had stopped mingling with her friends. JoAnn raised her glass. "To Lulu, bon voyage. We'll miss you!" Louise drank to herself and went back to looking at the yearbook and giggling.

The next morning, Louise warmly hugged her mom goodbye and loaded her bags into the car. As always, her father insisted on driving her to the airport and seeing her off. They drove in silence, Louise enjoying the last moments of George's parental presence. "Thank you for driving me to the airport."

"It's my pleasure."

"So, what was Michael doing here last night?"

"He was there seeing you off like everyone else."

"Then why did he spend the evening in your office?"

"It was work related, nothing to be worried about."

"Work related?" Louise feigned indignation. "You consider *me* work?"

"I don't, but Michael might." She slugged him in the shoulder.

"He's a good guy, Lulu. Maybe you should give him another chance."

Louise stared at him, more confused than miffed. "If I had known you were so fond of him, I might have."

"It's never too late."

At the gate, George gave her a fatherly hug. Then he placed a small amulet around her neck. It was an antique gold chain with a scarab pendant. Louise knew the object very well. She grew up hearing her father's stories of the ancient dung beetle, the *Scarabaeus sacer* or *sacred scarab*,[14] which bore a hallowed status among the ancient Egyptians. Louise was flabbergasted he would give her this cherished object.

"Daddy, this is your *most beloved treasure*. You used to tell me it has powers. I can't accept this."

"You are my most beloved treasure. And you have *powers*." He kissed her forehead and watched her as she boarded the plane. "Now go recreate yourself."

THIRTEEN

Louise fingered the scarab dangling from her necklace as she stood in the entrance of her new home where her bags had already been delivered. It was a furnished nineteenth-century apartment located on Boulevard Haussmann in the affluent 8th arrondissement. The building used to be the home of the French novelist and essayist Marcel Proust. The top floor was now a penthouse apartment, featuring upholstered walls, updated kitchen, and bathrooms to rival those in the United States, and a circular parlor overlooking the boulevard. The décor was mostly Louis XVI including a velvet chaise longue in the parlor and an elegant four-poster canopy bed in the bedroom. It was an ideal setting for her new life. She kissed the scarab and started unpacking.

The next day, Louise began her orientation into BCCI and preparation for her first meeting with Jörg Soros. She compiled a financial market analysis in three languages.

Louise loved working both with numbers and foreign languages. She had developed a unifying theory about her skill reconciling language and math. It is commonly believed that a high level of verbal fluency and memory accuracy is left-brain dependent (English, foreign languages, history, poetry), and that holistic problem-solving and imaginary manipulation is right-brain dependent (science and mathematics). However, Louise believed both sides of the brain were completely compatible if not interchangeable.[15]

Chinoy was so impressed with Louise's presentation that he made it the model for all the company's financial presentations. Within a month, Louise had positioned herself to gain top-level clearance at BCCI. The company assigned her increasingly important projects, giving her greater access to confidential information. It was an exciting time to be in international finance. She felt the rush from global economic growth and expansion, technological advances, and converging global economies. She had the opportunity to work with the top minds in business and finance.

Louise and two of her colleagues became fast friends. Both Diana and Simon were English with the kind of deadpan humor that seems even funnier delivered with an imperial English accent. As Louise exited the elevator and made her way to her office, she heard them talking.

"Off to work, Simon, you lazy article," Diana said.

"Filthy Americans, making us look bad," said Simon.

Louise made a U-turn back to Diana's office. "By all means, don't stop gossiping on my account," said Louise, holding a porcelain bowl usually used for coffee in France. "Tea, please."

"How rude," joked Simon. "Begging for tea with a great sloppy bowl."

"Have one of my teacups." Diana served Louise some Earl Grey with milk.

"Okay, what are you two scheming? You look like evil twins."

"Sorry? We don't look alike in the least." Diana seemed genuinely offended, yet dignified. Indeed, apart from them both having thick blond hair, blue eyes, and better-than-average teeth, Diana and Simon would never be mistaken for siblings. Diana had delicate features, whereas Simon had a rugged bone structure and big teeth. Diana had a reserved nature, while Simon was outspoken and prone to antics. But now they wore identical mischievous expressions.

It was strange and unsettling to work in a place where everyone had a secret. As a Wall Street veteran, Louise was no stranger to corporate secrecy. However, in the world of public companies and the Securities and Exchange Commission regulations, full disclosure and transparency are the norm. Even extremely confidential business strategies, trade secrets, corporate restructurings, mergers, acquisitions, and new technologies eventually became public knowledge. But BCCI was different. There was a definite lack of transparency that went beyond corporate strategy and trade secrets. It was an extremely cloistered corporate culture with an underlying presumption that the less one knows the better. It was a mafia mentality.

Louise went to her office and checked her calendar—and learned Diana and Simon's secret. She was booked on a flight to Budapest tomorrow to meet with Jörg Soros. He was so impressed with Louise that he declared he would work only with her. Inviting Louise to Budapest for a meeting was a big deal.

Soros was born in the *Kingdom of Hungary*, Budapest, to Hungarian Jewish Esperantist writer Tivadar Schwartz. The family changed its name from Schwartz to Soros in 1936, in response to growing anti-Semitism with the rise of fascism. Tivadar liked the new name Soros because it is a palindrome and also had a meaning. In Hungarian, *soros* means *next in line*, or *designated successor*. In Esperanto, it means *will soar*. The word Esperanto means *hopeful*. The now defunct language was invented in the late 1870s with the goal to create an easy-to-learn and politically neutral language that would serve as a universal second language to foster peace and international understanding. There is evidence that learning Esperanto may provide a superior foundation for learning languages in general, much like Latin. Soros's father had taught him to speak Esperanto from birth.

Now, Jörg Soros was instrumental in transforming the economic and political framework of Hungary, converting Hungary from communism to capitalism.

FOURTEEN

Louise left the next morning and arrived at the Gellért Hotel that afternoon. An impressive art nouveau building, the Gellért overlooks the Danube River and the beautiful thermal baths. From the hotel, she could see the Buda Castle of the Hungarian kings, completed in 1265, comprising the world's largest thermal water cave system with a total of eighty geothermal springs. There are still ruins of the enormous baths that were built by ancient Romans who established their regional capital at Aquincum so that they could enjoy the thermal springs.

The maitre d'hotel handed Louise her room key. "Mr. Soros is waiting for you in the lounge, Mademoiselle Moscow."

Soros was sitting at a private table. He greeted her warmly and asked her to join him. "Thank you for coming, Louise. I hope this trip didn't cause you too much inconvenience. But I wanted to see you in person and could not get away from my business here at this time."

"It is my pleasure. I have always wanted to visit Budapest."

"It is a beautiful city and well-deserved UNESCO World Heritage site. You must try the thermal baths. They work wonders on backaches, which are the key to my success."

"So, genius is one percent inspiration and 99 percent backaches?"

"That is a clever twist on the Thomas Edison quote from the girl from Edison, New Jersey."

"How did you know I am from Edison, New Jersey?"

"I know everything about you."

"I hope I'm not the source of your backache."

"Backaches or any other malady can be very telling if you know how to listen to them. I realized long ago that when I make the right decision, my backache goes away. For example, one of my major undertakings was in South Africa, but the apartheid system was so pervasive that whatever I tried to do made me part of the system rather than helping to change it. Backache.

Then I turned my attention to Central Europe. Here I was much more successful. I started supporting the Charter 77 movement in Czechoslovakia in 1980, and *Solidarity* in Poland in 1981. I established separate foundations here in my native country, Hungary, in 1984, then in China in 1986, in the Soviet Union in 1987, and in Poland in 1988. No backache."

"No backache after changing the world?"

"Exactly. Recently, I established a network of foundations that extends across more than twenty-five countries. Unfortunately, I believe we will shut it down because my back has started hurting again."

"Fighting dictatorships to promote tolerance and human rights can be taxing."

"Point taken. Perhaps, I should be less judgmental of my back. But I brought you here to tell you in person about my latest backache, which has made me decide to close my accounts at BCCI."

Louise was stunned. "But you just opened the accounts."

"The reasons will become clear to you eventually. For now, I want you to know that I am very grateful for your hard work and that I will always be there to help you, should the need arise."

"Does Chinoy know?"

"It is all taken care of. It has nothing to do with you." Soros rose and kissed her on both cheeks. "Now I will leave you to enjoy my beautiful city. I have hired a car for you. The driver will give you the grand tour and take you anywhere you like, my treat. Have a wonderful time. This is a day of great celebration."

"Not for me."

"For you and everyone in Hungary."

Despondent, Louise went to her suite. She stepped out onto the balcony to enjoy the view of the historic riverbank with its ancient spas and buildings in the evening sun. She heard festive music as people drank in cafés and relaxed in the hot springs.

"Louise!" a familiar voice said. There in the balcony next to hers was Diana. "Surprise!"

"Diana! What are you doing here?"

"Soros insisted I come to surprise you. Sorry I couldn't tell you."

"How wonderful! I could use a girlfriend right now. Let's go. I'm famished." Soros had sent a car to take them to dinner at Karpatia. Founded in 1877, it was located in historic downtown, on the Pest side of Elizabeth

Bridge. Soros even arranged to have champagne chilling at their table.

Louise raised her glass. "To Jörg. Man of mystery."

"So, what is this all about? Is it about BCCI? He's withdrawing his accounts?"

"You know I can't say anything. But I feel like a failure," said Louise.

"Trust me, he may be closing his accounts, but it has nothing to do with you. He's doing what's best."

"Is there something you're not telling me?"

"There's a lot I'm not telling you."

"Of course. Maybe I shouldn't have taken this job," Louise offered. "I'm glad you did. Let's not talk about work. Today is a special day."

"It seems like the whole town is having a big party. Is it always like this?"

"Not for one hundred and fifty years. Today the government declared the anniversary of the 1848 Revolution to be a national holiday."

Louise had been so busy she didn't realize they were smack dab in the middle of historic celebrations. As soon as the sun set, fireworks started going off all over the city. It was the culmination of events starting one year earlier when thirty thousand people demonstrated against the Communist Regime of Romania's plan to demolish Transylvanian villages. Now, more than seventy-five thousand demonstrators filled the streets of Budapest. Louise and Diana watched the events from the restaurant terrace.

"This is going to change things," said Diana. "The banking world will benefit from more open governments and economies."

They watched as thousands of Hungarians celebrated in the streets late into the evening. The demonstrations would lead Hungary to begin removing its barbed wire fence along the Austrian border, the first tear in the Iron Curtain, leading to the dismantling of the Berlin wall.

FIFTEEN

Louise immersed herself in the world of international banking, making time to socialize and network with others in the business. They were the modern-day banking counterparts of Sartre, de Beauvoir, Cocteau, and Picasso, drinking in Paris cafés, discussing creative accounting and fiscal philosophy. It was springtime and the evening air was refreshing, easing off the winter chill. She met Diana with her husband, Max, and Simon for dinner at a trendy bistro, Le Gourmet des Ternes, in the 8th arrondissement. Also joining them was a Russian-American, Vladimir Egger, whom Diana had invited as a set-up for Louise. Vladimir brought a friend, Greg Kessler.

Vlad was tall and slim with light brown hair and hazel eyes. Only his given name revealed his Russian origins. He had an entirely American accent with no trace of monotone, guttural spoken Russian. He was good looking but there was no immediate attraction between them. Louise usually trusted her first impression because it was a gut reaction to a person's aura. On the other hand, Louise's gut reacted immediately to Vlad's friend, Greg. He was also American with Cary Grant good looks, and he dressed the part.

The mixed company made for awkward conversation at first. Louise felt self-conscious and out of step with European social etiquette. In business, she was aggressive, goal orientated, and very direct, sometimes at the expense of decorum. Socially, she sometimes forgot to tone it down, and she came across as rude or *mal élevée*.

"So, Greg, how long have you lived in Paris?"

"About fifteen years. And you?"

"I just moved here a few months ago."

"Maybe I can show you some of the sights."

Diana hoped to get Louise to talk to Vlad, so she offered, "Vlad is Russian."

"Oh really? Vladimir, you don't sound Russian at all. Your accent sounds American."

"Yes, I speak American, not English."

Simon hoped to increase the tension. "Whatever happened to that su-permodel you were seeing, Vlad? What was her name?"

"Wasn't it Claudia Schiffer?" asked Diana.

"No one nearly as *super*," Vlad said.

Louise made an attempt to shift the conversation to the cultural differ-ences between the United States and France. For foreigners living abroad, this subject was a constant source of fascination and analysis. The British compared France to England, while Americans compared America to both England and France. The search for concrete answers seemed futile.

"What about bribery then?" asked Louise. "Isn't it actually legal in most countries to accept bribes?"

"Is there something you'd like to tell us, Louise?" asked Vlad. "And by 'us' I mean the U.S. government."

"I was just wondering."

Diana explained, "The short answer to your question is yes, bribery is legal. However, we prefer the term *commission*."

"And by 'we', you mean BCCI," quipped Vlad.

"As a legal advisor of BCCI, I am well versed in international banking law. BCCI provides a very valuable service to its clients, especially since the Foreign Corrupt Practices Act turned business upside down in the Middle East. Paying 'commissions' is the way they do business there, and it isn't considered bribery. The Saudis considered the use of 'agents' to be one way of redistributing the wealth. They are go-betweens providing a way to give loyal commoners a piece of the action. The way most commoners in the middle East got rich off the oil boom was through a simple system known as 'agency arrangements.' In order to sell a product or service in Saudi Arabia, you had to know someone in the royal family who authorized all expendi-tures. If you did not know a princeling or a royal cousin, then you hired an 'agent' who provided you access to a royal for a 'commission.'

"However, when the Saudis and the emirates outlawed the use of 'agents' and prohibited payment of commission in arms sales, the royal families were horrified at the thought of being embarrassed by accusations of bribery. So, BCCI solved the problem. We simply structure the agent commissions into the financing of the deal, so they aren't seen, and the bank in turn pays the commissions."

"So, the United States condones these so-called commissions?" asked

Louise.

"The commission often looks very much like a bribe or kickback, and the U.S. Congress spent much time trying to distinguish between the two. But it is the way business is done."

"It's a trade-off," Greg chimed in. "When OPEC raised the price of oil, the United States went along with it publicly. Privately, the United States threatened OPEC with the use of military force and a food embargo if the oil producers didn't invest their oil dollars in western banks and spend most of them on western goods. The biggest purchases have always been arms sales, and prior to the Foreign Corrupt Practices Act, you couldn't make a sale without giving a healthy commission to a U.S. agent."

"We help broker those commissions now too," affirmed Diana. "Even in the United States, commissions don't necessarily violate federal or state laws and are commonly paid on behalf of clients throughout the industry."

"As long as they are not paid to an official or employee of the federal government or to an official or employee of a foreign government," Greg finished Diana's thought.

Simon asked, "Greg, don't you sell commercial jets for a living?"

"Yes, and there is some overlap in the laws."

"Don't worry about the commissions," Diana assured Louise. "Believe me. We would let you know if there are any discrepancies."

"Oh, of course," said Simon. "We all know BCCI's practices follow the highest legal standards."

"Simon, there may be spies among us," Diana half joked. "Literally," teased Simon.

Louise wondered if one of them was a spy. Greg dealt in Aerospace, and Vlad hinted that he worked for the U.S. government.

"None of it matters if there's no one enforcing anything," Vlad said. "Since the stock market crash, bank regulations have become even more lax. Ironically, regulations were loosened in order to stimulate the economy after the stock market crash on Black Monday."[16, 17]

Vladimir mused, "Louise, didn't you work for J.P. Morgan during that corporate debt offering?"

"Yes, but not as a trader or hedge fund manager."

"Wasn't it Mark Twain who said, 'October is one of the particularly dangerous months to speculate in stocks. The others are July, January, September, April, November, May, March, June December, August, and

February.'?"

Simon smirked. "Vlad quoting Mark Twain? That's a first."

Diana's husband, Max, had been listening silently all evening. Normally, he showed interest only when the conversation turned to the arts or philosophy. He was a well-established Parisian artist of the chain-smoking, brooding, eccentric variety. He also spoke broken English, so when he joined Diana's social gatherings, most of the time, he was content to remain silent and maintain a mellow red-wine buzz. However, every so often he would fire off a remark, proving he was more than coherent. "Brandissez vos pistolets!" proclaimed Max.

"Max, old boy, we have no pistols to brandish." Simon laughed. "I have only my paltry repertoire of facts and figures. Did you know that, despite the crash of October 1987, the Dow was positive for the 1987 calendar year? It opened on January 2, 1987, at 1,897 points and closed on December 31, 1987, at 1,939 points."

"The stock market and the banking industry have received a boost from current political events," said Vlad. "The Cold War is ending, causing a surge in trade and economic development. Black Monday was a little over two years ago, and the Dow has already regained its August 25, 1987, closing high of 2,722 points."

"Thanks for ending that Cold War thing for us, Vlad," Greg said.

"I cannot take all the credit..." Vladimir said, bowing with a flourish of his hand, taking all the credit for ending the Cold War.

Louise said nothing. She just thought of the events she and Diana had witnessed in Budapest, which ultimately led to the dismantling of the Berlin wall, thanks to Soros.

Like a drunken boxing referee, Max grabbed Vlad's arm and raised it triumphantly. "Le vainqueur!"

Simon raised his own arm in the same fashion, "The vanquished!" and stood up from the table.

"Well, best be off." Diana also rose. "Early day tomorrow."

After a four-hour dinner and innumerable bottles of wine, they staggered out. They all shook hands or kissed each other twice, once on each cheek, as is customary in Paris. In a group, this process can last several minutes. As they stood outside the restaurant, clearly not all the men were ready to call it a night. But Simon was the first to give in and grab a taxi home. "À Dieu vat!" he exclaimed, getting into a cab and driving away.

"Godspeed!" Greg replied as he flagged another taxi. "Would you care to share a cab with Vlad and me, Louise?" Louise looked at Greg, then at Vlad, then back at Greg. "Vlad is staying at my place while he's in town."

"Although it would be fun to share a ride with you two, my place is not far from here, so I think I'll walk. It's a lovely evening."

On cue, Greg and Vlad stood back from the cab and held the door open for Max and Diana, who got in and drove off.

"Why don't we all walk together?" Greg said. "My flat is just around the corner. We could have a nightcap at my place and then walk you home?"

"Why not?" They left the restaurant, taking Boulevard de Courcelles near the Monceau metro stop. They walked through Parc Monceau past the Rolex boutique then turned into the *cour d'honneur* of a spectacular *hôtel particulier*. Whereas ordinary houses in Paris shared walls with the surrounding houses, filling the lot on both sides and splitting the depth of the lot with the house on the street behind, a hôtel particulier is usually free standing, and located between an entrance court and a back garden, taking up the full double lot between two streets. With limited real estate in European cities like Paris, a free-standing home was grand indeed.

They entered the charming foyer, and Greg sent his live-in *domestique* silently back to her quarters. They adjourned to the kitchen, which was elegant with updated appliances, white subway tile, marble countertops and cabinets, and an antique stone country basin. Even with the most tasteful table settings at dinner parties, human nature invariably leads us to the comfort of the kitchen.

Greg reached up to the liquor cabinet for a thirty-five-year-old cognac. He poured snifters, and the three clinked. The golden liquid burned all the way down to Louise's belly, and the bittersweet musty bouquet comforted her. She opened her eyes and noticed she was being watched. She muttered, "So, Greg, this is your house?" Vlad glanced at Greg.

"It was my wife's. I . . . inherited it."

"Oh, you're…"

"A widower. Yes."

"I'm sorry." Louise had not talked to Greg about his personal life at dinner, and now she felt like a heel. Vlad knew that Greg's widower status added to his charm. But he didn't begrudge him that. Something about Greg and Vlad gave Louise the impression they had much deeper ties than they let on.

Vlad sensed her curiosity, so he decided to make himself scarce. "Greg, I'll be leaving before you wake up, so could you . . ."

Without missing a beat, Greg went to the den, opened the wall safe and returned with two passports, which he gave to Vladimir. Louise noticed both passports were issued by the United States. However, neither one was dark blue. One was maroon, and the other one was black. They noticed Louise looking at the passports.

"Thanks, buddy," said Vlad.

"You noticed Vlad's passports?" said Greg.

Louise blushed.

"Black U.S. passports are for CIA agents."

She just smiled, thinking Greg was joking.

But Vlad didn't deny it. "Louise, it was a real pleasure meeting you. I'm sure we'll be seeing more of each other." Vlad kissed her on either cheek and disappeared into some corner of the massive house.

There was a scary and exciting mystique about both of them. But there was something about Greg that made her feel safe, while Vlad intimidated her. Greg had that certain combination of strength and vulnerability that widowers possess. Plus, he was extraordinarily handsome. He was about forty-five and in perfect athletic condition. He was the kind of man who always dressed in tailored suits and handmade shirts with French cuffs and a cufflink collection. He seemed to come from somewhere between the past and the present. She noticed a fairly recent portrait of him with his wife on the mantel, showing his hair completely brown, much darker than the striking grey hair he had now.

He noticed her quizzical look. "My hair turned grey all at once when she died."

"Do you always read women's minds?"

"Only the interesting ones."

He kissed her with reserved passion. The way he moved was instinctive, sincere, attentive. Louise wished she could stay, but she stopped him. "Walk me home?"

"Of course."

SIXTEEN

Driven by the new digital age, the global economy was poised to expand at a remarkable pace while simultaneously becoming more accessible. Digitalization opened international borders, and money poured in from developing nations, extremely wealthy individuals, moguls, and oil barons. Cash changed hands and crossed borders free of regulations. Large sums of money were being spent on everything from the Internet to infrastructures in Third World countries. It was a boom time in every industry from big-ticket luxury goods to the entertainment industry. With loosened international banking regulations, money made from the dealing of illegal arms and drugs could easily be laundered through the funding of businesses, movies, music, and the arts in general. Cash was put right back into the economy by big spenders purchasing luxury cars, jewelry, designer clothing, and travel.

Louise began to acclimatize to the BCCI corporate culture. The paid business travel, spacious Paris apartment, Mercedes-Benz sedan with driver on call, and cash were just *ordinary and necessary expenses*. Things were done differently at BCCI than they were at J.P. Morgan, and that was okay. It was an exciting time to live in Paris, which was central to it all. Paris fashion permitted Louise more creative freedom than Wall Street had. She relaxed her corporate attire and Patrician elegance and developed her own unique style. Her cash bonuses allowed her to build a fabulous wardrobe of the latest designers. She had open invitations to fashion week and access to private showings.

Her wardrobe also included some one-of-a-kind elements. Louise had inherited a collection from her great aunt, who had been the costume designer for the legendary film series, *The Thin Man*. Louise possessed many of the actual outfits made for Myrna Loy in the 1930s. Although Louise was thrilled when she received the collection from her aunt, in New York she rarely had the occasion to wear any of the pieces. But in Paris, some of the ensembles perfectly suited her business and social needs.

The overblown fussy style of the 1930s with frills, fancy sleeves, and elaborate hats was not Myrna Loy's style. She managed to stay streamlined and elegant without ever losing her femininity. The simplicity of the garments especially around the neck and shoulders made them fit right in with contemporary fashion. Louise decided to have the entire collection shipped to Paris where street fashion allowed her to take a gutsier approach to style. The stunning classic lines of the collection lent an instantly chic look that perfectly enhanced Louise's classic American features, blonde hair, and green eyes. When she had a meeting with a particularly high-profile client, she would dress in one of the elegant suits for added dramatic effect.

The rest of her work attire was comfortably chic. The weather usually determined her outfit and whether she would call her driver or walk to work, which she preferred. The BCCI office on the Avenue des Champs-Élysées was just a brisk stroll from her apartment. Today she dressed for comfort in a sleek black pencil skirt and turtleneck with flat black Gucci boots and a taupe lightweight cashmere overcoat. Louise stopped for coffee and croissant aux amandes at Le Madrigal café. She arrived by 9:00 a.m. at the office just in time to prepare for her 10:00 meeting with Nazir Chinoy regarding information about the National Bank of Georgia that Abedi had requested.

Louise went to Diana's office for gossip and a cup of her delicious English tea, which she always had brewing. Diana bought only the finest whole leaf teas costing upward of five hundred francs per hundred grams. Louise poured fragrant Earl Grey into her favorite teacup and added a little milk and one sweetener. "I brought you a palmier." Louise handed a flat brown paper bag containing the flaky crispy honey-glazed pastry to Diana.

"You're a life saver."

"No, you are," said Louise, savoring the aromatic tea.

"So?"

"So…" Louise knew what Diana was getting at, but unfortunately, there wasn't much to say. Diana's oxford English accent otherwise known as the *Received Pronunciation* (RP) or the *Queen's English*, along with her reticent nature gave her an irresistible charm. She was thin with billowy blonde hair, blue eyes, and white-toothed, rosy-lipped smile. "So, how are you and Greg?" Diana insisted.

"Ugh. He's so… beautiful, sweet, generous, sexy…"

"And…"

"And… nothing. I'm not sure what it is, but there's just something missing. What is my problem?"

Diana gave her a doe-eyed, dimpled smile. "I told you to pick Vladimir."

"You were probably right," Louise pouted. "Vlad definitely had more… *smolder*. Live and learn. Anyway, so tell me, why does Chinoy want to know about National Bank of Georgia?"

Diana, who had been a legal exec at BCCI for five years, had higher security clearance than Louise. Diana's innocuous appearance belied her vast insider knowledge. "I really can't say."

"You can't say, or you *can't* say?"

"I really don't know. But I do know that Chinoy needs the information for Abedi."

"Working here really puts a damper on our gossip."

"We can talk about Greg." More doe eyes.

"Ugh!" Louise rolled her eyes and left Diana giggling.

Louise got to her desk just as some flowers were being delivered, one dozen yellow roses. She read the card, but she already knew they were from Greg. She glanced at Diana's office and saw her grinning at her. She sniffed the roses and sat down in front of her computer. "Yellow. Figures."

Although the sex with Greg had been perfectly steamy, his cryptic life was tiresome. Louise suspected that Greg's stated profession of commercial airplane salesman was a front for some other line of work. But she enjoyed his company and that was fine for now. She checked her calendar and saw the addition of a business trip in two weeks to meet with the Panama branch manager in Panama. She grabbed her file on the National Bank of Georgia and gave it a once over, then headed to Chinoy's office. He got right down to business.

"What have you got for me on NBG?"

"Here is the due diligence you requested." She handed Chinoy the file she had assembled. BCCI had been hired to broker the acquisition of one U.S. bank—National Bank of Georgia (NBG)—by another U.S. bank, First American Bankshares (FAB). The deal had to be legally done at arm's length. Therefore, neither BCCI nor any of its major shareholders could have ownership in either bank. Louise was instructed to research any potential conflict of interest in the deal.

"What's the take-away?" Chinoy asked, not taking his eyes off the documents as he leafed through the file.

"The good news is First American Bankshares' corporate strategy has been to expand in the United States, so the acquisition of NBG is the opportunity FAB has been seeking. The bad news is that Ghaith Pharaon acquired NBG several years ago, and he is a BCCI shareholder, so BCCI will have to recuse itself from the deal. Also, I'm having trouble tracing the ownership of FAB. But so far none of the investors currently listed as owners of FAB are owners of BCCI or NBG and vice versa."

He stopped leafing through the file. "Okay, thanks. I'll send the file to Abedi. Great work."

Unbeknownst to Louise and Chinoy, BCCI had already acquired both banks. The way BCCI transferred ownership to itself was simple and elegant. It was also a felony under U.S. banking laws. BCCI used front men who would acquire stock in their own names, mostly using money borrowed from BCCI. In fact, BCCI had acquired FAB long ago with the goal of owning a bank in the United States. From December 1977 through February 1978, four front men bought up nearly 20 percent of the stock of FAB's precursor, Financial General, mostly from money loaned by BCCI, violating the law by failing to declare that they were acting as a group. The front men were some of the richest and most powerful people in the Middle East, including Sheikh Zayed bin Sultan al-Nahayan of Abu Dhabi. The owners of First General and the Securities and Exchange Commission sued the men who then signed a consent order with the SEC, agreeing to play by the rules and to make a public offer for Financial General as a group. The front men, who in actuality were acting on behalf of BCCI, retained the firm of Clifford & Warnke as counsel.

Clifford's presence in the 1978 takeover of Financial General quickly tipped the scales in Abedi's favor. After three years of infighting, Financial General had succeeded in forcing up the bid from an opening offer of $15 a share to $28.50. There was still a problem of regulatory approval, but then Clifford received a call from one of the principal stockholders in Financial General, Armand Hammer, requesting a truce. A day and a half later, the Arab investors completed the purchase of Financial General from its current shareholders.

Federal and state banking officials demanded a public hearing during which Adham told the regulators that he and his partners would be passive investors, and that BCCI would exercise no control over Financial General. When Financial General tendered its shares in 1982, it officially renamed itself First American Bankshares (FAB). In spite of Clifford and Altman's assurances to regulators that BCCI would have nothing to do with the management of First American Bankshares, the two would act simultaneously as lead U.S. counsel for BCCI, chief counsel for FAB, and chairman and president of FAB. In 1982 they began traveling as often as once a month to London, mostly to meet alone with Abedi on the subject of the management of First American Bankshares.[18]

In a similar acquisition during the same time period, BCCI was acquiring another U.S. bank, National Bank of Georgia, which was owned by T. Bertram Lance. He had grown up a poor boy who took a job as a bank teller in a small rural town, married the chairman's daughter, became president of the bank, then aligned himself with an ambitious state senator named Jimmy Carter, who assigned him to a cabinet post when he was elected governor. When Carter announced he was leaving the Georgia governor's office in 1974, he supported Lance as his successor. Lance lost that election, and therein began his problems, for he had financed much of that campaign through overdrafts at his bank. In 1975 he became chief executive officer of the National Bank of Georgia and borrowed another $2.6 million to finance his purchase of stock in the bank.

Abedi had found Lance through an appropriately shady connection: former Georgia State Senator Eugene Holley, a man with the distinction of being the first person prosecuted under the Foreign Corrupt Practices Act for paying bribes in the Persian Gulf state of Qatar. Lance told Abedi his National Bank of Georgia, in which he held a 12 percent stake, was looking for a buyer. He also told Abedi that a Washington-based bank holding company—Financial General Bankshares, Inc.—had a unique franchise. While most banks operated within only a single state, Financial General Bankshares owned banks in several states. Lance said that its shareholders had split into armed camps so the time would be ripe for a takeover.

Like Clark Clifford, Lance claimed that he had no inkling that he was being recruited by Abedi for nefarious ends. Yet in the critical years between 1977 and 1979, he became the lynchpin of Abedi's American strategy. He was replaced by others soon enough but not before he had given BCCI the means to enter the U.S. market. He was in most ways typical of Abedi's marks: a well-connected politico with identifiable strengths and weaknesses.

T. Bertram Lance was not only the best friend of President Jimmy Carter; he was also $5 million in debt and watching the value of his stock plummet.

When Abedi's investor Ghaith Pharaon agreed in late 1977 to purchase Lance's National Bank of Georgia, Robert Altman handled the negotiations. Pharaon was the first Arab to acquire control of a billion-dollar U.S. bank. Through him as front man, Abedi acquired Lance's stake for $2.4 million on January 4, 1978, at $20 a share, $4 over the going rate, a handsome price considering no one else wanted it. That same day, Abedi paid off Lance's troublesome $3.4 million loan from the First National Bank of Chicago. He did so by creating a loan in the same amount to Lance from the Cayman Islands, a loan for which there was no paperwork at all.

Louise waited as Chinoy pulled at his eyebrow. "Is everything okay?"

Chinoy looked up from the file. "Yes," he replied, not realizing he had been crumpling the documents as he read through the file. In fact, Chinoy had asked Louise to research the bank for his own purposes.

Nazir Chinoy, who had no direct involvement with the sale of NBG to First American, happened to learn of BCCI's real role in it only by accident when Abedi had come to Paris and lost a briefcase containing key documents regarding the sale. In January 1987, Naqvi and Abedi came to meet with Ghaith Pharaon in Paris and through a communications error, Chinoy was not there to receive them at the airport. They wound up having to take a taxi to BCCI's offices. When Abedi entered the bank, he said, "Where's my briefcase?" All the men looked surprised and realized it had been left in the luggage compartment of the taxi. Chinoy talked to a girl at the airport and offered a 1,000 Franc reward—about $100 at the time—to find it.

The next morning at 9:00 a.m., the taxi driver delivered the briefcase to Chinoy. Naqvi told Chinoy to bring it to London. However, Chinoy was leaving for the Ivory Coast and couldn't go. Naqvi told Chinoy to open the briefcase. When he did, he confirmed the papers, marked National Bank of Georgia, were right to the top. The following week Naqvi and Abedi returned to Paris for the briefcase. Abedi told Naqvi in Urdu, thank God the

National Bank of Georgia deal is done. Then Naqvi signaled to Abedi to keep quiet because Chinoy was in the front seat.[19]

Prior to moving to BCCI Paris, Chinoy had been stationed at the BCCI branch in Nigeria for the first half of the 1980s where he was tasked to establish a second bank for BCCI with the sole purpose of protecting BCCI against the possible expropriation by the government of the first bank. Chinoy had recently been transferred to Paris to set up the Paris branch to loan funds for BCCI investments elsewhere, on a "parked loan" basis under which the Paris office would take no credit risk. Chinoy set it up so that BCCI's Central office in London would broker the loans and would earn interest and commission, and the loans would be *parked* in the Paris branch.

"Would you like me to make a copy of the file?"

Chinoy snapped out of his reverie. "Yes, thank you. Please make a fresh copy to send to Abedi."

"I'll just print a new set of the documents and send them." But Louise hesitated to leave.

"Is there something else?"

"Well, I just saw on my calendar that I'm scheduled to go to Panama in two weeks."

"Yes. We need you there."

"It's just after the holidays."

"Of course, you can book the flight home first and go to Panama from there. The company will cover it."

"Thank you."

Louise returned to her office and prepared the file to send to Abedi. The phone rang, startling her. She let the call go to messaging and called the travel agent to book her trip.

SEVENTEEN

Louise booked the trip to Panama through New York to spend the Christmas holiday in Westchester County. Her father insisted on picking her up at Newark Airport. He greeted her at the gate with a big burly hug.

"Let me look at you," he said, locking eyes with her in the way that fathers do that would make most girls of any age tear up. "What? Not even a quivering lower lip? I must be losing it." Louise's training in international client negotiations had given her a somewhat thicker skin than when she was younger. However, she was far from invulnerable. "At least I don't see any sign of corruption in those pretty eyes."

"Daddy, you raised me better than that. Besides, there's no way my integrity could be compromised living under the sanctity of French socialism."

He put one arm around her and took her bag with the other. "A father can never be too careful." They walked out toward the parking garage.

"Actually, I think it *is* possible to be *too* careful, Daddy." She watched a departing plane glide up toward the sky, aglow through the winter clouds like Santa's sleigh. "But I don't mind. And for the record, you haven't lost it in the least." She leaned her head on her father's shoulder, her nose red and runny from stifled tears.

They got into the car and took off down the snow-banked pastoral roads. "Did I mention how proud I am of you?"

"Only once so far today, Daddy."

"Well, I apologize for my laxity."

"Laxity. I like that one."

"You don't see that one much on the *New York Times* crossword."

"I've never seen it on the crossword. Nicely done."

"So where are you headed after this?" Louise feigned a look of being clueless. "Come on, I know you plan your trips home around business."

"I have a meeting in Panama with the head of the branch there."

"Panama!"

"Don't worry, Daddy."

"Will you at least make time to see Michael before you go?"

"I fly out of New York so maybe I'll give him a call. Although at my going-away party, he was too busy talking to you to pay attention to me."

"He'd love to see you. I don't think he's quite over you."

Louise and Michael had met when she was an undergrad. Michael was four years older than Louise. Shortly after graduating from West Point with honors, Michael was recruited as an agent for the FBI while Louise was still in grad school. They broke up after she graduated due to conflicting goals.

Michael's father was a Spanish journalist and historian, and his much younger mother was a Chilean ambassador. His parents had moved to the United States not long after the Spanish Civil war, so Michael spoke four languages from birth. Michael's father, who was fifteen years older than his mother, died when he was twenty-one. Michael's father was a "Republicano" supported by the Communist Soviet Union and stood against the "Nationales" who received the support of Fascist Italy and Nazi Germany. In the aftermath of the Spanish Civil war, all right-wing parties were fused into the state party of General Francisco Franco's fascist Nationale regime.

With the United States heavily anti-communist, major American corporations including Texaco, GM, and Ford Motors had greatly assisted the Nationalist rebels with a constant supply of trucks, tires, machine tools, and fuel. The war had increased international tensions in Europe in the lead-up to World War II and had largely been seen as a proxy war between the Communist Soviet Union and fascist states of Italy and Germany. The Spanish Civil war had been dubbed "the first media war," with several writers and journalists wanting their work "to support the cause." Michael's father had been one of the foreign correspondents and writers covering the war. Other correspondents included Ernest Hemingway, Martha Gelhorn, and George Orwell.

Like most civil wars, the Spanish Civil war became notable for the atrocities committed on both sides of the conflict. The victorious Nationales had persecuted the Republicanos, forcing Michael's parents to flee to France. At the end of World War II, his parents moved to the United States. In the world of espionage and double agents, their communist leanings actually made them valuable to the United States. By expatriating and walking a fine line of activism and cooperation, American intelligence welcomed their service. Ever grateful to the United States for their new life, Michael's parents had instilled in him a great respect and loyalty for the U.S. government. Michael became an American citizen as a child at the same time his parents were naturalized. He grew up American and, aside from his perfect fluency in Spanish, Italian, and French, he gave off no hint of being anything other than American. George Moscow had gotten used to the idea having him as a son.

George had been sitting at a stop sign, watching Louise deep in thought when she felt his stare. "Promise you'll call him," he said. "Maybe Michael can talk some sense into you and get you to stop requesting missions to exotic locations. The world is not what it used to be. There have been terrorist bombings in the London Tube and Paris department stores. Who knows where next?"

"No promises, but I'll think about it."

"Fair enough." He drove the remaining two blocks home, and she continued gazing as they passed the elaborate Christmas lights decorating every single front yard until they arrived at their ranch. By choice, George commuted to New York City. Their ranch, which was on ten acres, had been built by his grandfather. After having been away for so long, Louise found the place breathtaking. She hadn't realized how beautiful it was because it had become familiar. She and her father looked at each other and smiled. They made the mental transition from business to family mode, and there would be no more talk of work in front of her mother.

Louise trudged up the walk and opened the front door, stepping out of the snowy cold and into the warm rustic living room with logs burning in the fireplace, country farmhouse décor, and a sparkling Christmas tree. Arriving from a completely different culture intensified that old Christmas feeling she always got coming home for the holidays. The scents and sounds were a shock to her sense-memory, and she was propelled back to another moment in the past that felt as real as being there: a flash of a familiar face, a table, a lamp, and then it was gone, like déjà vu, only more vivid. She breathed in, then out, and felt her father's arm around her shoulder. "Welcome home, sweetheart."

"Thanks, Daddy."

Mary peeked out the swinging kitchen door, eyes wide and ears perked up for a second until she saw Louise, then a beaming smile lit up her face. Simultaneously pulling oven mitts off her hands and brushing flour from her apron, she rushed to Louise for a long hug. "Louise May Moscow, how we've missed you!" Mary began fussing, and, in a single swirling movement, she waved for George to take Louise's bags to her bedroom, removed her coat, grabbed her arm, and led her into the kitchen. "We're just so happy you were able to be here for the holidays." Louise sat on the stool at the kitchen counter. Mary poured some hot spiced tea with a hint of brandy. "Just relax and don't do a thing. You must be exhausted from the trip and your high-powered career."

"I flew first class, Mom, and working in France doesn't require the kind of pressure we have here. My job is almost too cushy."

"Don't be modest. Your father is so proud of you. He brags at every opportunity. Why just yesterday..." Mary was interrupted by a knock at the back door, which gave Louise that surreal feeling, like a premonition that arrives a second too late. The door jutted open a few inches, the sound of snow being kicked off boots against the doorjamb, then the door slowly opened wider, and in walked Michael. Louise's heart fluttered for a split second.

"Michael!" Mary exclaimed. "What a surprise!" Michael raised his arms laden with a basket of apples toward Mary. Then out of the corner of his eye, he glimpsed Louise, who wore an expression of doubt and suspicion.

"Lulu," Michael said, genuinely surprised.

"Michael," Louise shot back.

"I came by to drop off some apples."

"I ran into Michael's mother in the city yesterday," explained Mary, "and I mentioned to her that we would love some of the delicious apples from their orchard for our holiday pies." The 'city' always referred to New York City. Mary and Michael's mother had become friends over the years. They used to shop together and probably still did. Michael's family home was up in Stamford, Connecticut, so they would sometimes meet in the middle. They still frequented the same places in the city, so it was plausible that they could run into each other. But Louise was still suspicious.

Michael kissed Mary on the cheek and placed the basket on the counter. "Mom asked me to deliver these with her best Christmas wishes." Michael was tall with dark brown hair, dark eyes, and an irresistible dimple when he smiled. "You are a darling. Well, since you're here, sit, have some delicious spiced tea." Mary showed Michael to a stool at the counter next to Louise and poured him a steaming mug. "I'll have to make apple cider now you brought so many apples."

Louise and Michael clinked cups in an awkward toast simultaneously saying, "Merry Christmas." They drank, grateful for the jolt of brandy underlying the comforting deliciousness.

Michael leaned in close to Louise. "It's great to see you, Lulu." He held there for a second, flustering her, then kissed her innocently on the cheek.

"It's an unexpected pleasure for me too."

"Well, I've got a few more deliveries to make," he said, getting up and turning to Mary. "Thank you for the lovely spiced tea." Then to Louise, "I'll be seeing you again soon."

"Merry Christmas."

"Please thank your mother for us," insisted Mary. "I'll be sending a pie over to your house before Christmas."

"We look forward to it!" Then with a wave of his hand, Michael was out the door. "Ho, ho, ho! Merry Christmas!" His words trailed off.

As though on cue, George entered the kitchen. "I thought I heard a man's voice."

"You just missed Michael! If you hurry, you can catch him," said Mary.

"I'll see him soon enough," George said. "Your room is all ready, Louise. I'm sure you'd like to get some rest?"

"Thanks, Daddy. You're like the wise old man inside my head." Louise kissed her father on the cheek and gave Mary a hug, then went off to her room.

EIGHTEEN

Louise bolted upright in her bed. It was dusk or was it dawn? She wasn't sure where she was or even what day it was. But she had a strange feeling. Her daily meditation had made her dreams more vivid, almost lucid. Meditation cleared her psyche better than any number of years of psychotherapy could have done. Her thinking was becoming sharper and less encumbered by doubts and fears. However, another result was she sometimes felt disoriented as though she could be almost anywhere in time or space.

She focused and got her bearings, then studied the bedside clock and decided it was eight in the morning. She picked up the phone, dialed, and listened. Then she changed her mind and quickly hung up. Although Louise's new Parisian life was ideal, she had no family there, no old friends, and no one who really understood her. At times she felt ungrounded. That and the cultural adjustments made her feel vulnerable, disconnected, as though she were watching herself, like an out-of-body experience. She thought if she could spend a little time with Michael, she might regain some equilibrium, at least temporarily. That would be her excuse to see him anyway. She decided to meet with Michael in New York City before her flight to Panama. She would give him a call tomorrow and make a plan.

For now, she threw on her robe and went downstairs toward the aromas of coffee, bacon, and maple syrup. With the time difference, she had gained six hours, so she was right back where she started. She had taken an evening flight and arrived in time to go to sleep the same evening and wake up in the morning as though nothing had changed except for where she was. It was Christmas Eve, and she hadn't made any plans, but she knew her parents had. She was just happy to be home to rest and regroup.

Louise noticed a freshly baked apple pie on the windowsill. "Mom, do you really have a picture-perfect hot apple pie cooling on the windowsill?"

"Lulu! What are you doing up? I thought you'd sleep in late the way the Europeans do."

"That's not an accurate generalization, Mom. I believe only the artists sleep in late. The workingman wakes up early and hits the café for an espresso and shot of red wine."

"Well, I don't have any red wine open, but I'll pour you a nice cup of hot coffee and make you a stack of pancakes with bacon layered between and maple syrup on the side, just the way you like it."

"My favorite: layer pan-cake." Mary served it up and Louise carved a perfect pie piece out of the buttery stack, revealing the layers of bacon between pancakes, and poured maple syrup on each bite as she ate it. The perfect combination of contrasting flavors, textures, and temperatures: hot buttery spongy pancake, crisp bacon, and sticky syrup, salty-sweet. One could argue that France had the best cheese, bread, and wine. But you could never convince Louise that there was better breakfast or dessert than in the States. You couldn't find this breakfast in Paris. And delicate French pastries are delicious, but to Louise there was nothing better than homemade strawberry-rhubarb pie or peach blueberry cobbler. "Masterpiece, Mom."

"I'm glad my little girl is happy. We didn't know you were coming home for Christmas until a few days ago, so we didn't make much of a plan for this evening."

"That's fine by me. I'll be happy sipping hot toddies in front of the fire, waiting for Santa."

"That can be arranged."

Mary was the perfect mom. She truly enjoyed taking care of her family. Who better to be a mom than someone who loved to cook and decorate her home? If Mary hadn't been completely content taking care of her husband and daughter, Louise was certain she could have been a gourmet chef. Everything Mary made was so completely and perfectly inspired: the seasonings, the balance and quality of ingredients, and the *cuisson*. Mary was also a creative genius using objects to decorate that most people would never think of using. She once found a chair in the garbage that she buried in the back yard so that the lawn grew over it forming a chair made of grass. It was so comfortable she continued to add pieces of old furniture until there was an entire living room made of grass in the yard. She even strategically planted flowers and vegetables to decorate the outdoor space, burying a pot on a table under the grass and planting flowers in the pot.

"We invited a few people to come by, so I'm roasting a turkey. We don't even know if anyone will come. We left it an open invitation, so they wouldn't feel obligated. But you know how that goes."

Yes, Louise knew how that went.

When Louise was growing up, the family house was where people could always find an open door. Not only because the family had been part of the community for three generations, but also because Mary was from the Midwest and that was just the way things were done. They never locked the doors, windows, or cars. Everyone knew Mary would be there if they came by, and if she wasn't, she would be back soon. However, the neighborhood had vastly changed since their family had first settled. It was now much more affluent, and new arrivals were petitioning to make it a gated community. Mary and George were against that because they felt no one should put a gate around nature. To them, it would be like having to get permission every time they wanted to come and go. But it was a losing battle, and it would be only a matter of time before they would be fenced into their own property.

Louise hadn't done any Christmas shopping because there was really no one to buy gifts for except her parents. She was an only child so no nieces or nephews, just aunts and uncles and cousins back in the Midwest. She had offered bottles of fine wine to her friends in Paris, and she and Greg were no longer seriously dating so no gift exchange there. "I think I'll go into town and do some shopping."

"Don't bother shopping for pa and me. We don't need a thing." Louise had never noticed how strong her mom's Midwest accent was before, another culture shock. After spending time with Mary, Louise's Midwest accent would tinge her speech. But having taken so many foreign languages classes, Louise's diction had become a mastery of phonetics. For each language, she was taught to speak according to standard rules of pronunciation. Therefore, phonetics was so ingrained in her language skills that it was impossible for her to pronounce any word without using the standard rules.

"Is there anything you need me to pick up?"

"We have everything we need. Your pa is picking up a few last-minute things, and he'll be right back."

"Well, if you think of anything call me on my cell."

"Call you on what?"

Louise wrote down the number of her Mobira Cityman 150, Nokia's latest mobile phone. She took it out of the pocket of her robe and showed it to Mary. "Call me."

"Wow! What is that? Some kind of new space phone?"

"It's the latest technology, Mom."

"Wait, let me call you now. I want to see that thing in action." Mary picked up the handset of their old Bakelite rotary phone, which still worked like a charm, and dialed the number. "There sure are a lot of numbers to dial. We might have to get one of those push-button phones." She listened in the earpiece and heard Louise's phone start ringing a loud high-tech ring tone.

Louise answered, looking at Mary, "Hello?"

"Lulu, is that you?"

"Yes, Mom, it's me. Okay?" They hung up.

"See? Call me if you need anything." Louise headed upstairs to shower and dress. When Louise came back down, George was sitting at the table, drinking coffee and reading the paper. "Good morning, Daddy."

"Good morning, sweetheart. Heading off to see your girlfriends?"

"No, just going shopping." Although Louise would have loved to see Renée and JoAnn again, she was in town only for two nights. Plus they were married with children and home preparing for Santa to arrive. "Can you think of anything I should pick up?"

"No, we have everything we need. But we have your mobile phone number if we think of anything." George was teasing her, but she just smiled and kissed him on the cheek.

"Like you don't have one for work," she whispered.

"Don't tell your mom. She couldn't handle it."

"Should I take the pickup?"

"No, take the Saab. It's a little slick out there."

"See you in a little while."

"See you when you get back."

Louise wasn't sure where she was going. She was still jetlagged and had that spacey feeling. Taking a drive in an old familiar place would bring her back down to Earth. Her cell phone rang, and she pulled over to answer it. "Hello?"

"Is that you, sweetheart?"

"Yes, Mom, it's me."

"Okay, just checking."

"See you in a little while, Mom." As soon as she hung up the phone it rang again, and she answered. "Mom, I'm trying to drive."

"Lulu?"

She recognized Michael's voice. "Oh, hi, Michael. Sorry, I thought you were my mom."

"Oh. Ha. Um. Is this a bad time?"

"No, actually I'm just going out for a drive. What are you up to?"

"Just running errands for my mom."

"Wow, an FBI agent running errands. Talk about overqualified."

"It keeps us on our toes."

"Right. So, what's up?"

"Want to grab lunch or something?" Michael asked.

"That would be great. Then I won't have to leave early for my flight."

"What?"

"Never mind. The usual place?"

"Yes, see you at noon?"

"How about noon thirty?" Louise said.

"Noon thirty? What the heck is that?"

"You know, half past noon."

"Oh. I get it, Franglais. Cute. Okay, see you then."

NINETEEN

Louise was looking forward to meeting at their old spot, the Grand Central Oyster Bar, located in the basement of Grand Central Station. It is an old-world architectural wonder, a 10,000-square-foot, custom-tiled structure built in the underground subway in 1913 that reminded Louise of ancient Roman baths. The thriving seafood restaurant in the subway has the same hundred-year-old charm. Louise slid onto the stool next to Michael at the oyster bar and selected her usual made-to-order New England clam chowder. Michael was already enjoying his usual half-dozen fresh oysters. The short-order cook never missed a beat as he dipped ladles into various steaming vats and mimed tipping his hat as he served it up.

Michael picked up his plate and their two shots of vodka. "Shall we?" Louise picked up her bowl of chowder, and they moved to the arched Guastavino-tiled dining room. The four-hundred-and-forty-seat dining room overflowed with patrons. The couple managed to find relative quiet in a remote corner.

"I've missed this place," said Louise.

"With all your fine Parisian venues of degustation?"

"It's not better, just different."

"Different good?"

"Different fine."

"So, what's on your mind, Lulu?"

"You called me remember?"

"No, you called me."

"No, you called me."

"But you were sending me a telepathic message to call you."

"No, I wasn't!" He gave her a look that she couldn't fight. "Okay, maybe inadvertently. I guess I felt bad about being so cold toward you yesterday when you brought all those apples to mom. But I thought you and she had set it up."

"I don't know why you don't trust me after everything we've been through. Aren't we passed all the bad stuff?"

"Are we? I mean I left you for a career. Not very nice of me."

"Come on. A lesser man would be upset, even angry. But I'm a trained professional," said Michael.

"You are a trained professional in heartbreak?"

"Aren't I?"

"Okay, so we are friends," Louise consented.

"Friends forever as far as I'm concerned."

"I feel like a heel. Here I was acting suspicious, but then I saw the look on your face, and you seemed just as surprised to see me as I was to see you."

"But I was glad to see you," said Michael.

"That was obvious too."

"Well, I've been worried about you living all alone over there in Paris. Is everything okay with work?" He had always been able to read her mind.

"My work? Why do you ask? Do you know something I don't know? Does the FBI know something I don't know?"

"I'm just being a good listener."

She had concerns about work that she couldn't share with her father. He would be overly protective, and she just wanted a sounding board for now. "No, it's a well-run company. I've learned a lot and I have amazing clients."

"Do you have access to a lot of sensitive information?"

"The corporate controls are pretty robust," said Louise. "It would be next to impossible to hack into the system. Only top administrators have access to client files. I know only what is directly related to my clients and only on a need-to-know basis."

"So, you don't have any real knowledge of what your clients or your superiors are doing." Michael watched her reaction and registered a glint in her eye, but she covered well. He changed the subject. "So, what's with this CIA agent, Vladimir Egger?"

This time she didn't conceal her reaction. Louise glanced around, scanning the bustling dining room, worried that someone was listening. But, even if someone wanted to eavesdrop on their conversation, with or without a parabolic listening device, it would have been impossible over the din of clanking dishes, loud conversations, and rumble of trains. "You're really not helping me here," she said.

"Oh, so you do need my help?"

Louise took a deep breath. "I'm just reaching out to an old friend who has known me for a long time and can reassure me that I am still me. It's very disorienting to live in another culture. How do you do it?"

"I don't," said Michael. "I have never lived an extended length of time in another country, not even when I was very young."

"But you speak several languages and adjust from one culture to another without even thinking."

"So do you."

"I know, I'm just... concerned about the impact of living in a foreign country on my psyche. I read that it is common for a person relocating to a new country to experience mild to severe culture shock."

Louise was referring to a common phenomenon. The trauma of living in a different culture could bring on psychological effects from a feeling of uncertainty and alienation to paranoia. It is even widely believed that visiting certain cultures can provoke psychosis and in extreme cases, delirium. For example, since the 1960s, India had been blamed for mental breakdowns by many of those who flocked there to experience hallucinogens. People from age eighteen to thirty-five are considered especially susceptible mentally, particularly if they have pre-existing conditions. It's called the 'Indian Syndrome.' That term, which came from the 'Paris Syndrome,' has been known to afflict some Japanese tourists visiting Paris. It can cause depression, paranoia, and hallucination. For instance, some have claimed to hear the voice of the Virgin Mary on visiting the Notre-Dame Cathedral.

Some studies have been conducted on causes of why westerners are attracted by India and, once there, are potentially driven crazy by some invisible force.[20] Although materially poor for the last two centuries, India has an inexhaustible wealth of spirituality. The Himalayas are a high-mountain abode for yogis and swamis. 'Spiritual Skyscrapers' may be encountered on any roadside. The characteristic feature of Indian culture has long been the search for ultimate truth and the disciple-guru relationship.[21] Culture shock works both ways and is not a phenomenon restricted to travelers to India or France alone. Anyone visiting foreign lands can be so acutely overwhelmed by their new environment that it impairs their mental balance.

"You're fine. The fact that you are aware of the culture shock means that you are controlling it. This is not about culture shock. Your work is making you ill."

"I have no one I can talk to," Louise admitted. "The company has strict rules. If I told my father, he would go nuts."

Michael took her hands in his and looked into her eyes. "Do you remember that time right after you graduated college, and I got recruited to the FBI? We got drunk and had that absurd conversation about international espionage. We even came up with an emergency code word…"

"Foliage," Louise said. It was one of those moments of psychic connection and pent-up emotion. They both burst into uncontrollable laughter. "We said if either one of us communicated our *code word* in any way, it meant we should meet at our designated secret location…"

"At twelve noon after the transmission thereof!"

"You taught me the protocol tactics for losing a tail, and how to ditch my car and take the train to our designated meeting place. Remember?" Louise said.

"We drove and took the train for two hours!"

"Then we couldn't remember where we left the car!" Louise laughed so hard that people started to look at them.

"Our code word was so obvious."

"I know! How corny!"

Then Michael became serious. "But, at the same time, romantic."

Louise snorted and giggled softly through teary eyes. "Yes. Very romantic." Then the emotion flooded out. Louise stared at the glass of wine the waiter had just placed in front of her. A tear barreled down her cheek and splashed onto her hands folded in her lap, then another, and another. The tears felt hot and heavy as though composed of mercury.

Michael placed his finger under her chin and lifted it. "Lulu, I'm here for you, no matter what. Remember that. Remember our code word. And don't hesitate to use it."

Michael walked her to her car. He had an apartment in the city where they could be alone, but he didn't suggest it. Instead he kissed her on the cheek and watched her drive away.

Louise drove home, feeling more centered albeit sexually frustrated. The drive down the snowy tree-lined roads at sunset was peaceful. She kept a watchful eye out for wildlife as she took in the scenery. White tail and Sika deer were known to dart out in front of traffic. The scenery seemed magnified after being away for so long. Everything looked new and more defined. The blanket of white snow glowed with the reflection of the golden red sunset. The same groves still defined the fields and orchards, but new details emerged that she had never noticed. As she passed the familiar grove of trees by the river she had known all her life, there was something different about it. Then she noticed two moving black objects. She pulled over and got out of the car.

They were American black bears, native to New Jersey, living in the forests throughout the state prior to European settlement. The black bear population declined throughout the 1800s. In 1953 the New Jersey Fish and Game Council classified the black bear as a game animal to protect it from indiscriminate killing. Since then, the black bear population had been increasing. In all her years living in Edison, Louise had never seen a black bear. Now she stood on the side of the road, watching a mother bear and her cub playing in the snow along the riverbank in Westchester County.

T W E N T Y

George was sprinkling salt on the driveway and sidewalk in anticipation of guests when Louise pulled in. "Did you see the black bears, Daddy?"

"Oh, yes, they were sighted last week in the grove by the creek. Mother and cub."

"They're so cute!"

"Sure, four hundred to six hundred pounds of cute."

"They won't come around here, right?"

"No, just don't go walking around in the wilderness, that's all."

"What time is dinner?"

"People will be showing up around seven. Not a sit-down dinner, just some food out on the table buffet style."

"Okay. I'll take a nap, so wake me, okay?"

"Sure, honey. Get some rest." She started to go into the house when George said, "How's Michael?"

"Daddy!"

"You did see him though, right?"

"Yes. He's fine. okay? Are you happy?"

"Yep."

Louise peeked in the kitchen. "Hi, Mom."

"Hi, sweetheart. How was your day?"

"Great. Need any help?"

"No, everything's done. Just need to get the turkey out of the oven in an hour and put the ham in."

"A turkey *and* a ham? How many people are coming?"

"What we don't eat, we'll have for leftovers."

"I'm going to take a little power nap."

"Power nap? Huh, I like that."

"See you in a little while. Wake me if I oversleep."

"Will do."

The sounds of Christmas music and laughter woke her. It was dark, making it more difficult for her to wake up fully. She breathed into the pillow, soaking in the comfort. Who would really miss her if she stayed in bed? After all, these weren't her friends. They were neighbors who all had completely different lives from hers. They were very nice people, but they simply had nothing in common. They would all ask her where she lived, and when she would answer "Paris," they would ask "Paris, France?" Then she would give her assessment of what it's like living in Paris.

Louise disliked talking about herself. She enjoyed talking about financial markets and business. But when it came essentially to giving an interview for the sole purpose of dispensing knowledge about her personal life, she was against it on principle. Partly, it was because she was protective by nature but more because her training taught her never to give out any more information than necessary. She was taught never to engage in conversations with a taxi driver or other strangers. Never ask someone a personal question because that invites questions in return. These were security tricks that Michael had taught her years ago. "You never know to whom you're speaking," he told her. That always got her thinking when she entered a cab or when a stranger began asking her questions.

There was a knock at the door and George opened it. "Are you okay, honey?"

"Hi, Dad. Yes, I'm just tired. I guess the jetlag hit me."

"Well, stay in bed if you're not up to it."

"No, I'll come down. But I don't really feel very sociable."

"Don't worry; it's just light conversation. No busy-bodies."

"Okay, be down in a minute."

George was right. The guests were mellow, down-to-earth local friends who enjoyed each other's company. The conversation never went beyond Christmas gift ideas, recipes, knitting, or sports. The fire crackled, and Louise sipped homemade hot apple cider with rum. The laughter subsided and the guests left. As Louise headed upstairs, Mary set cookies and milk out for Santa Claus.

TWENTY-ONE

Louise squeezed the small stuffed pig Santa Claus brought her and gazed out the window as the plane took off. Flying always felt like time travel. When visiting family and friends after being away for any length of time, she tended to resume previous conversations right where they had left off. Therefore, it felt like she was traveling *back* in time. At the same time, when she returned to family and friends after a long absence, the physical changes that took place in people and in the surroundings during her absence gave the impression of having traveled to the *future*. Both effects made her feel younger, relative to where she went and whom she saw. The plane transported her to another place in time while she still remained the same.

The flight from JFK to Panama City was approximately five hours and fifteen minutes. Louise had kept clothing at her family home, so she had packed only a carry-on bag. Women, whose clothing is usually smaller, have an inherent advantage over men when it comes to packing. In one carry-on she fit her charcoal grey stretch poly-wool blend suit, a couple classic blouses and tops, one light cashmere sweater, one pair of jeans, a Hermès scarf, one dress from her Myrna Loy collection (just in case), one pair of panties per day, and one pair of dress shoes in addition to the comfortable shoes she wore on the plane, and she was set.

Her plane landed at about 10:45 a.m., and a town car was waiting to take her to the hotel. Her driver, Jesus, provided by BCCI Panama, doubled as a security guard and would always be close by. Her meeting with the attorney of an important Columbian client was scheduled for noon the next day, so she could enjoy a day at the hotel spa and dinner with her old friend, Peter Edwards. He was an English ex-patriot who was one of the world's most prominent dealers of antique violins. After years of schlepping the priceless objects, he had retired to his idea of paradise—Panama City.

Peter was an old family friend. As Louise grew up, Peter became a mentor to her. He offered Louise objective career advice and introduced her to many affluent clients and colleagues, making her comfortable with the elite class. At one point, her college girlfriend, Suzanne Clark, dated Peter's friend Paul Childs, a first violinist for the Chicago Symphony Orchestra. Louise had introduced them when Paul came to New York on tour.

However, Suzanne was the polar opposite of Louise. Suzanne majored in English literature and was an aspiring writer. She came from a family of English teachers who were avid patrons of the arts and had season tickets to the opera, ballet, and New York Philharmonic. Suzanne's style was edgy steam-punk chic. She wore trendy boutique and thrift-shop treasures, mixing lace and linen with spikes and boots. She wasn't a classic beauty, but she was sexy and skilled at making the most of her features. Her long, wavy teased hair cascaded down her tall thin frame to dramatic effect. Her charcoal liner enhanced her piercing blue eyes and drew attention away from her prominent pointed nose. The way she painted her full lips red and applied a pale base to her skin gave her a Kewpie Doll quality.

Louise, on the other hand, was focused and driven to succeed in the world of finance. She came from a traditional family with a stay-at-home mother and a government-employed father. She was inspired by Suzanne's fashion tricks but honed her own more classic sense of style. Suzanne's long-distance relationship with Paul didn't last, and after the girls' disastrous college trip to Paris, Louise lost touch with Suzanne. Those days were long behind her, and she wondered where Suzanne was today.

Louise wore the Myrna Loy dress and pinned her tousled hair into a relaxed up-do. The town car pulled up to Peter's Panama home where he was waiting outside for her like a cuddly court jester. His rosy-lipped smile, fleshy cheeks, crystal blue eyes, and short cropped salt and pepper curls always made her happy to see him. She reached up and locked her hands around his neck, pressing her cheek into his chest.

"Moscow-ski. You *are* a sight for sore eyes." She curtsied, showing off her dress. "Wow, smashing. I'm afraid I just popped on these old rags."

"You look perfect. The tropics suit you, Pete-ski." Peter dressed with the casual elegance of a retiree living in the tropics, in lightweight white linen shirt and beige linen pants and espadrilles.

"Come on. Let's have a drink." They entered his open-plan villa, which overlooked the Gulf of Panama. The architecture was Mediterranean with terra cotta floors and stucco walls. The interior décor was an eclectic combination of beautiful locally crafted rustic wood furniture, exotic fabrics, exquisite antiques, and comfortable sofas. Louise walked into the center of the vast living room where breezes blew through windowless arches, cooling the room. She spun, letting her dress flare out. It was white silk with large floral print that tied in a bow on one shoulder.

"Here, this will complete the picture." Peter handed her a glass of champagne.

Louise closed her eyes and sipped. "How ingenious of you to move to Panama to retire. It has all the refinement of Europe but with sea air."

"And without the pretense," Peter said. "Oh, take a gander at my wine collection." They walked toward the kitchen, down three steps and opened a heavy wooden door to enter the wine cellar. He selected a bottle and dusted it off. "To start, a bottle of the Châteauneuf-du-Pape 1988, in your honor, my darling."

"Côtes du Rhône, my favorite."

"It's become quite the grape juice around here. Good value that, as well. Will do moreish after we've put paid to this one. You have a driver, don't you?"

"Of course."

Another bottle caught his attention, and he plucked it from the rack. "In that case, we'll need this 1976 Lafitte. Fitting bicentennial for my American beauty."

"I love it." They adjourned to the terrace dining area.

"So, Lulu, Paris? The protégée surpasses the mentor?"

"You flatter me."

"I immodestly take credit for most of your success, Moscow-ski," Peter said. For reasons unknown to Louise, Peter had decided to add 'ski' after her name, perhaps in honor of her half-Polish bloodline on her mother's side. Louise loved it.

"Rightly so, and I've got lots more to learn."

"At your service," Peter said, raising his glass. "Shall we dine and talk business?" They sat at the table, and Peter's domestic served several courses of homemade local cuisine.

"What are you keeping busy with these days?" asked Louise.

"Darling, they simply wouldn't let me quit."

"Violins? But I thought you retired."

"Only publicly. Privately, there is demand that only I can fill."

"And to think I had romantic visions of you writing your memoirs and picking up the cello again."

"Tendonitis precludes both, I'm afraid. Instead I have a very clever plan. But I'll need your help."

"Count me in."

"You haven't heard the plan."

"Okay, what's the plan?"

"The plan, my dear, is to set up a company in the Caymans for my very exclusive business."

"Then I can help. My boss will be pleased I've returned with a prestigious new client," said Louise.

"Glorious. That was part of the plan."

Two hours later, they had polished off two bottles of wine, and Louise found herself once again traveling through time. "When I was twenty-two, you put me on a plane to Chicago, schlepping a Stradivarius. The bow alone was worth $80,000."

"Very cost effective and more reliable than some diddling courier."

"You're welcome. Any time."

"Well, since you offered." Peter grinned slyly.

"Uh, oh."

Peter produced a violin case from under the table as if by magic.

"Oh, Pete-ski."

"How about a lovely port?" he offered.

"Just a small one; I'm here on business and need to be fairly lucid tomorrow."

Peter opened an aged port and filled small glasses as she ate the last spoonful of caramel flan.

Peter walked her to her car. "I'll call you when you're back in Paris to arrange delivery of that fiddle."

"Should I handcuff it to my wrist?"

"I trust you. It's only worth about $1 million. Irreplaceable."

"I'll guard it with my life."

"That won't be necessary. Cheers, darling."

TWENTY-TWO

Louise was jittery as she sat in the waiting room of the law offices of Hector Vargas, her client's attorney, absorbing the spectacular view over the Gulf of Panama and its islands. The minimalist elegance of the room reminded her of the graceful Italian décor of a charming hotel where she and Michael had stayed in Venice. Sleek olive wood and leather furniture, breezes billowing long voile curtains that tickled hardwood floors. She took a deep breath and drew positive energy from her surroundings, channeling it inward. By the time the paralegal ushered her into the attorney's office, she felt calm and relaxed.

"Señorita Moscow." Vargas smiled with Latin charm, shaking her hand. "How gracious of you to come all the way to Panama during the holidays."

"We are always happy to accommodate such an important client, Señor Vargas."

"We hope you can accommodate your important client by releasing his accounts."

"We should be able to work something out. As I understand it, the U.S. government has frozen our client's account in another BCCI branch due to a pending investigation," Louise said.

"The U.S. loves their investigations."

"It's fairly routine. I will broker the release of funds in the form of a loan to our client from the BCCI Paris branch that he will repay in full, once the funds with the other branch are released from the investigation. However, due to the international intricacies, we will have to assess a fee."

"BCCI is a bank. That would fall within generally accepted banking practices."

"The fee is 10 percent, if that sounds reasonable to you."

"Yes, $250,000 should cover the legal fees and your travel expenses to Panama, I expect," he said with no trace of sarcasm. "Drink?" She indicated no. Vargas went to the wet bar and poured a glass from a $5,000 bottle of

Cognac.

Louise had had enough experience dealing with BCCI clients to know how to get through an irregular negotiation process without blowing the deal. "I have the documents already drafted." Louise smiled warmly, removing the file from her briefcase and handing them to Vargas. "We should be able to get this taken care of right away."

Vargas was no pushover and intended to get as much customer service as possible. "I'm sure my client will find the terms acceptable. I shall review them today and meet you for dinner tonight with fully executed documents, provided there are no major modifications."

"I look forward to it. I'll leave you to your work." Louise turned to leave.

"My car will pick you up at 7:00 to bring you to my place."

"My car will drop me at the restaurant of your choosing at 7:30."

"Very well. La Casa del Marisco."

"Wonderful, I've heard about that place and am looking forward to it."

Louise sat in the steam room to relieve some of the stress from the meeting as well as the lingering hangover. She dressed in a simple but chic black dress from a local designer's shop. She put her hair in a relaxed up-do somewhere between sexy and businesslike. One of the things Abedi appreciated about her was her ability to walk the fine line between business and pleasure.

Jesus drove her to La Casa del Marisco. "Here we are, miss. I'll be right outside." Louise studied the outside of the restaurant, which looked like a private villa fitted with a fortified iron gate.

"Is this Vargas's personal residence?"

"No, I know this place very well. You will enjoy it," Jesus assured her.

Louise entered, and a woman immediately escorted her to Vargas's private table where he was already seated. Vargas stood and held her chair for her while the woman poured her a Chilean Syrah. La Casa del Marisco was exclusive and private. Only politicians and wealthy businessmen were granted reservations, which explained why the prices were extraordinarily high. The cuisine was authentic Spanish from Pay Basque region. A man and woman lavished attention on them, serving them tapas and preparing their table for the meal.

"Is this your restaurant?"

"No, the man and woman serving us are close personal friends of mine. They are also the owners."

"It's charming."

"Food and wine are my passions." They clinked glasses, and she tasted the wine, which, after last night, she was pleased had just the right balance of structure, fruit, alcohol, and secondary flavors.

She was served some of the best Spanish cuisine she had ever tasted. Hector raised his glass. "To your beauty." Louise raised an eyebrow, and Hector took out a large manila envelope. "The fully-executed documents, as well as a little something for you."

"Salud." She drank then opened the envelope and quickly checked the signed documents. She took out a sealed white envelope that she assumed contained cash and pushed it back over to him. "This is really not necessary."

"Please, I insist." The last thing Louise wanted to do was insult him, so she accepted the envelope, raised her glass to him, and drank. They spoke in both Spanish and English of everything from the global economy to bullfighting. Louise loved the Spanish culture. Having lived with Michael and traveled to Spain had made her fluent enough to carry a conversation.

Hector and Louise had a lively discussion about Panamanian culture, which pleased Hector. Two hours and two bottles of wine later, Louise had managed to leave the restaurant without making Hector feel the least bit cast-off. He kissed her hand and helped her into the town car.

"Thank you for waiting, Jesus," she said after they drove away. She heaved a sigh of relief then checked her bag to make sure she had the documents.

"No problem, Miss Moscow. Senior Vargas let you go early."

"I convinced him that the sooner I got home the sooner the deal would be complete." They drove in silence until they reached the hotel. Jesus opened her door and accompanied her into the lobby.

"Miss, you fly away tomorrow?"

"Yes, Jesus. Please pick me up at 1:00 p.m. Good night."

Jesus bowed. "I'm sorry to see you go. You are my favorite BCCI boss."

"Feliz Año Nuevo, Jesus."

Back in her suite, Louise slapped the envelope from Vargas down onto the nightstand and undressed down to her camisole and panties. She poured herself a small amount of the complimentary brandy and packed her bag except her toiletries and her traveling clothes. She picked up Hector's envelope and flopped down on the bed. While sipping the brandy, she took out the two signed originals of the contracts and checked the signatures. She then took out and opened the plain white envelope, which was thick with cash, just as she had expected. She flipped through the cash and placed it back in the large envelope along with the contracts. She noticed another envelope at the bottom of the large envelope. It was a sealed letter-sized envelope with no writing on the outside and the thickness of only a single-page letter. She opened it and read the letter, then read it again. She sat up and looked around, not sure why. Maybe she was looking for some sort of explanation.

She read the letter again. It was on official letterhead from the attorney general of Panama, who, at the time, Louise knew had been working closely with the United States on anti-drug trafficking efforts. The letter was not addressed to her. It was addressed to BCCI, ordering the release of her Columbian client's funds. This didn't make sense. The funds released were supposed to be a loan to the Columbian client. This letter indicated that the funds in the Columbian client's actual account would be released, and the letter would be placed on file at BCCI as confirmation of approval from the Panamanian attorney general. The signed loan documents were a charade, meaning that BCCI was going to report to the U.S. government that the funds were still frozen.

In preparation for the trip to Panama, Louise had done some research and learned that the United States was ordering certain Central American bank accounts to be frozen as a result of an anti-drug operation it had mounted called *Operation Pisces*. BCCI had publicly taken the position that accounts were being frozen as a formality and that it would cover any client funds for a 10 percent fee. She was assured that her Columbian client was not under investigation, and that the account had been frozen as a formality. But the letter from the attorney general of Panama meant that her client must have been involved in one of the drug rings under investigation. She suddenly realized that she had been sent as a pawn to facilitate the transaction with the Columbian client who was probably a drug trafficker. The letter had not been intended for her. It was given to her by mistake.

Trying not to panic, she decided to act as though she hadn't opened the letter. She took two new blank envelopes from her briefcase and sealed the letter inside one envelope, and the cash in the other. Then she took the contracts and the two sealed envelopes and placed them in a file folder. She would need to leave the hotel earlier than the scheduled 1:00 p.m. departure and called Jesus from the hotel room phone and asked him to come for her at 10:00 a.m. instead.

TWENTY-THREE

Louise was having coffee in the hotel restaurant overlooking the Gulf of Panama when Jesus arrived. The valet had already loaded her bag, and she got into the town car, carrying the violin case.

"Buenos días, Jesus."

"Buenos días, Miss. To the airport early?"

"No, Jesus, we need to make a stop before the airport. Please take me to the home of Mr. Sakhia."

"As you wish, Miss Moscow." Jesus took the detour to the beach house of the BCCI senior official for the Caribbean, Abdur Sakhia. It was about fifty miles south of Panama City in Playa Coronado. BCCI had purchased the property and built on it for the exclusive use of BCCI directors and guests.

They arrived and she got out, taking the violin case with her. She rang the doorbell and looked back at Jesus who gave her a reassuring nod. The property was extremely secluded, so it provided some reassurance to know that Jesus was waiting for her. The servant opened the door and invited her to wait on the terrace overlooking the private beach.

The house was bright and airy with fifteen-foot ceilings. There was a 160-degree view of miles of unspoiled verdant coastline with white sand and turquoise water. Stairs from the terrace lead to the water, and a refreshing ocean breeze cooled the outside temperature substantially. Looking eastward, she could see the spectacular Playa Grande, another two miles of undeveloped coastline. Westward the private beach continued along the unspoiled coastline, this time featuring spectacular high cliffs with inter-spersed private beach alcoves. Marmoset monkeys played in the trees, and toucans poked their heads out of tree holes, feeding on dates and other fruit. Louise drew from beautiful surroundings to raise her spirits.

Sakhia greeted her within moments of her arrival. "Ms. Moscow," he said, motioning for her to sit down. "I wasn't expecting you. Why didn't they let me know you were in town? I would have arranged for a more social gathering."

"Thank you, Sakhia. I apologize for the intrusion." Louise played along, even though she was sure Sakhia was aware of her trip. "The Paris office thought it would be unnecessary to disturb you while you're busy dealing with the Jamaica and the Florida branches." Sakhia was constantly traveling to Caribbean branches. Plus, since the loan originated through the Paris branch, it was best for Louise to handle the Columbian client.

"It is no intrusion. Please, how can I be of service?"

Louise took the file folder out of her satchel and handed it to Sakhia. "Here are all the documents that the attorney for our Columbian client gave me. He has agreed to the terms and signed the contracts. There were also other items that I wasn't sure about so I wanted to hand everything over to you to go through before I take the contracts back to Paris for finalizing."

"You have a first-rate sense of protocol, Miss Moscow." Sakhia took the folder and leafed through, absently checking the contracts and completely ignoring the envelope filled with cash. Then he plucked out the sealed envelope, opened it, and read the letter. "This all seems to be in order." Sakhia returned the file to Louise but kept the letter. "Thank you."

Louise smiled. "You're welcome. I'll process the transaction and file the documents." She picked up her briefcase and the violin case and rose to leave.

"Miss Moscow!" Louise paused, startled. "You play the violin?"

"No, not at all. I'm transporting it to Paris for a friend."

"How very kind of you. Please give Nazir Chinoy my warmest regards."

"Of course." Louise left, unsure about the situation but determined to act as if nothing out of the ordinary had happened.

Jesus opened the car door, and they quickly got back on the road to the airport. Louise breathed deeply and caught Jesus's look in the rearview mirror. "Everything okay, miss?"

"Yes, thank you, Jesus."

He pulled up to the curb of the international terminal and opened her door. He went to the trunk and placed her carry-on bag on the sidewalk. "It was a pleasure serving you, Miss Moscow."

Louise squeezed a hundred-dollar bill into his palm. "You are a good friend, Jesus. Hasta luego."

Through airport security, her additional carry-on drew quite a bit of attention. However, having impeccable documentation, the priceless violin caused more of a sensation than alarm. After some lively conversation and admiration of the fiddle, the security agents sent her on her way. Over the years of international travel, Louise had mastered the art of passing customs with ease. By wearing the look of an inquisitive American tourist, she could walk right through security almost unnoticed. Her pleasant-but-slightly-confused expression was so convincing that by the time customs agents had checked her travel documents, they had already made up their minds to let her pass. But under these circumstances, she found that look of inquisitive innocence harder to muster. Now that she had made it through the security check, she couldn't help smiling. Getting out of Panama and on the plane back to Paris, alive, was a great triumph.

TWENTY-FOUR

Louise closed the door of her Paris apartment, left her carry-on and the violin case in the foyer, and plopped down on the chaise longue by the circular bay window. She took a deep breath, but just as she was about to exhale, she held it. Something seemed out of place in her comfort zone. The change was so slight; it was detectable only by some gut-level sensor. She scanned the room carefully and found nothing out of place, at least not that she could tell. But she had a sense that someone had been there.

Over the ensuing days, she felt paranoid and suspected someone was following her. She checked for listening devices, cameras or any other surveillance equipment in her home and office. Finally, Louise decided to contact Vladimir. Louise still suspected that Vlad was a CIA agent, so she wanted to confront him. They arranged to meet at their mutual friend's wine bar in the Latin Quarter called Millésimes on rue Lobineau behind the Marché St. Germain. Located on street level of a sixteenth-century building, the tiny café was long and narrow with beamed ceilings, rustic tables, and chairs, and amber walls discolored by candle flame and cigarette smoke. The scent of chicken livers with Dijon mustard searing in a poêle always reminded her of the pungent smell of cannabis smoke. The hot chicken livers were then nestled over mixed greens to make the specialty, salade aux foies de volaille, her favorite.

Diana's husband Max had opened the little café, where he often did the cooking himself. He had bought it with the proceeds from his art to spite his family, who ridiculed him for shunning the family business and becoming an artist. He decorated the walls with his artwork and played the role of temperamental artiste/chef very convincingly. The old-world unpretentious charm, the small but excellent wine selection, and simple but delicious cooking drew a regular clientele.

The wine bar was Louise's home away from home. She swirled Bordeaux in her wineglass, stuck her nose inside, and breathed. She took a mouthful and quietly aerated it before swallowing. She closed her eyes and felt her courage mount. Vladimir plunked himself down across from her, and she opened her eyes. He leaned forward and they exchanged double bisous. Max was already at the table with bottle in hand. The two men shook hands, and Max poured Vlad a glass of the Bordeaux. Max left the bottle and went back to his frying pan, glass of wine, and cigarette. It was entirely possible that he could not do one without the others.

Vladimir gave Louise an icy stare. He was inscrutable the way a politician skirts questions from the press.

Louise's mother had taught her always to be completely candid with others. Contrasted by her father who had always admonished Louise not to be such an open book. Louise's mother was from Chicago—a big city located smack dab in the rural Midwest—and claimed to have an internal *bullshit meter*. Her father taught Louise to suppress her tendency to wear her heart on her sleeve. Louise's mom never found any fault with being totally honest, but she never had anything negative to say either. Louise's father never had anything to say at all, at least nothing revealing. Louise's tendencies leaned toward her mother's, so learning to hold her tongue was a challenge. She also had the habit of always trying to break through a person's veneer and get them to open up. The French expression often used by journalists, to *pull the worms from someone's nose*, means to get someone to open up.

Louise felt she was good at opening up others, and she hoped to get Vladimir to do that now. For the moment, though, he was sphinx-like.

She aerated more wine in her mouth and swallowed. "Thank you for meeting with me, Vlad."

"You're welcome. How's Greg?"

"Just peachy. Haven't seen him for a few weeks. I just got back from Panama two days ago."

"Ah, Panama. Lovely country. Spectacular seafood."

"Indeed." Louise took another sip of wine. "So, you've been there?"

"Yes."

She finally gave in to his stoic glare. "Look. I need to ask you a favor."

"You name it."

"This is going to sound strange. But I think someone is following me."

"Who?"

"I don't know. But in Panama my client's attorney gave me some documents, one of which was a sealed letter that wasn't intended for me. It must have been a mistake."

"Mistake?"

"You know, a mix-up," Louise said. "The document was supposed to go to someone higher up than me."

"But you think it may not have been given to you by accident?"

Louise suddenly got the sense that Vladimir knew more than he let on. "Exactly. I pretended not to read the letter. I resealed it and gave it to the head of the Panama branch. But I have the feeling he knew."

"Why did you call me?"

"You're a friend," Louise said.

"I'm really a friend of a friend."

"I was hoping I could trust you."

"We may be able to work something out."

"What do you mean?"

He leaned closer and whispered. "We have been investigating BCCI for several months, and you are well positioned to help the CIA," Vlad said.

"So, you are with the…"

He silently mouthed, *shhh*.

She whispered. "Me? Work for the CIA?"

"Unofficially, yes, you could do a lot. If you can deliver useful information, you could be spared."

"Spared from what?" Louise was shocked. "I haven't done anything wrong."

"We have evidence about your trip to Panama that could be very incriminating."

"That's ridiculous. I came to *you* for help."

"I am helping. Like I said, you are very well positioned and can be another asset for us inside."

"*Another* asset? Is Diana an asset?"

"I didn't say that. But what I am saying is, from where I sit, you would do best to cooperate."

"What exactly do you want me to do?"

"Nothing. Don't change anything in your routine. But you need to dig into the client files, computers, and accounting to find out whatever you can about the movement of funds to and from whom and where. We'll contact you sporadically to get updates. But…top secret." The blood rushed to Louise's cheeks, and he could see her struggling. For the first time he let down his guard. "You did the right thing coming to me."

Just then Diana walked into the bar, carrying New Year's Eve party favors. "Louise! When did you get back from Panama? Will you two be ringing in the New Year here with us? How nice to see you two together!"

"Sadly, I was stopping by only to wish you all Happy New Year." Vlad got up and gave Diana two bisous. "I have to be somewhere else at midnight."

"At least finish your drink," Max said.

"Sorry, have to run." Vlad shook Max's hand then leaned over Louise to ostensibly kiss her good-bye. "I'll be in touch," he whispered to her.

Louise felt powerless, like a teeny speck in an infinite universe, which in fact she was. We all were, literally. She tried to reassure herself that everyone, no matter how important, was just a teeny dot in the universe. But relatively she was an even teenier one than those in power. Normally, she was happy to fly under the radar and be the cog in the wheel. But now she was getting pulled into someone else's fight.

Diana sat in Vlad's chair. "Don't be sad, Louise. It's obvious that Vlad likes you. He probably just didn't know you would be here for New Year's Eve. Would you like some champagne?"

"That sounds good. Spending New Year's Eve drinking champagne in my favorite place with my closest friends bodes well for the New Year."

People started entering the restaurant for dinner and the midnight festivities. Diana poured Louise a glass of champagne.

TWENTY-FIVE

After having confided in Vladimir, Louise felt even more vulnerable and paranoid than before. She couldn't talk to Diana about anything, not even what had happened in Panama. She spent her first day back at the office at her desk and plunged into work. As instructed, she began to analyze all of her current and past clients, working for six hours, compiling a spreadsheet, populating it with information from documents, and setting up an algorithm to make connections within the company database. Finally, patterns became apparent. The more Louise studied her algorithm the more she saw a baseline for assessing BCCI's principal relationships with foreign governments. By analyzing the deposits it received from foreign Central Banks, there were so many Third World countries with deposits at BCCI that it became clear BCCI was the bank of choice for Third World Central Banks. What was troubling was that every central banker knew that BCCI, being a bank not based in any one country, had no *lender of last resort*. In other words, BCCI had no government that would extend credit in an emergency, leaving BCCI working completely without a net.

Even more troubling, BCCI had been able to avoid reporting audited consolidated financial statements of any of its branches. Normally, banks must undergo quarterly reviews and annual audits by accredited audit firms in the country in which they are based. Then the holding bank that owns a majority of all the foreign branches consolidates the various subsidiary audited financial statements into one consolidated audited financial statement. However, because none of BCCI's many international branches was over 50 percent owned by any one BCCI branch, no consolidated financial statements had ever been done.

BCCI also had a neat arrangement with auditors of its two main offices. By dividing its auditing functions between two auditors, one for Luxembourg and the other for Grand Caymans, BCCI's activities could not be monitored by any one auditor. Price Waterhouse, whose audits had given the bank a clean bill of health for years, was one of the world's largest accounting firms. Price Waterhouse wielded enormous influence, and a clean, or "unqualified" audit from the company meant easy access to credit and capital. It meant regulators kept their long noses out of the bank's business, and it gave depositors a sense of security. However, Price Waterhouse had never performed a worldwide audit consolidating the financial statements of all the BCCI branches. Thus, funds deposited in BCCI were potentially at very substantial risk for any Central Bank. If BCCI failed, the funds from Central Banks of many countries would not be protected. The funds would be treated like the funds of any other depositor. Dozens of countries placed their reserves with BCCI, in some cases, at very substantial and imprudent levels, despite these obvious risks. Failure of BCCI could bankrupt entire countries!

Furthermore, these Central Banks' deposits were hidden by BCCI from U.S. scrutiny. In the United States, documented BCCI repositories contained only records pertaining to deposits in BCCI Miami, and thus represented only a fraction of total deposits by Central Banks. For example, a number of the countries that had deposits at BCCI in the United States would also maintain larger deposits at BCCI in Panama, where they would be invisible and therefore protected from creditors.

Louise realized that if she knew all of this, then so did her superiors, as well as the CIA, the FBI, Interpol, and anyone else who had taken an interest. A completely unregulated banking system, coupled with a very willing clientele, made for a legally corrupt banking system. Since she had worked extensively with the highest ranked officers of BCCI, she knew how overconfident they had become. The high-level clientele that BCCI had been financing for anything from arms to drugs to politics were essentially self-insured by BCCI. And it was becoming more evident that BCCI would need to cash in on its insurance where it could, and soon.

Furthermore, the great windfall of OPEC was over. The OPEC countries, upon which BCCI depended for most of its deposits, had been spending as though it would never end. Saudi Arabia was a prime example. From a high of $119 billion in earnings in 1981, the kingdom's revenues had gone into free-fall. By 1984 revenues had fallen to $36 billion, by 1985 to $26 billion. The country's development program was reduced sharply, and the world's richest oil barony even started to run into budget deficits. The same held true for Abu Dhabi and the United Arab Emirates, clients that were

BCCI's once-golden and ever-renewable sources of working capital.

This was the first shattering blow against BCCI. Deposits were the life-blood of the bank, and, for its grand deception to function properly, BCCI needed an ever-fresh stream of new money. A Ponzi scheme in which new money is used to cover old losses crashes the minute the funds stop flowing. The second shattering blow was the bank's massive exposure to Gulf Shipping and Trading, the global shipping giant and its affiliates, run by Abedi's close cronies, the Gokal brothers—Mustafa, Abbas, and Murtaza—who had used BCCI money to build one of the world's great shipping empires.

In their late-1970s' heyday, the Gokals chartered more ships in one year than did the countries of China and India combined. By the late 1970s, a recession in the shipping industry nearly as bad as the later recession in the oil business, plus a series of bad investments in other businesses, had made it impossible for the Gokals to repay their BCCI loans, which topped out at $831 million in 1990. The third blow was an estimated $1 billion in losses incurred between 1977 and 1985 in the bank's treasury operations, the results of wildly imprudent commodities trading and outright theft. As a result, BCCI would take extreme risks, becoming sloppy and leaving paper and digital trails.

And now, Louise was tapping into those trails. But she needed more information, and she knew that Diana had the highest-level clearance at BCCI. She logged off her computer and filed all the documents she had retrieved back in their respective places.

TWENTY-SIX

Louise woke up early and made coffee, perused the *International Herald Tribune*, and started the *New York Times* crossword. As she looked out the open window over Park Monceau, she heard the birds chirping in the early morning air. It was unusually warm for January, so she got the urge to walk to work. She dressed in comfortable business attire and left for work, carrying the violin case.

The fresh air and pale golden sunlight evoked a sense of timelessness. The sunlight at this time of day made Paris appear the way Louise imagined it might have centuries ago. She took a detour walking through the Jardin des Tuileries toward the Champs-Élysées.[22]

Strolling in silent appreciation, Louise imagined what the park might have been like when they were still fields and gardens traveled by people in carriages and on horseback. She breathed deeply and closed her eyes but was jarred by the sudden whinny and clop of a hard-ridden horse approaching from behind her. She spun around, her black overcoat billowing and her Hermès scarf almost escaping upward into the breeze. Her blonde tresses came loose and tousled across her face, obscuring her vision of the horse as it reared to a stop.

"Pardonnez-moi, Mademoiselle. Je vous ai fait peur." His appearance was overpowering, a square jaw, eyes and hair dark under a black cap, his riding duster flaring open to reveal a tall muscular physique. He was dressed in a white banded hunt shirt, jodhpurs, and riding boots. "Permettez-moi de vous accompagner jusqu-a vos bureaux?"

Louise was stunned, being offered a ride to work by a man on horseback in the middle of the Tuileries Gardens. Even more baffling, he seemed to know who she was and where she was going.

"Who are you?"

"My name is Jean-Philippe de Villeneuve. And you are Louise Moscow, non?"

"Non. I mean yes. But non, merci. I prefer to walk." Louise turned and started walking fast, frightened.

"Entendu. À votre service, Mademoiselle. Au revoir." He rode off, disappearing as swiftly as he had arrived. She looked around to see if anyone was watching. She walked even faster toward her office.

Louise strode into Diana's office, silently placed pastries on her desk, and went straight to the teapot.

"Good morning," Diana said waiting for an explanation.

Louise gulped the tea, breathed deeply, and turned to Diana. "Sorry I didn't stop by yesterday. I had so much work to catch up on since my trip to Panama."

"I was beginning to wonder if you had run off to join the symphony the way you've been carrying that violin case around."

Louise had gotten so used to keeping the violin with her at all times that she forgot it was drawing attention. "Oh, Peter asked me to deliver it. I can't bear to leave it at home. If anything were to happen to it, I could never forgive myself."

"You saw Peter?"

"Yes, I had dinner at his villa."

"Just dinner?"

"Yes, of course," Louise said.

"Oh, you are a bore. How long will you be schlepping his fiddle around?"

"Someone is supposed to contact me any time now. I think Paul Childs or some other violin dealer."

"Paul Childs, the charming violinist?"

"Yes, but I'm holding out for top fiddle."

"Vlad doesn't play violin," Diana teased.

"Then he'll have to play second fiddle."

"Come on! What's going on with you?"

"I need a favor. No questions asked," said Louise.

"Is *that* all?"

"I'm serious. Someday I hope I can tell you."

"Is everything okay? Are you in some kind of trouble?" Diana asked.

"I really can't talk about it."

"Tell me but don't tell me."

"Could you just tell the IT department that you've asked me to do some routine maintenance on your computer? I need to log in with your clearance."

"Oh, Louise, that is highly irregular. It may raise more questions than if you just broke in."

"Great idea. I'll just break in."

"Goodness no! Let me sort it out."

"Think quickly because I'm going in." Louise sat at Diana's computer and inserted a floppy disk. Diana tried not to look panicked. "By the way, have you ever seen a man riding through the Tuileries on horseback? His name is Jean-Phillll…something…"

"Jean-Philippe de Villeneuve!"

"Yes. That's the guy."

"He's a bit eccentric, but he's considered a national hero in France. He fought with the French troops against Gaddafi when Libya invaded Chad as part of Opération Epervier. He was actually knighted and is a *Chevalier*. He believes he should honor his title literally, and that's why he rides on horseback as often as possible."

Louise stared at Diana in stunned silence. "Is that all? You didn't leave anything out?"

"He's somewhat of a celebrity in France. He comes from a very old line-age of the French aristocracy, a long line of commandants with the French Royal Navy, dating back to Napoleon I."

"So, he rides a horse in public because he's a knight?"

"He is also one of the *Immortels* of the Académie Française."[23]

"Really? An *Immortel*. That *is* impressive." Louise wasn't joking. She really was impressed.

"He's quite dreamy."

"So, you've met him?" Louise asked.

"He's actually a friend of mine. Why do you ask?"

"I met him this morning on my way to work. He offered me a lift on his horse. I said no, thank you."

"Next time, accept," said Diana. "In fact, if you're ever in trouble, you should call him and tell him that you are my friend."

"Wow, again, I'm impressed. But he already seemed to know who I was." Louise popped the disk out of the computer and took her cup of tea. "Please let my algorithm run. Don't touch it. I'll be back to check it."

"You do realize that there is nothing on our computers, no real information anyway."

"What are you talking about? This is an international bank," said Louise.

"An international bank with no formal record keeping, accounting system, or database," Diana said.

"How could we possibly track all the transactions?"

"They are being tracked, just not in the computer system."

"Then how?" asked Louise.

"I've said too much already. Just suffice it to say you should stop digging around."

"You know that will not happen."

"Then promise me this," Diana insisted. "You'll contact Jean-Philippe if things get out of hand."

Louise kissed Diana's cheek. "Love you."

As soon as Louise got back to her desk, Chinoy entered her office, startling her.

"There you are, Louise."

"Good morning, Mr. Chinoy."

"Don't get too comfortable, Ms. Moscow. You have a new assignment. We are moving the London office. You're going to South Korea."

"When?"

"Next week."

"Next week? That's not a lot of time to prepare."

"Please begin writing in integrated enterprise-wide database model right away. We are setting up an IT department as well that you will oversee. You will be the senior administrator providing independent oversight. Your clearance has already been increased, so you can get right to work."

"Yes, Mr. Chinoy." He left and Louise almost jumped with excitement. If management entrusted her with such a high-level project that meant the incident with the letter in Panama had not mattered.

Louise returned to Diana's office. "You can relax. I've just been given top clearance." Louise checked her algorithm on Diana's computer. "It's already finished processing. That can't be good. Let's take a look at what it found." They both moved closer to the monitor. Diana's eyes widened. "I'm going to print this," Louise said, clicking the mouse. A series of pages spewed forth from Diana's printer.

"I think we shouldn't be looking at this."

"No one will ever know," Louise said. "See you later at Millesimes?"

"Max and I will be there as always."

Louise felt like a great weight had lifted. She was just being paranoid that someone was following her. Plus, this put her in a better position to report to Vlad and cooperate with the CIA. Her new level of security clearance would give her some bargaining power. In light of all she was uncovering about BCCI, it was better to be on the side of the CIA. It made her feel like a slightly smaller speck in the universe.

TWENTY-SEVEN

Louise had been immersed in the project to migrate the UK servers to South Korea for a week. The migration was going smoothly, and she was scheduled to leave for Seoul tomorrow. Things at BCCI seemed to be back to normal. But she was still carrying the violin case around with her and was worried she would have to take it to South Korea. She entered her apartment after working late just as the phone rang.

"Hello?"

"Is that Louise?"

"Yes."

"Peter Edwards here."

"Pete-ski! How are you?"

"I'm great. How's the fiddle?"

"It's fine. I was wondering if you had forgotten about it."

"No. Just waiting for my associate to arrive in Paris. He's there now for a few days."

"Oh, I'm leaving for Seoul tomorrow."

"Oh, dear, we'll have to do it tonight then. Remember Roger Bing?"

"Yes, of course."

Roger Bing was the *Bing* of the renowned Chicago-based violin dealership Bing & Fushimi. Peter had worked with them for several years.

"Well, he's is in Paris now so would you mind taking it to him?"

"Perfect timing."

"I'll give him your number, and you two can arrange a meeting."

"Okay, darling," Louise said. "Have him call me right now. I'll take care of it. Don't worry."

Louise hung up and Roger Bing rang after a few minutes. They arranged to meet at Maxim's, where he would be dining with a client that evening. Louise left right away, hoping to drop off the violin before his dinner guest arrived.[24, 25]

The violin that Louise was delivering to Roger Bing was another from the Segelman collection. Bing was presenting it for sale to the client at the legendary restaurant, founded in 1893. Louise entered the landmark art nouveau building and immediately spotted the rotund Chicagoan in the dining room. Bing was having a pre-dinner snack of coq au vin. He broke off a piece of crusty bread and dropped it into the rich red wine sauce, stuck it with a fork, swirled it around, and plunged it into his mouth. His loosened tie hung around his unbuttoned collar and sloped down over his large belly speckled with a dusting of breadcrumbs. The host escorted Louise to his table.

"Hello. I'm Louise Moscow."

Roger invited Louise to sit down with a wave of his hand.

"Thank you," said Louise. "I don't want to intrude. I know you are expecting someone."

"Come, it's the least we can do for you bringing the fiddle all the way from Panama," he sputtered, his mouth full.

Louise politely sat down. "It was my pleasure. Peter is a dear friend."

"Right. Great guy." A consummate Parisian waiter arrived swiftly to take her order. "Please bring a bottle of Veuve Cliquot for my guest and me." Louise perked up. This was her favorite champagne.[26]

The career waiter had the bottle on ice and uncorked it in moments. They clinked glasses. "To Mary Portman."

"To Mary Portman." Louise was uncomfortable meeting Peter's business associate without him, so she sipped quickly. But Bing made conversation. "Peter tells me you're with BCCI."

"Yes. I'm a personal banker."

"We're establishing an offshore entity in the Caymans and need a banker."

"Yes, Peter mentioned. I'd be happy to help with that."

"We'd like you to be our banker. It's a question of provenance, you understand."

"Of course. I'll be in South Korea for the next two weeks. But I can fly to the Caymans after that."

"We are setting up the entity expressly in a venture with an important client, and your bank may be best suited to handle the transaction. The client will be here shortly, and it would be great if you could meet him."

"Perhaps it would be better to wait until I return from Seoul and discuss it with Peter."

"This was Peter's idea in order to save time and get the ball rolling."

"Yes, of course," said Louise.

"We'd like to do business specifically with you, and you would be doing us a favor by staying and hashing out some of the details tonight."

"I understand, but …"

"Our client is a high-level French official, and the violin serves as part of the investment capital investment. So, you see, it is a highly sensitive transaction involving a lot of money."

"Highly sensitive transactions are my specialty," said Louise. The words from her own lips struck her as strange and full of hubris. Her mother would not approve.

"That's what I wanted to hear."

"I'll do whatever I can for Peter." Louise finished her glass of champagne. "However, I must finish a few things before I leave for Seoul tomorrow." Louise stood to leave. "I'll have my office contact you to schedule something more formal in the Caymans."

Bing suddenly shot up, oblivious to the crumbs exploding from his chest, and waved to someone across the room. "There is my client. Please, stay and join us for dinner."

Louise wanted to leave but it was too late. She turned and was stunned to see that she recognized the client.

"Roger, mon ami. Bonsoir." Jean-Philippe de Villeneuve shook Bing's hand then turned to Louise. He was equally surprised to see her. "Je vous connais," said the knight on horseback that had startled her in the Tuileries Gardens. He took Louise's hand and kissed it, bowing. He looked much different with no hat and cloak. He had dark wavy hair and wore an impeccably tailored suit and elegant tie.

"Yes, you are Jean-Philippe de Villeneuve. We met briefly in the Jardin des Tuileries. You offered me a ride on your horse."

"Ah, oui. Vous êtes inoubliable." His flattery seemed altogether too genuine to be an act.

She blushed. "Encore une fois, vous m'avez fait rougir."

"I apologize, Mademoiselle Moscow, I promise not to make you blush again."

"You know each other?" Roger was flabbergasted. "Well, this is serendipitous!"

"I didn't realize you knew Mr. Bing," said Jean-Philippe. "I didn't realize you knew me either."

"Yes, our mutual friend Diana Burke told me about you."

"Ah, yes. My dear friends Diana and Max."

"Such a small world," noted Roger. "Please, stay and dine with us," he insisted, pulling Louise's chair out for her.

They ate and drank wine for hours, discussing fine instruments and the Cayman Islands venture. It was to be a holding company set up for the purchase of the violins and other antique instruments. Since the vast majority of sales were international, the funds could be paid to the offshore entity, and no revenues would be recognized in the United States, England, or France. All sales would be tax exempt, as long as the money stayed offshore. It was an ingenious set up and would be a big account for BCCI.

"Well, I have a morning flight to Seoul," Louise said. Roger paid the bill, and they got up to leave.

"May I take you home?" offered Jean-Philippe. "No horse, I'm traveling by car this evening."

"Thank you, but I can call my driver."

Roger interrupted, "I have to walk just a few steps to my hotel, so I'll leave you two to work it out."

"Roger, it was a pleasure meeting you. I look forward to working on this venture," Louise said, shaking Roger's hand.

"We will stay in close contact. Have a good trip to Seoul. Good night."

Roger waddled away.

"S'il vous plaît, allow me to personally see to it that you arrive home safely." Jean-Philippe was so courtly, she couldn't think of a reason to refuse him again.

"All right."

Jean-Philippe held the door to his Ferrari for her, and they sped off. He insisted on walking her to her apartment door. "I really do have a flight in the morning."

"Entendu." Jean-Philippe kissed her hand, this time more affectionately. Then he kissed her cheek, "Je vous souhaite bonne nuit," and the other cheek, "et bon voyage." He had that kind of sexy impassiveness that drove her crazy.

"Mercy. I mean, merci." She mustered her own impassiveness and stepped into her apartment, leaving him standing in the hallway. She watched breathlessly through the peephole as he motioned to knock then changed his mind and walked away. She blushed once again.

TWENTY-EIGHT

The next day at Charles de Gaulle Airport, Louise made her way to the Korean Air gate. After passing through security with no trouble, she started to get that strange feeling again. She slowed her gait and casually swept her eyes over the crowd until she saw him. She went over to the duty-free shopping where Vladimir was waiting for her. She picked up a magazine from the rack and pretended to read.

"How did you know where to find me?"

"I know everything."

Louise rolled her eyes. "What do you want?"

"Did you bring me anything?"

"That depends." Louise had been carrying the floppy disks of the accounting reports and list with her. She didn't know where else to keep them.

"On what?"

"Why should I help you? What are you going to do for me?"

"You're knee-deep in shit here, Louise. I'm trying to help you."

"Help me? By making threats?"

"You are seriously implicated in this," said Vladimir. "It's in your best interest to work with us."

"I'll give you what you want if you give me complete immunity."

"We'll do better than that. You will have asset status effective immediately, and if you continue to cooperate, you will be considered for more official status."

"I want it in writing."

"You will receive word to drop off any new information you gather in Seoul, and you will get automatic upgraded travel status."

"I'll think about it."

"Or should I take that list now?" said Vladimir.

"What list?"

"The list of BCCI clients that you printed from Diana's computer." She couldn't conceal her surprise. "Louise, we know everything."

"How?"

"Let's put it this way. You easily passed through security, but that doesn't mean you're certain to get on that plane. Or back in the country for that matter."

"You can't do that."

"We can and we will," Vladimir asserted.

"Go to hell." She was at the end of her rope. Just when everything seemed to be back to normal, the CIA was threatening her. She put the magazine back and walked away. Vlad followed her.

"Louise, it doesn't have to be like this. I strongly recommend that you cooperate."

"I didn't say I wouldn't. But I want it in writing first."

"You'll be contacted in Seoul."

"Very well." Louise had little patience for manipulation. Her father warned her that her righteous indignation was a character flaw she had picked up from her mother. But he also told her to trust her instincts.

"By the way, you should try the Korean barbeque restaurant just across from your hotel. It's a local favorite." With that he disappeared.

TWENTY-NINE

On her first day in Seoul, she went to the Korean barbeque, or *gogi gui*, across from her hotel as instructed. An agent, posing as a cook, made contact with her. He fried up her selection of thinly sliced beef, chicken and pork, bean sprouts, and a medley of other greens on the large grill at the center of the communal table. His only communication to her was through an origami that he folded and placed in front of her at the end of her meal. Back in her hotel room, she unfolded the note and read the message. She was instructed to be at the great market district of Myeong-dong and wait alone in front of the only antique shop at noon on the last day of her trip.

Over the next ten days, her solid performance on the project in Seoul earned her praise and the directors' complete trust. She excelled at assessing the technicians' flowcharts and keeping the migration of the database to the new mainframe on schedule. She sent daily reports to Abedi and Chinoy, keeping them apprised of progress. Abedi and his top official in Seoul, Naqvi, asked Louise to attend a world Bank meeting and assist Alauddin Shaikh, the head of the London branch.

Shaikh was based in London but had flown to Panama two or three times a year to meet with General Manuel Noriega, the military dictator of Panama since 1983. Alauddin even transferred his assistant, Amjad Awan, from the BCCI London office to BCCI Panama, with the sole purpose of acquiring Noriega's account. His relationship with Noriega became very close. General Noriega had once given a copy of an ancient handwritten Koran to Alauddin Shaikh. When Noriega visited London, Shaikh entertained him with dinners and other gatherings, and soon thereafter Noriega assisted BCCI in obtaining a license to open a bank in Panama, the very branch of Louise's Columbian client.

Shaikh was in Seoul, having just returned from Cannes where he had hosted a party in the fifteenth-century chateau that BCCI had purchased the previous year. His annual party during the International Film Festival was always one of the hottest and most exclusive invitations, offering the best setting, atmosphere, celebrities, champagne, bribes, and hookers, outdoing all the other industry galas including that of *Vanity Fair.*

The palm greasing continued here in Seoul at the World Bank party. The cash gifts, although a staple of BCCI corporate policy, were kept top secret. But, with Louise's high-level security clearance, they could rely on her to help with the tracking and disbursement of the cash. Her assignment entailed writing amounts, names, and associated companies and banks as Shaikh handed out cash in the hallway. He shook hands and greeted people as though it were an Amway convention. Louise took careful notes as Shaikh handed envelopes to the entire staff of the Central Bank of Nigeria.

"Abedi's philosophy was to appeal to every sector," Shaikh told Louise. "If you were religious, he would help you pray. If your brother-in-law needed a job, he got a job, as did your mistress. If your son needed to get into a certain university, he got in, provided of course that you were one of BCCI's key clients."[27]

Louise gave the list of names and amounts to Shaikh at the end of every event. But only after committing it to memory, so she could recreate it when she went back to her room every night. At one point, Shaikh gave her his master list to hold for a while, and she immediately memorized it. She couldn't believe the names. It was a log of all the payments to political figures from BCCI's headquarters in London. She realized that only Shaikh, Abedi, and Naqvi knew of the list. It was a worldwide list of people who were being paid off by BCCI: the family of Indira Gandhi, President Ershad of Bangladesh, General Zia of Pakistan, and many of the leaders of Africa.

On the morning of her last day in Seoul, Abedi announced that she was being promoted to regional director of the Paris branch. Her dreams of becoming an international corporate executive were coming true, but not on her terms. She thanked Abedi and returned to her hotel to prepare for her departure.

Living a double life was not natural to Louise. In her hotel suite, she placed a copy of the list into her bag along with the floppy disks and went to the great market district of Myeong-dong and waited in front of the antique shop. By a quarter after noon, no one had made contact. Resisting the temptation to shop, she started to walk slowly back to her hotel. She had a flight to Paris that evening and had been anxious about having new travel clearance. But no one had contacted her as Vladimir had promised, leaving her worried about the deal she had struck with him.

She made it through security easier than ever, so she wondered if she had been given the upgraded security clearance. She sipped champagne in the first-class cabin and fell asleep.

THIRTY

Louise arrived in Paris in the early evening about two hours later than the time her flight had taken off from Seoul, having gained eight hours with the time difference. She felt exhausted so she dumped her bags in the entrance of her apartment, grabbed a glass of Badoit, and went to bed.

In the morning when she awoke, she felt disoriented, not sure what city she was in, what date or even what year it was. The jetlag and difference in natural light between Seoul and Paris played on her psyche. It was as though during sleep she had drifted to another state of awareness. She wiped the sleep from her eyes and slowly returned to earthly consciousness.

After brewing some coffee and opening the morning edition of *Le Monde*, she was able to focus. As she skimmed over the world news, she found herself drawn to a small headline in the local section. It was a murder, and at first glance something in the details caught her eye. Her stomach sank, and she was overwhelmed with a sense of dread. She threw the paper into her satchel, scrambled to get her things, and headed to work. The dismay that had been building on the way to work was now jammed in her throat as she rode the elevator to the second floor. She was ashen and her palms sweaty when she entered the office. Everyone looked at her, and Chinoy immediately led her into his office and closed the door. He remained silent, watching her and waiting for her to react.

"It was Diana," Louise muttered. "The murder in the paper this morning, it was Diana."

Chinoy helped her into a chair and took a seat directly in front of her, looking her in the eyes. The article hadn't confirmed the name of the victim, but Louise knew who it was. A single phrase gave the victim's identity away.

Woman attacked while entering her Range Rover on Rue Lobineau. Diana had been so proud of her Range Rover, even though the car was much too big for Paris. And Max's café was on Rue Lobineau.

"Yes," said Chinoy. "The police say that some thugs, who had spotted her jewelry while she was walking down the street, followed her and attacked her in the garage." Hearing it out loud made Louise shudder, and she gave a kind of whimper. "I am so sorry, Louise. I know how close you two were."

But to Louise the police explanation made no sense. For one thing, violent crime in Paris was practically non-existent and unheard of in that neighborhood. Louise lost it. Glaring at him, she shot up out of the chair. "What have you done?" Her anger brought her body temperature up by at least one whole degree and caused her face to flush red.

"What have *I* done?" Chinoy seemed genuinely confused by her accusation.

"You had something to do with this."

"Louise, I assure you, this is as devastating to me as it is to you. Diana was not just a key employee to us. She was very much a member of the family."

Louise saw that Chinoy had tears in his eyes. Her emotion shifted from anger to sympathy then to anguish. Tears flooded her eyes and rolled down her cheeks to the floor. "I'm sorry," she said. "You're right, I'm distraught."

Chinoy patted her on the shoulder in deflated consolation. "Go home. Get some rest. The police are investigating this, and we will not rest until we know exactly what happened."

But none of that mattered anymore. Her friend was dead. Louise breathed deeply, trying to get air to her brain. She felt drained but took his advice. She shuddered a second time, got up, and walked out without stopping at her office. Some of her colleagues approached to console her, but she just gave a feeble nod and continued out toward home.

She got into her chauffeured sedan, her mind racing to make a connection between Diana and everything else. As she focused, it all started to shuffle into a cohesive order. It was Diana who had introduced her to Vladimir. She had been working at BCCI for many years. Was Diana also an informant? Diana knew that Louise had accessed the mainframe database and downloaded something ruinous about the company. Louise suspected someone was trying to send her a message through Diana's murder. There were high-level powers at play here.

Louise had lived her life, happily taking advantage of every situation for her own gain and advancement without regard for the consequences. She did not care about power, money, or recognition. It had been a game to her, to see if she could do it. She enjoyed the challenge of getting ahead in the complex male-dominated world of finance, to prove she was just as capable as any man. But, in reality, she preferred a simple existence. Now she had no idea how to protect herself against something she brought on herself. She was too ashamed to go to her father. Her only option was to reconnect with Vladimir.

She arrived home and unbolted the door, opening it slowly, lingering at the threshold. She waited before entering, frozen, as though taking one step inside she would pass through the looking glass. Just as she entered the foyer, she felt his presence.

"You're late." Through the foyer partially obscured by the wall to the salon she could see a man sitting on the chair at the far side in front of the fireplace.

She entered the salon to find Vladimir. "I didn't know we had a date."

"You look beautiful."

"Anguish becomes me," said Louise.

"Mourning became anguish?"

"I have no patience for mourning."

"Now you're becoming interesting."

"Your work is affecting your judgment."

"Snap judgment is my specialty," said Vlad.

"Enough. I did everything you wanted. In Seoul, I made contact with your Korean barbeque but got nothing. And now Diana is dead."

"What if I told you that the cook was not one of our agents, and we aborted the Seoul mission?"

"Then I would have to find a higher building than this one to jump off."

"As an expert in psychology, I could take that for suicidal tendencies," Vlad said.

"That's not the only thing you'd be mistaken about. I've had it with your lies and miscues. Do whatever you want. I am no longer cooperating with the CIA."

"Look, I've always liked you. It's because of me that you still have a high-profile glamorous career."

"Oh, really? Is it because of you that Diana is dead?" Louise said.

"That was not us; it was some punks."

"Never believe what you read in the papers."

"That's the official finding."

Furious, Louise ran at Vladimir, trying to claw at his face. "You killed her! You killed her! How could you? She was my friend! She was *your* friend!" Vladimir easily subdued her. Holding her wrists, he forced her down onto the chaise longue. He smothered her sobbing with a passionate kiss. Somehow it was the only thing that felt right to her now. She responded, taking then giving back control. She had had the power all along, but she didn't realize it. It was pure, not a bargaining chip, which made her even more powerful to him. Vladimir lifted her effortlessly. He was stronger than he appeared, strong enough walk to the bedroom and lay her down with the ease of fluffing a pillow.

She let herself go, and he synced into her rhythm. He pressed his body against hers, unzipping the side of her skirt and sliding it off her hips. He slipped his hand down the small of her back then squeezed her perfect butt cheek as he kissed her deeply, then he took hold of her slender waist, feeling her skin as soft as silk. His firmness pressed hard against her lower abdomen, almost bringing her to climax. She unzipped him, and he entered her and held still for a full minute, the emotion building. He moved left, then right, and she was completely freed. It was rare to find a woman who let go in that way. All her thoughts melted away; the more she blocked them out the more she opened up, until her body responded. He sensed that she was completely open and gave a final thrust. She wondered if she screamed; she couldn't hear herself over the orgasm. She had never felt so satisfied. No words. Just sleep.

THIRTY-ONE

She had no idea how long she had slept. When she awoke, he was watching her.

"I'll protect you," he said in her ear then kissed her fully. Then he pulled away and disappeared, seemingly down a zero-mass black rabbit hole.

She lay there alone between asleep and awake, her favorite state of mind. She could tap into spiritual and creative energy in that state, a kind of super-lucidity. It was especially intense in her Paris apartment, which emitted so much energy from the past, in the architecture, décor, even the smell. She slipped into a meditative state. Ever since her experience on the airplane, she was now fascinated with her heightened senses during meditation. She was convinced that if she kept practicing, she could feel the movement of Earth's rotation, as though riding on an enormous merry-go-round.

She came out of her meditation, slowly opening her eyes and focusing. She admired the beautiful Pierre Deux fabric that covered the walls. Decorating walls with fabric started in the medieval times. People used fabric to cover walls and windows in order to gain additional insulation and keep drafts out. In European castles, palaces, and affluent homes, these fabrics were elaborate tapestries. The walls throughout her apartment interior had been covered with large fabric-covered panels that had been custom fitted and fastened down, resulting in beautifully upholstered walls. She listened to the birds chirping outside, taking in the patterns of the elegant gold Provençal fabric walls.

One of the crevices between two of the panes had always drawn her attention because it was slightly wider than the others. It was her compulsive nature that caused her to notice such imperfections. It might have been the lucidity of the moment, but this time she was compelled to investigate further into the telltale crack in the wall. She could almost hear a beating heart behind the wall as she approached. But she realized it was her own. Upon closer inspection, she saw that there was not only a gap between the panels but also a gap in the wall behind it. She went to the nightstand and took out a flashlight. When she aimed it into the crevice, she saw the beam of light pass all the way through to a dark chasm. She pressed her hand flat against the crack and felt it give slightly on the left side. She pressed firmly against the left panel and, feeling it give, shoved her whole body against it, triggering a spring lock.

The door opened outward, releasing a miasma of dust. She panicked at first about the mess, but then the dust settled, and she was drawn in. Daylight revealed an empty chamber. She checked every corner with the flashlight and was satisfied she had found nothing more than some additional storage space. As she turned to leave the chamber, she spotted another crevice at the baseboard in the corner. It had been painted over many times and was hardly noticeable. She went to the kitchen and rummaged for a screwdriver then returned and began chiseling away at the crevice. Soon she loosened the bottom and sides but had to press her foot against the section of baseboard to create enough force to trigger another spring lock. It opened like a drawer, the inside of which appeared not to have seen the light of day for decades. It was empty except for what looked like an old manuscript. She dusted it off and leafed through. She wondered if it could have been an unpublished work by Proust who was believed to have occupied the apartment. She read an excerpt:

Perched safely on the cliffs of Thera, high over the southern Aegean Sea, her screams of anguish were heard by no one as she witnessed the massive wave wash away the entire civilization.

She jumped to another random page:

The sole female scribe during the time of Tutankhamun, she wore the same robes as the men. Monotheism was the creed of the day. She had come from a line of scribes and was enlisted to transcribe all the great ancient stories of Egypt reworking them so they would inspire thinking toward a unified consciousness but include the various pagan gods. She was the only female scribe commissioned to listen to the great stories and write them down in collaboration with other writers. These stories were the *first classics*.

Another random page:

The French language was jealously guarded. French was the diplomatic language. Because of its poetry and precision, it allowed for maximum stability in the telling of Egyptian stories. She listened and transcribed the lore into written French.

She closed the chamber door and set the manuscript on the nightstand, not giving it another thought. Then as if snapped back into self-awareness, she remembered Diana and went back into survivor mode. Despite his promise, Louise didn't trust Vlad. She needed to take further precautions for her own protection. She got dressed and walked down to the bar tabac to use the payphone. She made a collect call to her ex-fiancé, Michael. She told the operator to say it was from *Foliage*. Michael declined to accept the charges. Their communication was completed. She went back upstairs and called Chinoy to request a few days leave of absence, which he granted, no questions asked.

THIRTY-TWO

Louise booked the first flight to New York to leave that evening, taking only a small carry-on to go through security. The agent at the checkpoint slowly reviewed her passport. He checked it against the log as well as the small device on his desk that she surmised was a database station. The agent asked her to wait and left his booth to speak to his colleague. Louise forced herself not to over-think the situation. She would cooperate with the authorities, assured that Michael would get involved if she did not show up. Since she had not notified Vladimir about leaving the country, she wondered if he had placed some kind of alert on her credentials. She remained calm, playing the role of an American tourist heading home.

When the agent returned to his booth, Louise let a calm innocuous smile shape her face. He spoke to her in English. "I apologize for ze wait. I had to verify somesing in zee seestem."

"No problem," she replied in English.

French security tends to speak English to English-speaking travelers in a show of authority. She appreciated his efforts. As a rule, very few French people speak any English, despite the standard six years of English classes required of everyone through the twelfth grade. It remained a mystery to Louise why the French didn't speak better English, but she assumed it was poor learning tools, a lack of competent English teachers, and an overall cultural apathy.

The agent handed her passport back. "Thank you. Au revoir."

She smiled and quickly moved on. As she walked through the terminal to her gate, she stayed in character, not losing the silly-tourist expression until she reached the first-class lounge, ordered a glass of red wine, and took a big gulp. All the little survival techniques she had developed as an international businesswoman dealing with preconceived notions about her nationality and looks were now being tested. She could hear her father's words of encouragement to use common sense and strength of mind to resist negative influences. But more than anything he had said, nothing matched the innate sense of confidence he instilled in her. It was almost an entitlement it was so engrained in her not to doubt herself. Now however, for the first time in her life, she was fighting waning confidence and waxing self-doubt.

She landed at JFK International Airport, picked up her rental car, and headed due north on the I-87 Interstate. She ditched the car at the Poughkeepsie Amtrak station and bought tickets for the train and bus to the Ashokan Reservoir in West Hurley, located in the lush Catskill Mountains of Ulster County. As she paid for the ticket and read the departure city Poughkeepsie, she couldn't help but smile. When Louise and Michael were a young couple, they had picked that train station as their secret departure point because of its charming name. She had since learned that the name was derived from the Delaware Indian word *apokeepsingk* meaning "safe and pleasant harbor."

The long journey by plane, train, and bus had allowed her to organize her thoughts. She left the bus and walked down a path to the reservoir, stirring a gaggle of wild turkeys. At the shoreline, she breathed deeply, the view inducing her to relax. She had no idea when or even if Michael would show. They could have spoken on the phone, but their agreement was conceived to ensure no one could trace their meeting. Albeit overly precautious and puerile, the ritual provided some sense of security. She waited over an hour before Michael strolled up behind her as she waited on a tree stump, her shawl wrapped tightly around her neck against the coming evening chill.

"Clever girl."

"I can't believe our secret code word worked."

Michael dragged one of the metal rowboats out from beneath the trees. They launched it, and Michael rowed them out to the middle of the reservoir. There was only one other rowboat on the water with two men fishing in the distance. The reservoir always took Louise's breath away. In the fall, the rolling hills and changing leaves were rich with colors that the absconding sun torched in gold. The shifting colors of red, orange, yellow, and what she would describe as the hazel of Michael's eyes, seemed animated.

She drew her eyes away from the scenery to Michael's eyes.

"You look beautiful," he said.

"I didn't come thirty-six hundred miles for a romantic tryst."

"Why, is there someone else?"

"What do you mean?" she asked.

"Is there?"

"No."

"But you have something important to tell me," said Michael.

"That's right. I do have something to tell you."

"That there's someone else?"

"Will you stop with the false insecurity!" said Louise. "No, there is no one else."

"Oh, because I would have sworn there was something going on between you and Vladimir Egger."

"What do you know?"

"I know everything."

"So, if you already know everything, why do you keep asking me about my sex life instead of asking about my friend Diana?"

"I'm sorry about Diana," said Michael.

"Was she murdered?"

"I can't talk about it."

"Bullshit!" Her voice echoed through the hills, startling several geese into flight.

"Diana wasn't murdered by thieves."

"So, it was BCCI?" she asked.

"Yes and no. She was part of what we call an FBI dangle operation. She was a decoy."

"The FBI actually dangled her in front of the bad guys?"

"So to speak."

"Why her?"

"The other option was not an option." She understood by his look to mean that *she* was the other option.

"Was Diana a double agent?" Louise asked.

"No, but she was connected to them."

"*Them?*"

"Ghost surveillance."

"Ghost surveillance?"

"Extremely discreet and seemingly omnipresent surveillance, working mostly out of the view of the target. We have no idea who they are. But

Diana agreed to be a decoy to distract their attention off of you."

"So, she sacrificed herself for me?" Louise asked, incredulous.

"So it seems. The good news is you are safe."

"From the ghosts?"

"All signs indicate that the ghosts have moved on," said Michael. "They were trailing you in Seoul, but they backed off. Then, whether you meant to or not, you timed your trip here perfectly. It actually looks like a cover stop."

"A *cover stop*?"

"It's a tactic to take the FBI off your trail. To the FBI, you appear to have gone home to the comfort of your family after the death of a friend."

"But you're the FBI."

"Yes, but I'm also your friend," said Michael.

"I'm confused. You are saying that some ghost surveillance was tracking me, so the FBI dangled my friend Diana to take them off my trail?"

"That's correct."

"And now the FBI, who has been tracking me, think I came home to be with my family, not to meet an FBI agent?" Louise asked.

"Yes."

"Does the FBI know about Vladimir and me?"

"Yes and no. Vladimir placed an alert on your credentials, so *I* cleared you through customs."

"*You* cleared my credentials. Not the FBI?"

"You should be careful with Vladimir."

"So, you're saying I can trust you, but I can't trust Vlad," she said.

"The CIA is monitoring your movements."

"Was the ghost surveillance the CIA?"

"We're not sure who the ghosts were. It could have been BCCI or the CIA or someone else."

"Okay, I get it. Watch out for BCCI and Vlad."

"You had sex with him," said Michael.

"What business is that of yours?"

"You've been cooperating with the CIA. The CIA refuses to cooperate with the FBI on the BCCI case, so we have to assume you will be uncooperative with the FBI."

"*The BCCI case*? How long have you been investigating BCCI?"

"Since before you worked there."

"Does my father know?"

"This case goes all the way up to the highest-level public officials, who have been protecting BCCI, who are in turn protecting BCCI's key clients. That includes everyone from leaders of countries, including the United States, to drug dealers and arms dealers."

"This is a cover-up?" Louise asked.

"This may be difficult for you to believe."

"Try me."

"Joe Biden, chairman of the Senate Judicial Committee, has refused to follow up on reports of corruption. John Sununu who works under George Bush is also believed to be protecting BCCI. Even Jimmy Carter is close friends with Abedi and has accepted millions from BCCI for his charitable organizations. The CIA and the White House refuse to take action. The greed, power struggles, and campaign funding run on both sides of the aisle. The only official who has made a serious effort to investigate allegations is Senator John Kerry. I have been working on behalf of the New York County official enlisted by Senator Kerry to bring charges, Jack Blum."

"Jack Blum, my dad's boss?"

"Yes."

"What if the CIA finds out that I talked to the FBI? What could they do to me? They already forced me to cooperate under threat of arrest."

"You're in deep," said Michael. "Whatever you gave to the CIA, you'll have to share with the FBI. We don't share information, and this corruption is making the country vulnerable to terrorists."

"Terrorists? You can't be serious."

"It's a question of national security. If you don't cooperate, I can detain you for drug trafficking or charge you under the Racketeering, Influence and Corrupt Organizations Act, directly related to your work at BCCI."

Louise knew the RICO Act could cripple BCCI, but she had no desire to protect them at her own peril. She just wanted to fix the mess she was in. "I came to you for help and now you threaten me?"

"You have no idea what kind of pressure I've been under," said Michael. "You have been very lucky to have me on your side. I've been protecting you against the CIA and BCCI. According to our sources, the CIA has used BCCI extensively. The National Security Council, which is an arm of the White House, was using BCCI to channel money to the Contras through Saudi Arabia, even before Oliver North had set up his network for making illegal payments to them. Abedi will stop at nothing to keep expanding

BCCI."

Louise listened as Michael informed her of how much influence Abedi had procured over the past twenty years. "In order to influence Jimmy Carter, Abedi played his old themes of charity, philanthropy, and financial and technological assistance to the poor countries of the developing world. This was precisely what interested Carter in the years following his defeat by Ronald Reagan in 1980. Abedi befriended Carter and made a striking demonstration of his sincerity, donating $500,000 to help establish the Carter Center at Emory university in Atlanta. In 1985 Abedi began pumping millions into Carter's Global 2000 Foundation to provide health care to the Third World. During the 1980s, BCCI gave $8.1 million to Carter, while orchestrating the donation of another $2.5 million from Zayed through the Abu Dhabi Investment Authority. In exchange, Abedi raised his stature to that of close associate with a former U.S. president whose relatively enlightened policies toward the developing world had made him enormously popular there. For Carter, there was an apparently unlimited source of money to fund his new global philanthropies.

"The corruption had not been limited to one political party. Five months after the purchase of First American Bankshares by BCCI, the director of Saudi Arabia's General Intelligence agency, Sheikh Kamal Adham, inexplicably decided to give a public insider's defensive appraisal of BCCI to an Arab audience. There were so many things that were done through BCCI that were regarded by the Third World as achievements—like funding the Pakistani atomic energy program. For the Pakistanis, whoever helped them was a hero; since India had an atomic bomb, why not Pakistan? It was the only way to defend itself."

Louise listened in silent amazement.

Michael continued, "That was an astonishing statement, made by one of the most powerful and knowledgeable players on the Middle Eastern stage, acknowledging that the Pakistanis had their own atomic bomb and that Abedi and BCCI had helped them get it. Adham was defining BCCI not so much as a bank, but as a geopolitical entity designed to siphon petrodollar deposits away from Western banks. Such an entity could forward the Islamic cause unfettered by the dictates of any superpower. Adham may have been sending a message directly to President George H. W. Bush by speaking so boldly in public, reminding the President that Kamal Adham knew far too much to be trifled with.

"For the first time, the Bush administration had been dragged into the BCCI scandal. American political reporters, who had generally ignored the BCCI affair, had a brief field day with its implications. When a reporter questioned Bush about Adham, President Bush snapped, 'Ask him. I don't know anything about this man, Adham, except I've read bad stuff about him.'"

"Upon saying that, the President had just told a certifiable lie. Someone in the White House press corps asked again, and the President confirmed that he knew nothing about Kamal Adham. The reporters were incredulous. Adham had been the director of Saudi Arabia's equivalent of the CIA in 1976 when George H. W. Bush headed the CIA. The American agency had been helping to modernize Saudi intelligence during Bush's tenure, and Kamal Adham had been Saudi Arabia's main liaison to the CIA.

"The Reagan administration was intent on continuing military aid to Pakistan during the Afghanistan war and had turned a blind eye since U.S. law prohibited aid or military sales to non-nuclear countries known to be developing nuclear weapons. The situation was even stickier for the Bush administration: In 1988 and 1989, in the face of overwhelming evidence to the contrary, President Bush was constrained to certify that Pakistan still did not 'possess a nuclear explosive device' to justify continuing massive U.S. support for Pakistan, which was by then the third-largest recipient of American aid, after Israel and Egypt. The official excuse was that Pakistan had only the unassembled components of a bomb. Then in 1990, with the Soviets pulling out of Afghanistan, it was declared that possession of unassembled components violated the rules: Bush refused to give Pakistan another clean bill of health, and U.S. aid was abruptly shut off.

"Adham may have been suggesting that it would not be in the Bush administration's self-interest to probe too deeply into how Pakistan and BCCI came to possess such military capacity. The sheikh, more than almost anyone, was in a position to know that BCCI was the creation of a real-life Dr. No, whose empire brokered ballistic missiles, satellites, illicit pharmaceuticals, stolen military secrets, heroin, and hot money, leaving a trail of corruption across two decades and seventy countries. And of all people, Adham had reason to know that the White House knew it too and had known about it for years."

Michael continued explaining how Abedi then courted the Reagan-era white House. "After the mid-1980s Texas oil business crash, George W.

Bush's energy company, Arbusto, which is Spanish for Bush, was purchased in 1988 by a little-known Dallas firm, Harken Energy, which was primarily in the business of buying up old refineries. George W. was named a director of the company. Harken Energy's fortunes exploded when the company— which had no offshore drilling experience—unexpectedly won an offshore drilling rights from the Gulf kingdom of Bahrain that was potentially worth billions. Harken Energy's stock soared on the basis of the miraculous deal in the state of Bahrain, while oil industry giants like Amoco were cut out. According to his 1997 personal income tax returns, George W. Bush earned $271,920, but in 1998 that figure swelled to $18.4 million. Most of the difference came from the sale of Bush's stake in the Texas Rangers baseball team. However, Bush was able to build up that stake as a result of the suspicious sale of 212,140 shares in Harken worth around $850,000 (a typical daily trade in Harken stock was around 1,000 shares) immediately prior to the 1991 Gulf war. Bush informed the Securities and Exchange Commission eight months after the normal deadline for filing details of the transaction—when Desert Storm had come and gone—but there was no SEC investigation.

"Abedi's $20 billion 'bank' is in fact a vast, stateless, multinational cor- poration that deploys its own intelligence agency, complete with a paramilitary wing and enforcement units, known collectively as the Black Network."

Louise was stunned to hear Michael use that term. Vladimir had told her about the *Réseaux Noir*, or Black Network, and how a ring of enforcers hired by BCCI were likely the ones had been following her. Vlad told her about incidents of bank officers who had been threatened and intimidated to keep them quiet.

"You know about the Black Network?" Louise asked.

"Of course. BCCI is extremely powerful and corrupt. BCCI's Black Net- work was known to do a lot of intelligence operations even with the CIA.[28] It maintains its own diplomatic relations with foreign countries through 'protocol officers' with limitless amounts of cash to pursue Abedi's goals."[29]

"You know about the protocol officers too? That's top secret."

"Not anymore," said Michael. "Abedi's goals include development of a 'Muslim bomb' as well as transactions that have often upset the uneasy techno-military balance sought by the United States and other major powers engaging in government-to-government weapons sales.[30] Abedi will kill to get what he wants. So far, sixteen deaths around the world are related to the BCCI investigation."

"So, you have been protecting me. Vladimir said he was protecting me. I don't know who to trust. It's hopeless. Not even my father can help me now."

"You are not powerless here," Michael said. "As a primary informant to the CIA, you are very well positioned and an important asset to the FBI regarding this case. Therefore, you are under my protection."

"Then why don't I feel safe?"

"Go back to your parents' house for a few days and lay low. I'll come see you there."

"So that's it? I have to take a bus back home?"

"Hitchhiking is very safe in these parts too."

Louise looked around at the surroundings, which now brought to mind the movie *Deliverance*. She shivered. "I'll get a hotel in Woodstock for the night."

"Sounds cozy."

"Want to join me?"

Michael smiled and took her hand. "I'd love to but…" She understood that to mean he had to remain professional.

Louise walked back to the bus stop and waited. Despite Michael's disturbing tales of international intrigue, being in nature had a healing effect. Even being completely exposed to the outdoor elements, for the first time in months she felt safe. This was the closest to nature she had been in years. As a child, she used to lie beneath the evergreen bushes and gaze at the lilies of the valley. The perfection of their tiny white bells evenly spaced along the elegant stems. Nature's beauty was still magical to her.

The wild turkeys paraded along the brook that trickled beside the dirt road. The white bark of the aspens was striking against the blaze of yellow leaves. The glassy reservoir and the old stone bridge spanning it seemed in elegant harmony with it all. The reservoir was designed to enhance the natural surroundings. However, under the waters lay the ruins of hundreds of homes and even cemeteries that were destroyed for the project around 1910. There were still areas of the reservoir where one could see chimneys of homes that were there before the valley was flooded.

She got off the bus about ten miles north in Woodstock, the town made famous for the three-day music festival in 1969, which actually took place about forty-three miles southwest in adjoining Ulster County. When the number of tickets sold approached five times the original fifty thousand expected, the original venue canceled, and the concert moved to the six-hundred-acre dairy farm in the town of Bethel, New York.

Louise entered the first cozy bed-and-breakfast she found. The accommodating owners fed her a hot meal in the rustic dining room after which she had a cognac in front of the fire then headed up to bed. As she turned the key and opened the door, she thought room service must have lit the fireplace. Then she saw his silhouette in the glow of the hearth. "So, you couldn't stay away," she said.

"I opted for the element of surprise," replied Michael. The warmth of the fire combined with the chilled air was the perfect ending to a long day. He had only to see her smile for them both to know the power he had over her. She couldn't resist him. It was like they had never been apart. One thing was certain, their lovemaking would be spectacular. They shared an eternal flame that nothing or no one could extinguish, and Michael knew it. All the intrigue and adventure between them only heightened the sexual tension.

The next morning, Louise had momentarily forgotten the feeling of foreboding that had been clouding her psyche for the past few days. She wished she could stay right there forever. But Michael was already gone, and the peaceful night in the country had given her the fortitude to take the long journey back to civilization.

After a few days rusticating at her family home to ensure her *cover stop*, Louise decided it was safe to return to Paris. During the flight, she did her meditation, and her affirmations reminded her that everything she needed in life was available to her if she just opened herself to the universe.

THIRTY-THREE

Louise landed in Paris and went back to business as usual. First order of business was funeral services for Diana the morning after she arrived. The service was held in the same place Diana and Max were wed, the Benedictine Abbey of Saint-Germain-des-Prés.[31]

How surreal for Louise to come back to this place where she first visited Paris with her college friend Suzanne! It was nothing like her first impression of mystery and excitement. It now seemed *familiar*.

Much like Westminster Abbey in London, notables including René Descartes and Jean Mabillon are buried in the chapels that line the interior walls of the church. As she entered the abbey, Louise's eyes adjusted for the dim light. She moved to the front where Diana's husband, Max, stood, inconsolable. As she feared, Max was a brooding mess. While Diana's family wept quietly seated before the choir, Max absentmindedly leaned against the sixth-century pillar and lit a match for his cigarette. A monk approached and silently squelched the flame then made a gesture of blessing. His kindness calmed Max slightly.

Louise kissed Max on both cheeks then led him to be seated in the front row. The service began and Max walked to the podium. A man of very few words, Max gave the briefest of eulogies, "I miss you already, Diana," and sat back down.

As the service ended, the tower bell rang, and the mourners rose to shuffle out. Louise remained seated next to Max to buttress him. Then after most everyone had left, she helped him up and escorted him up the aisle. Out of nowhere, Chinoy appeared and bowed to Max.

"We wish to offer you our deepest condolences. Diana was part of our family, and we will miss her terribly. Please accept this gift." Chinoy held out an elegantly decorated sealed envelope.

Louise took it for Max, certain it was a generous offering. "I will make sure he gets it."

Chinoy bowed again and left.

Then as though waiting for Chinoy to leave, Vlad appeared. "Max, please let me take you home."

Louise shot him a look. "That won't be necessary."

"I'm sure Diana would have wanted me to."

"Not a chance."

"Je ne rentre pas." Max broke free from Louise's grasp and marched up the aisle, past the guests and out the door toward his wine bar, just steps from the Abbey. Louise placed the envelope in her bag and followed Max.

"More gifts from BCCI?" she heard Vlad say behind her.

Louise turned back and moved her face to within inches of Vlad's. "Do what you want with me. But leave Max alone. He's been through enough." She continued after Max, brushing past Greg without acknowledging him.

"Max has the right idea," Vlad told Greg.

"Drinks on me," said Greg. They left together and followed Louise and Max. Soon most of Diana's close friends were at the wine bar. There was solemn toasting and reminiscing. Being together, forgetting all other concerns, even just for a while, was enough to help ease the pain. Max turned the music on loud. The song "Évidemment" by France Gall played. Every person in the room was in tears, singing along, even Vlad.

THIRTY-FOUR

Louise's mother's words rattled around in her head: *After losing someone close, the best thing to do is go back to your life where you left off. Let everything take its natural course, and you'll figure out what to do.*

She went back to work and told Chinoy she needed to fly to the Cayman Islands to help Jean-Philippe de Villeneuve set up an offshore entity.

"Jean-Philippe de Villeneuve? We have been trying to land his account for years! How did you do it?"

"Jean-Philippe is forming an offshore entity with my friend in Panama, and they asked me to be their personal banker in the Caymans," said Louise.

"That's wonderful news."

"I'd like to leave as soon as possible. Tonight, I'm dining with Jean-Philippe at Taillevent, and we leave for the Caymans tomorrow. Would you like to join us for dinner tonight?"

"Thank you, but I have plans. Please take Monsieur de Villeneuve to dinner on behalf of BCCI. Insist on paying. Don't let him pay."

"I will try my best."

Louise arrived at the renowned restaurant, Taillevent[32] in the 8th arrondissement, not far from her apartment.

Although Jean-Philippe had insisted on sending a limo, Louise arrived by her own private company car. Her next challenge would be getting Jean-Philippe to let her pick up the tab. He was already there when she arrived. They started with a toast to Diana and then for hours discussed food, wine, American versus French politics and culture, and life in general. The latter was Louise's favorite topic of conversation. Intellectual discussions were a particularly strong character trait attributable to her Russian blood. Her father, a Russian American, had once told her that when he read Dostoyevsky's *The Brothers Karamazov*, he felt as though he was reading the story of his own family. Louise became an avid reader of Soviet literature, her favorite of which was the writings of Alexander Solzhenitsyn.

Jean-Philippe listened intently as Louise went into a passionate citation. "Solzhenitsyn once said, 'If I were asked today to formulate as concisely as possible the main cause of the ruinous revolution that swallowed up some sixty million of our people, I could not put it more accurately than to repeat: men have forgotten God; that's why all this has happened.' Twenty million Soviets were killed under Stalin. Russians were imprisoned, tortured, and killed indiscriminately, never knowing what had condemned them to the Gulag. It was a diabolical psychological game designed for ultimate control and power. The sense of absolute randomness left everyone with an utter sense of emptiness. This deep-rooted sense of meaningless existence has been shown to be carried on genetically from generation to generation."

"Genetically?"

"Yes," Louise said. "I believe that personalities and character traits are genetically passed on. The word *trait* comes from the Latin *tractus*: the act of drawing a line. A distinguishing quality—an inherited characteristic—is drawn from generation to generation. I also believe that the Russian persecution germinated the seeds of existentialism, which became popular in the years following World War II. Central to existentialism is that 'existence precedes essence' meaning that the most important consideration with regard to the individual is the fact that he or she *is* an individual, an independently acting and responsible conscious being, *existence*, rather than labels, roles, stereotypes, or other preconceived categories the individual fits, *essence*. The philosopher Kierkegaard posited that the individual is solely responsible for giving meaning to life and for living life passionately and sincerely."

"Living life passionately and sincerely seems to be your distinguishing character trait," said Jean-Philippe.

"You seem to know me so well. But I am presumptuous to discuss the human condition with you, a worldly gentleman."

"Nonsense. I am only human."

"You have a way of making me feel very comfortable," Louise said.

"You give me too much credit."

"Not at all. It must be a character trait of truly enlightened people. Whatever their background, they don't make others feel inferior."

"It's simpler than that. I just like you."

Louise felt they shared a connection that she hadn't felt since Michael, but it was even more profound. They were drawn to each other. After hours had passed, the server approached and politely asked in proper French without a hint of the guttural Parisian slang, "May we offer your something else? A digestif perhaps?"

Jean-Philippe realized the restaurant was empty and looked at his watch. "Mon Dieu. Please bring the bill."

"It has already been taken care of by Mademoiselle."

Louise smiled. "When I left the table, did you think I had gone to powder my nose?"

"This is unacceptable."

"This is non-negotiable." Louise looked at her watch. "My driver is waiting to take me home." The server bowed as they got up from the table.

"This is a precedent that must be undone. How will you make it up to me?"

"Unless you have a time machine, I'm afraid…"

"Here is what I propose. Your driver takes you home tonight. But tomorrow we fly to the Cayman Islands together."

"I already booked a flight and was going to meet you there."

"I insist, you accompany me on my private jet."

"You drive a hard bargain," Louise conceded.

"I'll send a car for you in the morning."

THIRTY-FIVE

The next morning, Jean-Philippe's driver was waiting promptly to take her to his private Gulfstream GIV at Orly Airport, which beat the hell out of going through customs. She would find his lifestyle as comfortable as her favorite little black dress. Although her tastes dovetailed with Jean-Philippe's lifestyle, she had always been low maintenance, practicing an ease of living that provided comfort no matter where she lived. She set her standards to a level so that if she were to lose everything and could afford only a studio apartment, she would be just as happy. Solzhenitsyn said, "Own only what you can always carry with you, know languages, know countries, know people. Let your memory be your travel bag."

Given her character, there were two things she could never do: marry for money or compromise her beliefs. She felt intense attraction for Jean-Philippe, but she wanted to maintain a professional relationship and was determined not to give in. She needed to avoid going down the path of romance that he was so clearly leading her to.

For the flight, she dressed comfortably chic and took one carry-on bag. They greeted each other with cheek kisses. "Vous êtes belles comme le jour." His use of the formal "you" when calling her *as beautiful as the day* took her determination down a full peg.

Six hours and a two bottles of champagne later, the private jet landed at the Owen Roberts International Airport, located on the largest of the islands, Grand Cayman. The stunning white sand beaches and sea air further weakened her defenses.

The Cayman Islands, located in the western Caribbean between Cuba and Jamaica, did not regulate any bank chartered there. Their lack of regulation was precisely the inducement for banks to charter themselves. Likewise, BCCI's operational home—the United Kingdom—also did not regulate BCCI's activities: The UK regulator, the Bank of England, considered BCCI to be a foreign bank, based in Luxembourg and the Grand

Caymans, and thus regulators in those respective countries were responsible. This neat arrangement by BCCI, together with its division of auditing functions between two unrelated firms, one for Luxembourg and the other for Grand Caymans, ensured that BCCI's activities could not be monitored by anyone.

Louise and Jean-Philippe spent the first leg of their trip on Grand Cayman, establishing the new fine antique instrument business. It took several days to set up the offshore entity. In order to open the bank account, they needed to draft the articles of incorporation and other documents for the company. They fastidiously hashed out the business structure and respective ownership of each shareholder. This required several conference calls between Louise, Peter, Bing & Fushimi, Jean-Philippe, and their respective attorneys. Once they had established the corporate structure, Louise set up an office and an accounting system, so they could begin operations immediately. That required renting a furnished executive suite, purchasing a computer and printer, and then hiring and training a part-time accountant who would process and track all transactions. All administrative and accounting functions actually had to take place on the Cayman Islands in order to maintain the corporate veil. Abedi had learned quickly that geography was the name of the game, so Louise had learned from the best.

The stateless Eurodollar, really nothing more than an imaginary construct that allowed banks to "place" certain portions of their assets "offshore," was the currency. Eurodollars were a bookkeeping trick that everyone, including the regulators, agreed to play along with. Eurodollars are "time deposits denominated in U.S. dollars at banks outside the United States and thus are not under the jurisdiction of the U.S. Federal Reserve. Consequently, such deposits are subject to very little regulation compared to similar deposits within the United States." The beauty of the system was that banks could park deposits and loans in odd places like Nassau, Bahamas, and the Cayman Islands, and by so doing conceal them from any meaningful regulatory supervision.

BCCI was incorporated in Luxembourg, the virtually unregulated financial haven that lacked even a central bank, such as the U.S. Federal Reserve or the Bank of England. All forty of BCCI's shareholders came from the

Persian Gulf. Its headquarters were in London and its principal branches concentrated in the United Kingdom and the United Arab Emirates. No other bank presented such a spatially dislocated profile. In the late 1970s, the Bank of England prevented BCCI from further branching and refused it "authorized status" as a British bank. Abedi's solution was to take a further step outside the boundaries of international regulations, a move that would effectively make BCCI a bank that was "offshore at all points." The bank was owned and controlled through a Luxembourg company called BCCI Holdings. In 1976 Abedi incorporated International Credit and Investment Company Holdings (ICIC) in the Cayman Islands through which much of BCCI's growing business would pass.

The sunny, paradisiacal Cayman Islands are at once a shining example of what is wrong with the world of finance and the reason no one wants to do anything about it. Beneath the veneer of respectability carefully polished by the big banks with offices there, the islands thrive on three principal commodities: money from legal and illegal tax evasion; money from drug sales and other criminal activities; and illegal capital-flight money coming out of the Third World. The tax games played so aggressively by the world's largest corporations needed a playing field, and if places like the Caymans, Monaco, Liechtenstein, the isles of Jersey and Man, Panama, and Andorra, did not exist, one could argue that they would have to be invented to accommodate a very certain need.[33]

The criminal element fit snuggly behind the reputable corporations and used the same mechanisms for their own ends. In turning to the Caymans for secrecy, Abedi and Naqvi were merely mimicking what their larger and more respectable First World counterparts had been doing for more than a decade. By 1991 the tiny island of Grand Cayman contained five hundred and fifty banks and trusts and $400 billion in "offshore" deposits, making it the number-one offshore financial center in the world. Forty-six of the world's fifty largest banks had Caymanian licenses. In all, twenty-two thousand companies were registered in the islands, engaged in everything from shipping and trading to insurance, real estate, and finance.

To understand how the Caymans work, one must understand the artificial banking practice called "booking." Booking is a special concept, having to do with the actual "location" of money. Let us say a bank in the United States makes a credit card loan in the state of New York. For tax purposes or other reasons, the bank decides to "book" or locate the loan in North

Dakota. This is done by a stroke of the pen. The bank simply decides that North Dakota is where the loan will be. The same can be done with deposits, and the concept can be just as easily transferred offshore. It is that simple. Most large banks have similar arrangements. Of the five hundred and forty-eight registered banks in the Cayman Islands, only sixty-eight have actual offices and staff there. *Booking* is a fiction, as are most offshore corporate branches and Eurodollars. For BCCI, the Caymans were merely a bookkeeping device used by men who sat at desks in London. The accounts booked in the Caymans remained invisible to European authorities.

BCCI's Cayman branch, ICIC, constituted a bank within the larger bank and was by far the largest of the rabbit holes down which funds vanished. It seemed a small step at the time. After all, most major American and European banks had some sort of operations in Nassau or the Caymans. Yet by doing so, Abedi effectively created the world's first truly stateless multinational corporation, a bank with offices all over the world, incorporated in Luxembourg and the Cayman Islands, run by a "joint personality" executive that had "no geographic location." BCCI was both everywhere and nowhere, a Third World bank operating out of a First World city.

Most offshore havens of the world's largest and most reputable banks offered similar services. Someone looking for secrecy in Panama, for example, would do just as well at various Swiss banks. BCCI was merely mimicking the state-of-the-art practices in the respectable west. The difference was BCCI's aggressive marketing strategy, known within the bank variously as the "Dollar Deposit Mobilization Program" or "External Marketplace Program" (EMP). The EMP targeted not only millionaires who wanted to hide profits, but also criminals, drug lords, arms dealers, and smugglers. Within BCCI, these banking services were highly systematized, coordinated from the top, and constituted the primary engine of the bank's deposit growth.

The EMP began with a referral from a customer or a BCCI officer. Once referred, the customer would then be shown, in precise detail, how he or she could bury his or her wealth so deeply in offshore tax havens that no governmental authority anywhere would ever be able to find it. To maintain secrecy, the bank provided confidential courier services, numbered accounts, and false offshore addresses to which account statements could be mailed. Bank officers could also provide, within a matter of days, "nominee" corporations based in Panama or Europe, creating "loans" that were really just transfers of money backed by false collateral. Once clients were given their Panamanian front companies, false addresses, false loans, and numbered accounts, the customers were assured that no more than two BCCI officers would ever know their real names. They were also assured that their accounts would be kept apart from the regular accounts of the bank, literally locked in the manager's drawer. Customers were told that no authorities anywhere would ever learn of the existence of those accounts, let alone the names of the persons holding them. Only an unprecedented global seizure of the bank could allow a glimpse into these so-called "hot money" accounts.

It was this marketing strategy that kept BCCI pumped full of deposits during the years after the fall in oil prices in the early 1980s. Because of the EMP's wild success, BCCI took pains to establish its own internal controls. First, "local" employees were never allowed to conduct such transactions. This role was restricted to "men of confidence," all of whom were Pakistanis who spoke Urdu. These men kept few tangible records of their transactions. They rarely wrote anything down, relying instead on telephone conversations conducted in Urdu or handwritten notes written in Urdu, kept locked away in personal safes. They were purposely not trained to comply with U.S. laws, so that they could claim ignorance of those laws. BCCI even maintained a corps of internal inspectors whose job it was to travel to branches and make sure that the proper levels of secrecy were maintained. The EMP was taken very seriously throughout the 1980s. The performance of these "men of confidence" was measured mainly by their success in generating EMP accounts.

It was alarmingly demonstrative of the mechanisms by which billions of dollars flee the United States each year. BCCI was a paradigm of the way much of the world worked, and nowhere was this truer than in its activities in the Cayman Islands. BCCI had become the world's leading "underground" bank, performing services and making money off *underground economies* from Pennsylvania to the Pacific Rim. Underground economies are mainly those parts of the economy that, in response to regulation, taxation, or law enforcement, have managed to remain invisible to the authorities. For example, one of the fastest, easiest, and least traceable ways to pay bribes is in the form of cashier's checks. They cross borders easily, can be endorsed to third parties, and are as good as cash. In one instance, thirty-one cashier's checks totaling $765,000 were issued on a single day out of

BCCI's branches in Boca Raton and Miami. BCCI would also set up accounts in one country in the names of phony Panamanian coffee companies expressly for the purpose of helping clients evade U.S. income tax. The client could thus make "payments" to these "vendor" accounts, which were then deducted as expenses from taxable income.

In the United States, the size of the underground economy in the 1980s was estimated to be $350 billion to $500 billion a year, equivalent to more than 10 percent of the U.S. gross national product. That represented $100 billion or more in lost tax revenue for the U.S. government. Economists at the World Bank and the International Monetary Fund estimated that a similar 10 percent of the Western European economy and 70 percent to 80 percent of the economies of the former Soviet Union and Eastern Europe were "black." Most of the money was completely untraceable.

To illustrate how completely off in the stratosphere and beyond the purview of anyone all of this activity is, one need only consult the Balance of Payments tables. These tables track global deficits and surpluses—a minus in the U.S. balance sheet is matched by a plus in the Japanese ledger, and so forth. By definition, the world must be in balance with itself. Yet from being approximately in balance in the early 1970s, an inexplicable black hole deficit of $20 billion had developed by 1978, and in 1982 the deficit hit $110 billion.

How damaging was capital flight to the Third World? In the years 1976 to 1985, $200 billion was transferred offshore by citizens of developing countries. Of that, between 1983 and 1985, the worst years of the debt crisis, $53 billion moved out from the countries that had the hardest time paying off their debt: Mexico, Venezuela, and Argentina. It has been estimated that as much as 96 percent of dollars borrowed abroad by these three countries for things like infrastructure projects and factories ended up in the offshore accounts of private citizens, many in the very same banks that had lent the money in the first place. In 1986 Morgan Guaranty Trust, which later became J.P. Morgan, estimated that of the $375 billion in new debt taken on by the ten major Latin American countries between 1975 and 1985, almost half vanished forever as flight capital.

THIRTY-SIX

After a week of grueling work, Louise and Jean-Philippe had tied up the remaining loose ends of the offshore entity. Louise had been staying at a luxury hotel provided by BCCI. However, with their work finished, Jean-Philippe insisted that she move into his family villa that overlooked Seven Mile Beach. Jean-Philippe dismissed the staff, leaving them completely alone. Finally, able to relax, they watched the sunset snacking on caviar and champagne. Louise threw off her caftan and lounged in nothing but a bikini bottom. Her favorite thing was a view of turquoise waters and powdery white sand. Jean-Philippe's favorite thing was a view of Louise lying on the white linen sunbed, in a turquoise bikini bottom.

Louise felt more natural undressed than dressed. As a child, she often discarded her clothes and ran around the yard naked until her mother could catch her. The French cultural norm of sunbathing topless suited her, but she wasn't sure about the rules in the presence of aristocracy. Nonetheless, she enjoyed torturing Jean-Philippe. He took the bottle of Cristal Champagne from the ice bucket and refilled her flute. Standing over her, he said, "May I ask you a question?"

"Sure."

"May I sit?"

"Why not?" she replied, barely moving over.

He sat beside her legs, facing her. "May I ask you another question?" She nodded. "Vous faites de la plongée?"

"Do I scuba dive? Yes, I was certified in Greece a few years ago," Louise replied.

"Parfait. Tomorrow we will dive the wall at Cayman Brac. It is one of the best dives in the world."

"How many hidden talents do you have?" Louise asked.

"Perhaps enough to keep up with you," he replied.

After the week of business, the sexual tension between them had become almost unbearable. Jean-Philippe exhibited a smoldering attraction to her, but his approach was old-fashioned, restrained.

He took her hand. "Ma chère Louise, mes sentiments ne doivent vous échapper." She was nonplussed by his sudden seriousness. He looked into her eyes and kissed her hand softly, causing her tummy to flutter. Then he said it, slowly, "Je…Je vous aime."

Until that moment, she had taken his romantic gestures as harmless flirtations. It may have been his strict use of the formal *you* not just toward her, but also when addressing everyone from a relative to his chauffeur. Or it may have been because she felt so at ease with him. Or perhaps it all seemed too good to be true. She had been acting under the assumption that he had been amusing himself with her. But now she could see in his eyes that he was laying bare his soul. No armor protected this knight. She suddenly realized that her feelings for him were more intense than for any other man she had known.

As soon as he said *I love you*, she knew that she had been lying to herself. It was an epiphany. He was not the type of man to *fake* anything. His integrity was unquestionable, *noblesse oblige*. He was probably one of the last modern noblemen in the true sense of the word. He was a *danrée rare*, a rare commodity, in the world today. For the first time in her life, she felt unworthy. How could she not have seen this coming? The implications of a serious relationship with him were dizzying. Her life would change forever.

He took her in his powerful arms, instantly comforting her. This was no flirtation. He was authoritative but openhearted, as though he needed to prove himself worthy of her love. To that end, he sensed what she really needed now was rest and a chance to assess her feelings for him. Making love to her in this state would be opportunistic. He kissed her intensely with the purity of first love. Then lifted her just as a balmy breeze carried the scent of jasmine, sparking an image in her mind of a knight sweeping her off her feet.

Louise had often mused about what sex might have been like during the Renaissance. This seemed as close as she would ever get. The sumptuous surroundings of the villa, its décor and the pastel sunset, were like a movie set from a period piece, his aristocratic manner further channeling the era. He carried her effortlessly, as she squeezed her arms around his neck, pulling her mouth feverishly to his lips and her body against him. She wanted him to set her down, but every time he tried, he stood back up not daring to lay her down for loss of control.

He carried her to the master suite, the charming décor reminiscent of an Impressionist painting. Placing her on the bed, he kissed her gently, then more deeply. He tore himself away and contemplated her longingly, but then composed himself.

"Je vous laisse dormir, ma belle." He left her to sleep.

Louise was dumbfounded and frustrated, but, overcome with exhaustion, she snuggled up in the bed. Her thoughts raced. It had been fine settling for fleeting passion her whole life. But nothing before compared to this. There would be no more questioning, no more doubting, no more taking him for granted. From now on, she would worship him. She would let herself be vulnerable and exposed. She fell into a deep sleep and didn't awake until morning.

THIRTY-SEVEN

The next morning, Jean-Philippe was waiting for her on the terrace where breakfast was served. She had fallen asleep before dinner and devoured the food, enjoying a rush of palatal pleasure with each bite. Her hunger heightened the flavors, evoking sighs of satisfaction. They both giggled at their own gluttony, while they stared into each other's eyes, all senses now fully engaged.

Then they put on their swimsuits and walked down to the private pier. His private seaplane flew them to the smaller islands about eighty miles away, making a water landing right in front of the private dock to Jean-Philippe's 170-foot live-aboard yacht. The state-of-the-art vessel had six luxury cabins, each with ensuite heads and queen-sized beds. It also had a large sky lounge on the bridge deck, an air-conditioned main saloon with a full bar and dining area, and a well-stocked gourmet galley. A crew of fourteen maintained the yacht year-round.

The captain, Timothy, also served as the dive master and maintained scuba gear for ten. Timothy looked like a California surfer with sun-bleached shoulder-length hair, sunbaked skin, and a sinewy physique. Wearing a short farmer John wetsuit, he greeted them with an enthusiastic smile.

"Ahoy! You guys might get lucky! Great weather and amazing visibility, perfect conditions for the *rays*."

"The rays?" Louise asked.

"If we're lucky, you may find out," Jean-Philippe said, taking the helm. He ran at 10 knots to the famous Cayman Brac[34] wall for a day of diving.

Just fourteen miles long and one mile wide, Cayman Brac lies between Grand Cayman and Little Cayman and has a population of one thousand. Its impressive pristine subaquatic limestone cliffs run along the middle of the island from west to east. At the eastern tip, the bluff ends in a dramatic one-hundred-forty-foot drop.

They anchored and suited up. In preparation, Timothy summarized the dive. "We'll essentially be floating over the tips of coral-covered underwater mountains rising from thousands of feet below the water's surface. Look for tarpon, turtles, barracuda, eels, spotted rays, and maybe a few reef sharks."

They plunged in. The waters were clear and calm with almost ideal eighty-foot visibility. Diving down to one hundred feet, Louise watched her Renaissance man explore the depths, more interested in the micro life than the bigger animals as he wiggled a finger at a bright yellow frogfish hiding in a notch in the reef. After their tanks ran down below 500 PSI, they came aboard for a snack.

Having gone down as far as one hundred and twenty feet on the first dive, they would need to wait an hour before the next dive and refrain from diving deeper than seventy or eighty feet.

Jean-Philippe skippered the boat over the blue water that was four miles deep at some points. The crew switched out the empty air tanks with full ones, and they put their buoyancy compensator vests back on.

"This time there is no reef, but you might be amazed at what you see," Timothy said.

They plunged back in and descended slowly, Louise squeezing her nose and clearing her ears repeatedly to manage the pressure. As she descended, it didn't take long for her to see the "rays" that Timothy had mentioned. Jean-Philippe was only a few yards from her, and the clear calm water gave way to flawless visibility. It was like they were floating in the air. The sun's rays pierced straight through the water, making it possible to see the bottom thousands of feet away. It was a miraculous sight. Louise was further stunned when she noticed the sun's rays bouncing off of Jean-Philippe, creating an incredible halo or star-like effect.

They boarded after floating for half an hour. "You looked completely in your element, like an angel in heaven," Jean-Philippe said.

"Can we go back down and see it again?"

"You were lucky to have seen it at all," said Timothy. "You brought us luck."

"So that doesn't always happen?" Louise asked.

"Maybe once in a lifetime, my love," Jean-Philippe said, kissing her gently. "We did two dives today, so we will come back again tomorrow."

They headed to Timothy's nearby home where the water was deep enough to anchor just a hundred yards from the beach. Timothy was a descendant of an old Cayman Islands family. His parents had moved to the United States to raise him and his brother when they were children, but they still owned a historic home on Cayman Brac. His brother became a successful New York attorney. Timothy made it through law school, but instead of a life in corporate law offices and a home in the suburbs with two cars, two kids, and a dog, Timothy chose the road less traveled back to his family legacy. He moved into the beautiful but neglected family home ten years ago, slowly doing renovations.

They lowered the skiff and motored ashore for lunch on the terrace. The house was about one hundred and fifty years old and built above the ruins of a seventeenth century stone port. Despite the rundown state of the home, it still held incredible charm. The terrace was made of old re-purposed stones that receded into the white sand beach. Rustic furniture made of driftwood collected over the years still served its purpose comfortably. They dined open-air style on fresh conch salad tossed with juice from homegrown limes and a touch of Scotch Bonnet hot peppers. It was served with dense soda bread and a crisp French rosé. Timothy didn't have a wife and kids, but he did have several dogs that he had adopted over the years. They were well-mannered, lying patiently at his feet for the occasional offering or accidentally dropped tidbit.

"Now this is what I called civilized," said Louise. "The last time I dove was a year ago, and I forgot how much I love island life."

"There's no comparison to city life," said Timothy. "I don't miss it at all."

"This must have been a wonderful place to grow up as a child," said Jean-Philippe.

"Yes, I highly recommend raising children here. The schools are better now than when my parents moved us away."

Louise raised her glass. "To living in paradise."

After lunch, they took the skiff out to the seaplane and flew back to Jean-Philippe's villa. Louise was exhausted from the dive and the wine. Jean-Philippe led her to the master bedroom, drew a bath for her, and left her to plunge into the warm waters beneath the foamy bubbles.

The next morning, they were up at sunrise and had breakfast. They took off again on the seaplane for another day of diving. Timothy was even more enthusiastic about the conditions.

"There is a lot of activity if we go a little deeper today, one hundred and fifty feet. Do you think you're up for it, Louise?"

"Sure, my ears cleared, and I got plenty of sleep last night."

Jean-Philippe kissed her. "Of course, my little dolphin is up for it!"

They geared up and plunged into the Caribbean at The Wall. Carefully equalizing as she descended, Louise quickly went down to one hundred feet where she saw all kinds of creatures. A dolphin swam right by her then weaved back and forth playfully overhead. Two black tip reef sharks scouted for food below her. She descended another twenty feet, when suddenly Louise felt some strange symptoms that didn't make sense. At first, she wondered if she was in narcosis. However, she hadn't gone deep enough for a sustained period. Narcosis, also known as *the martini effect*, is a reversible alteration in consciousness that occurs while scuba diving at depth. Narcosis produces a state similar to alcohol intoxication or nitrous oxide inhalation, and usually does not become noticeable until depths beyond one hundred feet.

However, having trained in nitrox diving, she knew her current symptoms didn't apply to narcosis but rather to nitrox sickness from diving too deep under nitrox. It is not a deep-diving gas mixture because of the increased proportion of oxygen, which becomes toxic when breathed at high pressure. The maximum operating depth of about seventy feet is not to be exceeded. She had memorized the acronym VENTID-C, which stands for Vision (blurriness), Ears (ringing sound), Nausea, Twitching, Irritability, Dizziness, and Convulsions, which seemed to fit her current symptoms.

Louise fixed her eyes on a nearby clownfish lurking in a brightly colored sea anemone, a common trick to keep from panicking while diving. Her gauge showed a safe 1,500 PSI of air, but it also showed she was at a depth of one hundred and twenty feet, which is dangerous for nitrox diving. She squeezed the underwater signaling device hooked to her BC vest. The clicking sound brought Jean-Philippe next to her in seconds. Not sure what signal to give, she made the hand signal for 'no air,' a flat horizontal hand movement in front of her neck like cutting off the head.

Louise took her regulator out of her mouth as Jean-Philippe removed his regulator and placed it in her mouth. She took two calm breaths, and they started floating slowly upward to the surface together, passing the regulator back and forth. After a five-minute safety stop at fifteen feet, they surfaced near the yacht to find a commotion. One of the crew was frantically radioing the Coast Guard as the rest of the crew searched for someone out in the water. Two of the crew helped Louise and Jean-Philippe aboard.

"Qu'est-ce qui se passe?" asked Jean-Philippe, demanding an explanation.

"Frédéric s'est sauvé," said one of the French crewmembers.

Timothy came aboard. "What the hell's going on?"

"Frédéric suddenly unloaded one of the Jet Skis and took off on it," said another crewmember.

"Louise's tank was empty, so we had to come up," said Jean-Philippe.

"No, my tank wasn't empty, but I didn't know the signal for nitrox sickness."

"That's impossible. I loaded your tank myself." Timothy inspected her tank. "What the hell! This is a nitrox tank! Who put this on her vest?" All hands pointed out to the fleeing Jet Ski. Timothy looked around for the missing crewmember. "Frédéric?" All heads nodded *yes*.

"Frédéric must have swapped out your tank. If you hadn't come up, you could have had convulsions and drowned." They quickly pulled up anchor, and Jean-Philippe took off after the Jet Ski.

"Do you have any idea why Frédéric would do this?" Timothy asked Jean-Philippe.

"Yes," Jean-Philippe said, accelerating.

"He has been part of my crew for ten years. I've never had any trouble with him before," said Timothy.

"There are people with a lot of money who are willing to spend it."

"Life-changing amounts of money," added Louise.

"This would have been the perfect scenario to do away with Louise," Jean-Philippe said. "It is very difficult to prove foul play in scuba accidents. When he saw us both resurfacing, he must have panicked."

Jean-Philippe noticed Louise was shivering and terrified. He signaled for Timothy to take over the helm. "Keep tailing Frédéric." He wrapped a plush towel around her and held her. She resisted at first, not sure whom to trust. "It's okay." Louise held back tears as the boat bounced over the turquoise waters like a skipping stone. Timothy raced to regain the fleeing Jet Ski following one wake then another, but it was gone.

They arrived at the seaplane. "I'm going to have to pay Chinoy a visit." Jean-Philippe was visibly irate. "We'll leave immediately."

"We just dove," Louise pointed out.

"You were down for only a few minutes," said Timothy. "And it has been twenty-four hours since your last dive, so you should be okay to fly."

When surfacing after diving, residual nitrogen in the body poses a health risk and could result in decompression sickness, also known as the bends. This also applies to ascending in an airplane if there is residual nitrogen in the body after a dive. The change in air pressure when a plane ascends is roughly equivalent to fourteen to sixteen-foot depth of water. The risks of decompression sickness are the same. Flying after diving could result in extremely painful gas bubbles forming in the joints and flesh, or, if in the blood, could lead to an embolism and even death. It is best to wait at least nine hours after diving before flying.

Not stopping at the villa, they took the seaplane to the private jet and went straight back to Paris, still wearing bathing suits. Fortunately, Jean-Philippe always kept dry clothes on the plane. Six hours later, they were in Paris. Louise looked like a little girl in the back seat of the limo wearing Jean-Philippe's baggy clothes. "You are staying with me tonight…and every night from now on."

"You will get no argument from me."

THIRTY-EIGHT

"Pierre will take me to BCCI and come right back for you," Jean-Philippe said. Louise went up to her apartment to shower and change, and when she came back down, Pierre was waiting for her in the limo. When she arrived at BCCI, Chinoy was serving café au lait and croissants to Jean-Philippe in his office overlooking *les Champs*.

She stopped outside the door and listened just as Chinoy asked Jean-Philippe, "When was the last time I saw you?"

"At your party in Cannes last year. I heard you purchased that villa."

"Yes, it's a great write-off for the company, and it's worth a fortune in rental income."

Louise stepped into the office but remained silent. How could she not have known they were so well acquainted? She blushed trying to control her emotions. Jean-Philippe picked up on her reaction and walked over to her.

"Excuse me." She rushed out and Jean-Philippe followed, getting into the elevator with her, just as the doors were closing.

"Where are you going?" he asked.

"I don't know. Home I guess."

"I need you here."

"I don't want to be here. I don't want to be with you."

"Don't say that. Come back to the office and finish what we started."

"First, tell me how you know Chinoy," Louise demanded.

"I'll explain later. Right now, we must let him know that we are, as you Americans say, *an item*. This will all work to our advantage."

"Why should I trust you?"

He raised her hands to his lips and kissed her fingertips. "Because, I love you."

When they returned Chinoy's office, he smiled and politely, welcomed them back. "There you are. I hope everything is all right?"

"Everything is fine, Monsieur Chinoy," said Jean-Philippe. "We have a confession to make, which should explain everything." Louise followed his lead. Jean-Philippe turned to her and lowered to one knee. "Louise Moscow, will you do the honor of becoming my wife?" The blood rushed to her face. Louise was stunned, excited, and confused. Was this real or made up for Chinoy's benefit?

"Yes," Louise replied, timidly.

"Bravo!" Chinoy said, shaking Jean-Philippe's hand. "Felicitations!"

Louise smiled nervously. Champagne appeared and popped open so quickly she wondered where it could have come from. She stared at the five-carat diamond ring Jean-Philippe had placed on her finger. It looked real enough. Had Jean-Philippe been carrying it with him this whole time? Had he been planning on proposing to her in the Caymans?

Chinoy grabbed Louise, hugging her and kissing her on both cheeks. Glasses clinked, and the cool bittersweet bubbly liquid never tasted so good.

"Take the rest of the week off," Chinoy said. "Go somewhere and relax. Don't worry about such boring things as banking and international finance."

"Mr. Chinoy, are you sure? I'm in the middle of quite a few projects," said Louise.

"Nonsense. You work faster and more efficiently than a dozen French staff. You could take a month off and still get more work done than them." She could hear the indignant huffs of her French colleagues just outside his office. However, Chinoy's charm let him get away with such cultural gaffes. "And now, I have an announcement," said Chinoy. "There have been some major changes at BCCI. Abedi and Naqvi have been terminated. Zafar Iqbal has been appointed as the new BCCI president."

"This is very unexpected," Louise said, genuinely alarmed.

"I trust my business with BCCI won't be affected," Jean-Philippe said.

"Not at all. This is all part of the BCCI expansion. Out with the old, in with the new. Customer service is our number one concern," said Chinoy.

"Well, if you're sure you can do without me for a week during this change," Louise said, "I will gladly accept your offer of a short vacation."

"Yes, by all means. Take care of our distinguished client," said Chinoy.

"With pleasure," Louise said. She kissed Jean-Philippe brazenly in a rare public show of affection. She beamed as they left the office hand-in-hand. Even if it had all been for show, she wanted to enjoy the feeling for as long as possible. She was engaged to marry the man of her dreams.

Finally, in the limo, they stared into each other's eyes. "You know what this means, don't you?" said Louise.

"That you love me?"

"No," Louise said, completely ignoring his question. "It means that Chinoy wasn't the one trying to kill me."

"I know. When I spoke to him, it was clear he had no idea," Jean-Philippe agreed, but then gave her the most pathetic wounded puppy dog look. "Is that all this means?"

She kissed him passionately. "I love you."

Jean-Philippe's eyes opened wide. "You do? You do!" They kissed, practically devouring each other. Pierre had never seen Jean-Philippe this way and closed the limo divider window. They embraced and she laid back, his hips pressing into hers, almost driving her to the brink.

"Wait. Not like this," Jean-Philippe said.

"Ugh! I don't care," Louise gasped. "I can't take it anymore."

"No," he said, kissing her firmly then softly, again bringing her to the edge. "I want to take you away." The limo pulled up to Louise's flat. "I will come back to get you in two hours. Pack your bag."

One more kiss then she practically stumbled out the door and up to her flat. She sat down in front of the vanity in her bedroom, staring at the ring, then at herself in the mirror. Her attention was suddenly drawn to the manuscript that she had found in the secret chamber and left on the table. She picked it up and put it back in the cubbyhole inside the chamber, returning it to its hiding place. She didn't think about her action. She did it unconsciously.

THIRTY-NINE

Michael had been typing at his computer when his closed-circuit cell phone rang. Only one person had the phone number, so Michael didn't even need to answer. He knew it was time to meet George Moscow. He gathered the research he had been preparing and left to bring his updates to George.

Michael entered the back door to the kitchen and gave Mary a kiss on the cheek. "How's my little girl?" Mary asked.

"She's safe but I can't say any more."

Mary handed him a cup of coffee the way he liked it, black with a little sugar. "That's all I need to know then."

"Thanks, Mary." Michael went straight into George's office where George and another man were already talking.

George rose and shook Michael's hand. "Thanks for coming over so quickly while I have these guys here. Michael, this is William Ryback, head of the U.S. Federal Reserve's international supervision division, and Virgil Mattingly, general counsel to the Fed."

William shook Michael's hand. "Call me Bill."

"Hi Bill, Virgil. Thanks for coming." They sat and Michael distributed some printouts of his latest research. "Okay, on October 3rd, 1990, I informed George that Price Waterhouse presented their audit report to BCCI's board that contained the records of immense loans to 'nominees,' which were actually front men, proving that BCCI owned First American Bankshares."

George interjected, "BCCI's attorneys, Clifford and Altman, had repeatedly assured me that there were no proprietary connections between the two banks. But Clifford was the chairman of First American Bankshares, and Altman was the president."

Ryback chimed in, "Now I have some information for you. Right after you informed me of this in December 1990, I went to London and spoke to the new BCCI president, Iqbal Zafar, and asked to see the audit."

"And he gave it to you, just like that?" asked Michael.

"Not exactly. I stopped just short of a full-scale threat by the U.S. Federal Reserve. BCCI still operated two large agencies and an office in the United States, holding hundreds of millions of dollars in assets in U.S. banks, so they did not want an irate Fed. They let me see the particulars of the fraud. What jumped out at me in the October 1990 audit was more than $1 billion in loans to an entity coded XYZ Corp. The loans were all secured by stock in XYZ and not a dollar of the loans had ever been repaid. I asked Iqbal if XYZ was really First American and if the loans were made to front men. He said yes. But neither Iqbal nor the head of the Bank of England, who also possessed a copy of the audit, would let me bring it back home. The Bank of England knew I would give it to Bob Morgan, and they were in the middle of negotiations with Zayed and absolutely could not afford to let that happen."

"So, we held off telling Morgan," said George.

"Excuse me for being blunt, but how did they convince you to keep quiet?" Michael asked.

"They have their ways," Bill said. "But we got the documentation soon enough. Right after I returned in December 1990, Virgil here received an impromptu visit from Sheikh Zayed's American attorney, Sandy Martin. He walked right in and told us in detail about the shareholder loans through which BCCI gained control over First American Bankshares. Zayed had Martin go to Abu Dhabi to obtain some of Naqvi's most damning and privileged documents, including records of the worst and most complex of BCCI's manipulations, and bring them to us. Sandy Martin also gave us documents that showed money lent to BCCI's American attorneys, Clifford and Altman, to buy shares in First American."

"He gave me a list of shareholders that had been filed in the most recent report," said Virgil. "He said 60 percent of the stock of Credit and Commerce American Holdings, or CCAH, the holding company that owned First American, was pledged in loans and that the loans were nonperforming. I was shocked. This was highly unusual that someone would come in and admit something like this. I mean, a lawyer walks into the general counsel's office at the Federal Reserve Bank and admits this stuff? I told him that BCCI was in violation of the Bank Holding Company Act."

"We called Robert Altman into our office," Bill continued, "and explained that we had seen evidence that BCCI had acquired the stock of First American. Altman stuck to his story that he knew nothing about any shareholder loans to anybody. Altman walked right into the trap, neglecting to mention that he and Clark Clifford had received $18 million in BCCI loans to purchase shares of stock in CCAH. Nor had he said anything about the $10 million in profits that the two men had made from the subsequent sale of that stock to another BCCI front man, Mohammed Hammoud."

"That made me mad more than anything else," said Virgil. "We immediately made a criminal referral to the Justice Department and ordered BCCI and First American Bankshares to cease and desist from any interaction or funds transfers. Once Altman had stepped on the tripwire, the Fed geared up for a full investigation."

"Okay, it's now March 1991. What's the plan?" asked Michael.

"The Fed is dispatching a team of three officials to Abu Dhabi to secure documents," George replied. "A large chunk of the prosecution's case will focus on the deal Altman and Clifford made with BCCI to purchase First American stock. Shares were bought in 1986 and 1987 at no risk with loans from BCCI. In 1988, roughly twenty months after the First American Bankshares stock was initially purchased, some shares were sold at a 300 percent profit, producing a pretax profit of $9.8 million for the two men. BCCI bought those shares."

"And you need me to make sure Louise is safe during this operation."

"That's correct, Michael," George said. "Where is she now?"

"As you can see from my report, she just returned to Paris from the Cayman Islands. Chinoy has authorized her to take a vacation to the south of France with Jean-Philippe."

"Keep us apprised of her whereabouts. You need to stay within striking distance at all times and be ready to move when it's time to bring her in."

FORTY

Jean-Philippe whisked Louise off to his family's twelfth-century chateau in Dordogne. Her very first trip to France had been to this region. Louise was excited to be back there with Jean-Philippe. His family chateau was located on a remote hilltop and the sight of it seemed vaguely familiar. Perhaps it was one of those that she had admired on the bus ride to her college summer program, which now seemed a lifetime ago now. The castle, with its long and eventful history—having played an important role in the Hundred Years' War with England—had been designated a historic national monument. At one point, Richard the Lionheart had seized the castle by scaling the cliffs below and entering through the 'toilet holes' that were suspended over the cliff. Centuries later, Jean-Philippe's family would claim the chateau for restoration. In addition to its impressive location, it had several ancient rooms including dungeons, kitchens, and living quarters hidden within the castle. It also had various open courtyards and views across the miles of surrounding Dordogne countryside.

Except for the bustling staff, Jean-Philippe and Louise were alone. He showed Louise to her bedroom where she could freshen up and relax. Then he dismissed the household staff to their quarters and opened the fridge.

Jean-Philippe had called ahead to have some classic American food prepared specially for Louise. He made sure everything was ready then brought Louise to the kitchen. With boyish pride, he revealed his surprises from the fridge and oven. As if by magic, he produced every American delight, from peanut butter and jelly sandwiches to macaroni and cheese and chicken noodle soup.

Louise sat in the medieval kitchen and snacked on comfort food. It was heavenly. They drank delicious wine from his family vineyard and chatted for hours. After a few glasses of Bordeaux, they opened up to each other about their personal lives for the first time.

"I haven't been completely forthcoming with you about my work,"

Louise confessed.

"Nor have I."

"Me first."

"Okay."

"I have been working under cover with the FBI on an investigation of BCCI," Louise said.

"I know."

"You know? How do you know?"

"That is what I have wanted to tell you. But please continue."

"During my business trip to Panama where I had to arrange for some funding for a client, I inadvertently received a letter that was meant for the head of the Panama office."

"Did the letter come from the Panama attorney general?" Jean-Philippe asked.

"Yes."

"Was your client an attorney representing Noriega?"

"Yes. But I didn't know it at the time."

"I know."

"How do you know?" Louise asked.

"I am an intelligence agent with the Directorate-General of External Security."

"You're a spy?"

"I am an agent. Are you a spy?"

"I'm not even an agent," said Louise. "I have been doing undercover work for the FBI and the CIA."

"So, you are an agent," said Jean-Philippe.

"No!"

"Yes, you are. It's just not official yet."

"How did you know about the letter?"

"I didn't. But I know all about Panama." Jean-Philippe told Louise about the photos he had taken at the Cannes Film Festival party in the chateau that BCCI subsequently purchased. It was the photo of the Panama attorney general shaking hands with Noriega's attorney. "The reason they sent you to Panama was because Amjad Awan, the former manager of BCCI Panama who handled Manuel Noriega's personal banking, was about to be arrested in Tampa, Florida."

"Was he arrested?"

"Yes, but he immediately defected and cooperated. He will do jail time, but he has given up a tome of information in exchange for a reduced sentence."

"So, you and I have been working on the same case?" Louise asked.

"Yes, and for the same side."

"Lucky for you. Otherwise I would have to kill you."

"Very funny." He said it in that adorable French accent that sounded like vereee fuuneee. "Seriously though, it is important that you remember what I am about to tell you. You are safe with me. But if ever the worst-case scenario happens when you are alone in Paris, there is a place you can always go. My friend is part of a clandestine group that will take you into the Catacombs and protect you."

"The Catacombs?"

"You don't know the Paris Catacombs? It is a very special place. You must memorize what I tell you." He gave her an address in 18th arrondissement in the south end of Paris. Finding the location consisted of navigating alleyways and secret knocks on doors. "You must commit this information to memory right now. He will show you to safety."

"Can I ask you something?"

"You are wondering if my proposal of marriage is real or if it is part of the operation?"

Louise nodded, her lower lip quivering.

"You really aren't much of a spy," Jean-Philippe said.

"You mean spies aren't supposed to cry?"

He took her in his arms and kissed her finger wearing the ring. "You see this ring? It is from my great, great grandmother. It is almost two hundred years old."

"Do you want it back?"

Jean-Philippe laughed affectionately. "This is why I love you. You're so unassuming, and yet you have such keen instincts and profound wisdom."

"Half the time I feel completely clueless."

"Do not underestimate your power," said Jean-Philippe.

"So, you don't want the ring back?"

"It is yours until you pass it on to our children."

"I love you." Their kiss was hotter than the meatloaf in the oven.

"Come on." They walked arm-in-arm through the medieval halls to one of the master bedroom suite. It was the perfect setting for their *first time*.

Louise felt beautiful, wearing a vintage Myrna Loy peignoir. It was of pale lavender georgette silk that formed to her figure, with perfectly placed pleats and lattice shoulder straps. Her femininity was offset by the ancient medieval surroundings. They sank into the four-poster canopy bed with down mattress. Finally, with nothing holding them back, they melded with each other, with their surroundings, with the universe. They awoke hours later from a deep sleep, nestled in each other's arms. He kissed her.

"I want you to stay here as long as you like. But in three days, I have to go to Paris to meet with someone."

"I'm coming with you," Louise said.

"Very well. If you insist."

The chateau overlooked spectacular vineyards and hillsides. The natural golden hue of the region mystified Louise. She wondered why natural lighting there would be unique to that part of the world. She had seen a similar phenomenon in Rome. From atop Janiculum Hill, all of Rome seemed to have been lit by a cinematographer with a pale orange lens gel and dry ice misting the orange groves, giving the city the appearance of a Renaissance painting. The ancient setting seemed impossible today. In the United States, this landscape might have already been ploughed over to make room for a giant mall or amusement park. And yet, in much of Europe, life continues the way it has for centuries, with the land almost completely unchanged and no desire for modern upgrades. The only comparable places in the United States would be the working ranches and cowboys in Montana, Wyoming, and other western states.

She sipped café au lait and munched a delicious freshly baked croissant on the terrace. Normally, she wouldn't indulge in a whole croissant. But this was a real croissant. At least five layers of paper-thin pastry dough, each slathered with butter then stacked, rolled, and baked, the steam separating each layer until the outer one was crispy brown. When she tore it apart, it unwound like a party favor. She added locally made butter and jam and took a bite.

Jean-Philippe admired her technique. "You give new meaning to playing with one's food."

"It is your fault if I lose my figure."

"Don't worry. We'll work it off. Get dressed into something comfortable."

FORTY-ONE

Louise's heart raced as their helicopter floated over the Great Dune of Pyla. They approached the town of Andernos Les Bains, which is on the north side of the Arcachon Basin about 60 kilometers west of Bordeaux. They made their way around the bay to visit the massive sand dune.

The Dune du Pyla is the highest dune in Europe—currently around 107 meters high; however, being a dune, the height changes slightly as the sand is blown around. They trudged up the wooden staircase to the top and took in the view. This was the way Louise had originally seen it on her first trip there during college. The area extends about 500 meters inland and 2500 meters along the coast. On a very clear day, it is possible to see the Pyrenees mountains in the far distance. It offers a spectacular 360-degree view over the Atlantic coast, the inlet to the Arcachon basin, and inland over the tops of the pine forest.

During the eighteenth and nineteenth centuries, the region was planted with pines in an attempt to stabilize the sand and for timber growth, making it the largest pine forest in Europe called La Forêt des Landes. On the coastal strip, the foredune is constantly on the move. Palisade fences were built, and grasses planted to try and halt the inevitable movement of the sand. The dune's age can be calculated by studying the dark lines of sand and other debris, which run through the dune. Layer Paleosol three, between 20 meters and 40 meters from the base, has been found to contain bronze coins and other evidence from the sixteenth century. But due to the forces of nature another 20 to 30 meters of sand was blown into place to form the current dune's height around the beginning of the twentieth century. So, the current Dune du Pyla has only been in existence for around one hundred years. Louise listened to Jean-Philippe describe the history of the dunes.

"When we were kids, we called it la *colline affamee*," he recalled.

"The hungry hill?"

"The dune's movements devour anything in its path. About 8,000 square meters of forest are covered each year, and last year a road was devoured by an avalanche of sand. Someone built a villa near the dune in 1928 and even though the owners tried everything to stop it, the house was completely buried by the sand in 1936."

"So, is it safe to be here?"

"Perfectly safe. It is also a very safe place to fly hang gliders."

Louise could see people on the giant kites, jumping off the top of the dune and floating gently over the Atlantic Ocean.

"Étienne!" Jean-Philippe called to one of the hang gliders.

"Vous voila!" Étienne approached, shaking Jean-Philippe's hand. "You must be Louise. Ready to glide?"

"Don't I need to take classes or something?"

"Not if you fly tandem!" Jean-Philippe took Louise by the hand and showed her how to harness into the hang glider for two people. He explained the directional apparatus for steering the glider.

An hour later they were at the edge of the dune. "Ready! One...two... three!"

Rushing off the edge of a cliff had seemed par for the course to Louise these days. She wondered if her life hadn't been so unpredictable and tenebrous lately, would she so easily have been compelled to hurl herself into the dizzying void. But as soon as her feet left the ground and after her stomach came out of its somersault, she knew this was exactly what she needed. The helicopter ride seemed like no more than a B movie compared to the peaceful, weightless, bliss of this experience. How perfect being held by the man who made her feel the same way whenever she looked into his blue eyes. They drifted over the waves turning back toward the shore as children below waved and shouted to them. Jean-Philippe guided her hand to show her how to change directions. Taking the controls to turn just a few degrees gave her a sense of power. Landing was nothing short of miraculous. The controlled descent felt like falling, then catching an updraft that prevented the fall.[35]

To fly, Louise had to do two things: maintain a constant speed and keep her direction in a straight line. She had to sense her airspeed, using no instruments. If she was moving too fast, she pushed the control bar away from her to slow down. If she was moving too slow, she pulled the control bar toward her to speed up. Always flying in a straight line. If she veered to the right, she had to shift her weight to the left to get back on course.

To land the hang glider, she had to stall it. As she approached the ground, she pushed the control bar as far out as she could. This tipped the glider nose up, slowed the glider down, and eventually stalled it so she could land upright on her feet. The experience of stalling and landing on her feet struck her profoundly as though experiencing gravity directly.

Étienne removed their gear, and Jean-Philippe took Louise in his arms. "You are amazing."

"I feel amazing." Her feet back on solid ground, they had hardly gotten their balance when Pierre bounced over the sand in a 1971 Citroën Méhari. They got into the utility off-roader, a type of fast-running "dromedary camel" car. It was named after the Méhariste, a French African Army cavalryman who used camels. It had excellent off-road qualities due to the lightness of the vehicle. Jean-Philippe had brought it back when he returned to France after his military duty. It reminded Louise of the Volkswagen 181, known as *The Thing* when it was sold in the United States in the 1970s.

Her hair floated in the wind as they drove up the Atlantic coast to the small port city of Arcachon in the Gironde department in southwestern France. It is a popular bathing location thirty-four miles southwest of Bordeaux. The mild climate and soothing waters are said to be favorable for invalids suffering from pulmonary complaints. When hygienists began to recommend *thalassotherapy*, or sea bathing, some entrepreneurs established seawater centers specifically for the Bordeaux bourgeoisie. The Romance language of Occitan is still spoken by some in southern France. Parts of France, Italy, Monaco, and Catalonia are sometimes known informally as Occitania.

They parked at a magnificent wooded spot overlooking the lush valley of lavender fields and vineyards. Pierre spread out a gourmet picnic and left them alone. Louise devoured the lunch, impressing Jean-Philippe with her appetite. "L'émotion, ça creuse."

"That expression is so true," Louise agreed. "Emotions dig a hole my stomach, making me very hungry."

"Emotions make you beautiful," said Jean-Philippe.

"The hang gliding was very freeing. With everything that's been going on, it gave me a whole new perspective."

"You can stay here and live in the lap of luxury. Forget all the drama." Jean-Philippe's perfect English was tinged with just enough of a French accent to be exotic.

"You should know by now that I'm not the type to sit around being fed macaroons."

"Maybe you could get used to it."

"Not a chance."

"It's *fatiguant*, your work, non?" Jean-Philippe asked.

"Yes, my work is tiring. But what choice do I have?"

"You have many choices."

"Like what?"

"I could help you. There's an operation. Your involvement would be very beneficial."

"Will it get me out of this situation with BCCI?" Louise asked.

"If it goes accordingly, you will have protected status all over the world. You can keep your identity and your life. But you wouldn't be working for the United States."

"I'd be working for France?"

"No. Interpol," Jean-Philippe said.

"I don't know."

"It could be your best chance to get out of this mess."

"What would I have to do?"

"The less you know the better for now. Trust me." He took her hand. "Je t'aime."

"Moi aussi, je t'aime." Louise leaned into Jean-Philippe, her chest rising. He fluttered the back of his fingers across the soft skin of her cleavage. She moved closer, her lips brushing his, their tongues lightly fluttering together. She felt completely uninhibited. The little alcove hid them from the road. She straddled him and took a sip of champagne then kissed him, letting the cool bubbly liquid trickle into his mouth. In an effortless maneuver, she slipped one leg out of her shorts and panties as he unzipped. He masterfully slid inside her, sitting motionless. When he felt her release, he moved slightly, precisely applying pressure to cause her to completely let go. Afterward, they lay there, looking up at the sky.

"Where to now?"

"We'll catch the helicopter back to Paris. Tomorrow there is an important diplomatic dinner that I must attend. That is where you can help. I have arranged for you to be fitted for the occasion."

"You mean, like a ball?"

"Indeed, a black-tie affair, but official business."

"Undercover?"

"Very top secret. Your first mission, should you decide to accept it…"

FORTY-TWO

Jean-Philippe served Louise breakfast in bed at his Paris home. The café au lait was perfection. She poured foamy steamed milk from a pitcher, creating a creamy liquid cloud that emulsified with the fine coffee grounds of the rich espresso. She plunked in a sugar cube and drank the combination of flavors that comforted and awakened her at once. She dunked the buttered baguette and crunched into it.

"Allez, ma chère. On risque d'etre en retard."

"We're late already? Where are we going?"

"Surprise. Habillez-vous." She jumped up, and he smacked her firm bottom.

"Are you always going to vouvoyez me?"

"Of course, it is de riguer. I even vouvoie my mother. Allez!" Another smack on her butt.

Louise had the gift of getting ready in a flash while achieving a fresh look of simple elegance. She quickly showered and blow-dried her hair, leaving it slightly damp and twisting it into an updo. She threw on one of her more casual Myrna Loy outfits and was so well put together she could have walked right onto a photo set for a magazine cover.

They pulled the Bentley up to the Chopard boutique in Place Vendôme and were escorted to the private salon for exclusive clients. There the two-time Oscar winning Italian costume designer, Milena Canonero, greeted them.

Jean-Philippe kissed her cheeks. "Ciao bella! Come stai?"

"Ciao bello." Upon seeing Louise, Milena was stunned by her chic appearance. "Who is this creature? She wears something magnificent."

"Ciao, I'm Louise." Double cheek kisses.

"Louise, this is Milena Canonero."

"Forgive me, but I must know where you acquired these vesti? I know these. They are from the movies, no?"

"Yes. My great aunt was a costume designer for the *Thin Man* films."

"Your great aunt was Dolly Tree? Spectaculo! You are si fortunata, bella ragazza. Come, I dress you like a princessa."

Milena took Louise into a dressing room where special clients were fitted with designer clothing and jewels for red carpet events. The racks of one-of-a-kind gowns made Louise gasp. She went straight for a Chanel.

"May I?"

"Certo! You pick first. Then I choose. We work together."

Jean-Philippe sat down with a newspaper and talked on his phone as he waited for the fashion show. Louise tried clothes from Hermes, Gucci, and Yves Saint Laurent. She came out first in a black Givenchy pencil dress looking like Audrey Hepburn. Jean-Philippe and Milena nodded approval.

"We keep this on the short list," Milena said.

Then Louise reappeared in the Chanel gown by Karl Lagerfeld, of white silk satin with metallic embroidery, reminiscent of the *full dress* of the eighteenth-century royal court, only with an updated twist. It was floor length but slit all the way up the front with a matching mini skirt beneath, sleeveless with detachable off-the-shoulder embroidered long sleeves, worn with thigh-high white silk boots.

"Spectacular. But, too flamboyant," said Jean-Philippe.

"Too flamboyant for what?" Louise pouted.

"Suivant!" Jean-Philippe said, ignoring Louise's question.

Finally, she appeared in a Christian Dior gown by Gianfranco Ferre. It was a rose-colored, strapless, knife-pleated silk organza gown with a majestic silk taffeta overcoat that attached underneath the arms at the back, creating a seductively revealing off-the-shoulder look. She really did look like a *princessa.*

Jean-Philippe and Milena said in unison, "*La voila.*"

"Une minute. Il manque quelque chose." Jean-Philippe left and returned a moment later with a red jewel case. He opened it revealing an emerald necklace and earrings. He placed it around her neck as she put on the earrings. It was a lattice necklace with several tiers of gradually larger emeralds interspersed with diamonds from Chopard's *Haute Joaillerie* collection. It was one of their most expensive works made with some of the most beautiful emeralds of Columbia. It totaled 191 carats in emeralds, interspersed with 16 carats in diamonds. The deep emerald color worked beautifully with the rose-colored gown.

Jean-Philippe kissed Louise on the cheek. "I'll pick you up tonight from the day spa."

"Day spa?"

"You have a six o'clock appointment. Your wardrobe will be there. You just need to show up."

"What do I have to do tonight?"

"Just be yourself. The rest will take care of itself." Jean-Philippe left her wondering. She turned and looked in the mirror.

"Alora! I take the clothes. You go home. Rest. See you at the spa, six o'clock." Milena left her to change.

When Louise came out of the fitting room, Milena was holding her camera ready to take a picture. "I must have a fotografia of you, per favore. I love these Myrna Loy clothes." Louise instinctively struck an old-style glamorous pose, and the camera flashed.

Once outside, Louise put on her oversized black sunglasses and got into the limo. As a child, her father used to joke that they were descendants of Ivan the Terrible. Louise dreamed of being a princess, waking every morning, waited on by maidens, bathed in warm aromatic waters, then dressed in the finest silks and satins before being privately tutored in literature, music, and art, and then courted by the most dashing of men. She came out of her daydream as the limo arrived at her apartment.

After a long bath, she tied her hair up in a Hermes scarf and flopped down on her chaise longue with a book and dozed off. Her internal alarm clock was infallible, and she awoke at 5:30. She jumped up to leave. But, not knowing what to expect that evening, she picked up the phone and dialed Michael.

"No questions. Just listen. If you don't hear from me by tomorrow morning, please find out what happened to me."

"What's going on?" But all he heard was a dial tone.

FORTY-THREE

Milena greeted Louise at the day spa and took her to the Hammam. Located in the 5th arrondissement La Mosquee de Paris was a Turkish bathhouse with high ceilings and mosaic tiled archways and columns. There were several chambers for different services centralized around a warming hearth, and an ice-cold dipping pool for relief from the penetrating heat. The alternating hot eucalyptus-scented steam rooms and healing saltwater treatments soothed her. She lay down for a very abrasive rock salt scrub administered by a robust eastern-European woman. She was certain that the jagged sea salt was drawing blood as it burned her tenderized skin. But when she rinsed in the cool shower, she saw that her newly exfoliated pink skin looked fresh and healthy. Next she went for her manicure, pedicure, and facial. Like a modern-day princess, she had her hair and make-up done by world-class stylists. Her elaborate updo with layers of curls was topped off with a small and graceful Tiffany's tiara. She put on the gown and Milena gave her the final accessory.

"Bellissima. Here is your clutch. Attenzione, do NOT push this button. Use only in an emergency," she said, indicating the clasp on the clutch purse.

"What will happen?"

"It will not kill, but it will definitely maim."

"Are you serious?"

"Yes. You just aim it like so," Milena closed one eye and aimed the clutch at an imaginary bad guy with sharpshooter skill. "Then press the clasp here. Also, your tiara is a tracking device."

"Who knew? What about my necklace?"

"That little bauble doesn't do anything, but it is worth a fortune, and it is on loan. So be careful."

"Milena, do you know what my mission is tonight?"

"All you have to do is get yourself introduced to the Sultan of Brunei and invited to his palace."

"Oh, is *that* all?"

"You are irresistible. He will want you in his cortege. But as a woman, you will not be considered his equal, so it will take some *comedia* on your part to be not so strong female."

"So, I should *not* be myself. I should act subservient."

"*Acquiescent*, nicer word."

"Do you also work for…you know…" Louise asked.

"Yes. Since Midnight Express." Louise had heard that film industry professionals sometimes doubled as agents because of their easy access to people and situations. "Don't worry. You are a natural."

Jean-Philippe was waiting for her in the lounge when she came out. "Vous êtes exquise."

"Exquisite enough to meet the Sultan of Brunei?"

"Exquisite enough to be the Sultana of Brunei."

"I'm nervous."

"Just remember to keep your eye on the fish, and don't panic," he said, referring to the scuba diving trick for calming oneself.

"So, it wouldn't bother you if I went to the palace of the Sultan of Brunei alone?"

"Who said you would be alone?" He took both her hands in his, brought them to his lips, and kissed her fingers. As he looked in her eyes, he eased the engagement ring off her finger and placed it in his pocket. "Just until after the party. You can put it back on as soon as we get home."

"I don't know if I can do this."

"I would not ask you to do it if I didn't think you could handle it. Think of it as a game."

"Is that what I am to you?"

"Yes. And you are the grand prize."

FORTY-FOUR

The gala was held at the residence of the United Arab Emirates ambassador to France to promote investment in Greater Dubai, which offered numerous opportunities. The ambassador chose the evening of July 14, also known in France as Bastille Day, which commemorates the storming of the Bastille on July 14, 1789. The holiday is the French equivalent of the Fourth of July, Independence Day in the United States. The storming of the fortress-prison remained a symbol of the modern nation, bringing down the constitutional monarchy that had ruled France for centuries.

Celebrations traditionally end with an impressive fireworks display over the Eiffel Tower. The home of the UAE ambassador in the 16th arrondissement overlooked the Eiffel Tower and provided a spectacular vantage point for the fireworks. The United Arab Emirates[36] were becoming a well-established influence in the world economy. The ambassador would spare no expense for his very wealthy and influential guests.

Tonight's gala would be filled with dignitaries from these emirates. The current UAE ambassador's home had security that rivaled any embassy. The previous UAE ambassador to France, Khalifa Abdel Aziz al-Mubarak, was assassinated just outside his apartment a few hundred yards from the Eiffel Tower. It was believed that the Israeli intelligence agency, Mossad, hired the leader of a militant Palestinian group, Abu Nidal, for the job. He had begun his long and bloody career in the PLO, only to become a bitter rival of Yasser Arafat and then a contract killer. It was a situation that the Mossad would seek to exploit. It is generally accepted that Abu Nidal worked for Mossad and may have been working on his next hit, hence the airtight security at this gala.

The new ambassador went only by His Excellency to help maintain anonymity. His Excellency's Paris home was located between the Trocadéro gardens and the Bir-Hakeim Bridge, in a building directly overlooking the Eiffel Tower. The construction of the building was in the Art Deco style of the late nineteenth century. The entrance to the building was on the quai that runs along the Seine River. Security guards lined the entrance hall of the Parisian mansion, and a digital door code secured the entrance.

Jean-Philippe sensed Louise tensing as they approached the armed guards. "Do not worry. You have no detectable devices on you." Jean-Philippe stepped aside to let Louise enter first. "Après vous, mademoiselle."

Louise handed her clutch to the security agent next to the metal detector and stepped through, causing it to beep.

The guard looked through her clutch. "Please remove any metal and place it in this container."

"It must by my tiara." Louise smiled sweetly and plucked the tiara from her hair, placed it in the container, and stepped back through. This time, the metal detector remained silent. The security agent handed her clutch and tiara back to her. As she waited for Jean-Philippe, she opened her compact mirror and gracefully placed the tiara back in her hair.

Jean-Philippe passed through security and took her hand. "Bien joué," he whispered, and they entered the villa.

She never imagined such an expansive residence could exist within the confined streets of Paris. The residence was about seven thousand square feet and spanned the entire top two floors of the building, plus about one thousand square feet of staff accommodation. The armored door opened onto a vast entrance with parquet flooring that delineated the occupants' area from the staff area. On the left, they passed a grand lounge and dining hall, separated by four pillars. On the far side, the large lounge had African teak parquet flooring, a very wide fireplace, and four double French windows with a direct view over the Seine, the Bir-Hakeim Bridge, and the Eiffel Tower. On the other side, the dining room in the same style as the lounge had two large stained-glass windows decorated with floral motif from the Art Deco period.

At the end of the corridor, they descended a forty-foot bowed staircase to make their entrance into the great room. All eyes were on them. Many guests wore traditional clothing from around the world, made of magnificent fabrics, beading and jewels, which added to the glamour. The room was filled with some of the most powerful glitterati from the Middle East, including rulers of four countries, princelings from Saudi Arabia, and fabulously wealthy *commoners*. Each one represented BCCI's deposits, which came rolling in from their petrodollar-rich treasuries. Jean-Philippe was a celebrity in France, but Louise's appearance drew more attention. She was used to being looked at, but this venue was intimidating. A server offered them champagne, which Louise sipped gratefully.

She was so radiant it didn't take long before the Sultan of Brunei approached her. He was accompanied by Mohammed Abed Al-Jabri, the contemporary Moroccan critic and professor of philosophy. Al-Jabri was excited to see Jean-Philippe, and they greeted each other with a customary kiss on each cheek. Jean-Philippe introduced Louise to both men. Al-Jabri graciously bowed to Louise who returned a slight bow.

"What a pleasure to meet the charming friend of Mr. Jean-Philippe."

"Mohammed Abed Al-Jabri is a foremost philosopher of Middle Eastern thought," Jean-Philippe told Louise.

"Sayyed Mohammed Abed Al-Jabri,[37] I am a great fan of your writings," Louise said, smiling modestly. "Congratulations on your Baghdad Prize for Arab Culture from UNESCO," she added. The men were visibly impressed with her knowledge of Al-Jabri's work.

"I spent a semester abroad at Mohammed V University in Rabat during my graduate studies. After the semester, I spent the rest of the summer in Marrakech." Louise's experience in Morocco had initiated her immersion in classical Arabic, the language of the Qur'an and the official language of Morocco.

"You have the eyes of a thinker," said Al-Jabri. "Are you a philosopher as well?"

"Far from it. My university philosophy professor told me that my sole purpose in life was to be looked at. He motivated me to surpass his expectations."

"Fascinating."

"I wish more of your work would be translated into English," said Louise. "Your *New Averroism*, separating theology from scientific and philosophical thinking, was groundbreaking. It left western philosophers scrambling." Al-Jabri had a childlike sense of humor and his eyes sparkled with delight.

"*Scrambling philosophers*," Al-Jabri repeated. "The imagery of the English language is wondrous."

"You are American visiting Paris?" the Sultan of Brunei asked.

"Yes, your Highness. Actually, I am an American *living* in Paris."

"Ms. Moscow is my personal banker at BCCI," Jean-Philippe said.

"May I ask why you are not *my* personal banker, Sayeeda Louise Moscow?"

"I will ask my boss, Sayyed Chinoy, first thing Monday."

"Sayyed Chinoy will be here tonight, and I will request for you to visit my home in Brunei for a meeting."

"I would be honored, your Highness."

"Salam alaykum."

"Wa alaykum as-salam," Louise said, wishing him peace. They exchanged a long handshake in a show of respect.

Jean-Philippe and Louise distanced themselves to speak privately under the din of the music and conversation.

"Well done, my love," Jean-Philippe whispered.

"Piece of cake," Louise said, finishing her champagne.

"Do not be modest."

"If I understand correctly, that was only a very small first step. I don't even know what my mission is."

"It was a very big first step being invited to the sultan's home."

"To do what? On whose behalf?" Louise asked.

"As far as you are concerned, you are working for BCCI."

"I'd rather be working for someone that can protect me instead of put me in danger."

"I will protect you."

For the remainder of the soirée, she followed Jean-Philippe's lead and they pretended to be engaged in lively conversation. In reality, Jean-Philippe was giving Louise the background of political and social figures in the crowd. In turn, Louise filled him in on the finance industry professionals she recognized. She pointed to the famed American financier, Michael Milken,[38] and relayed some facts she had learned from her father, notably his role in the development of the market for high-yield bonds, also called junk bonds, during the 1970s and 1980s, earning him the nickname *Junk Bond King*.

Jean-Philippe pointed out BCCI front man, Ghaith Pharaon, pronouncing his first name 'raith.' Pharaon was short, stout, bewhiskered, and elegantly dressed. And filthy rich. His very name means "pharaoh" in Arabic and his pharaonic good luck began with his birth in 1940 as the son of one of the most influential figures in the history of Saudi Arabia, Dr. Rashad Pharaon. He had served as physician to the founder of modern Saudi Arabia, King Abdul-Aziz ibn Saud, who happened to be a hypochondriac. The king welcomed the elder Pharaon to the royal inner circle, which he never left, becoming the king's closest adviser and a confidant of four successive Saudi kings. The Saudi people liked Ghaith's father, but they didn't like him. It was a cultural Bedouin thing. One may be given the title of sheikh, but he takes it reluctantly; he doesn't assume it himself. But Ghaith Pharaon gave himself the title of sheikh.

Despite his unpopularity, Pharaon successfully launched himself into the construction business in Saudi Arabia in 1965. With the 1973 Arab oil embargo and skyrocketing oil prices, he was positioned to be one of the prime beneficiaries of the $150 billion Saudi building boom that took place in the 1970s. Pharaon accumulated wealth and property, which included the palatial Chateau de Montfort in the Dordogne region of France, Henry Ford's mansion in Richmond Hill, Georgia, and his own headquarters in Paris, which occupied the choicest location in the city on the Place de la Concorde, flanked by the American embassy and the Hotel Crillon on one side and the Tuileries gardens on the other. BCCI needed Pharaon as a front man to acquire a substantial stake in many U.S. banks, such as CenTrust, so they made him a 'nominee' and shareholder.

Louise was listening to Jean-Philippe intently, just as Pharaon approached them.

Jean-Philippe bowed graciously. "Monsieur Ghaith Pharaon, may I present Louise Moscow?"

Pharaon shook Louise's hand. "You work with BCCI?"

"Yes, in personal banking," Louise replied.

"I have heard wonderful things about you."

"Thank you."

"I hear you will be traveling to Brunei," Pharaon said, making it clear that he already had the inside scoop.

"If my boss approves."

As if on cue, Chinoy approached them. "If your boss approves what?"

"Hello, Mr. Chinoy," said Louise.

"I must intervene before my favorite executive is stolen from me." He gave Louise a kiss on the cheek. "You look ravishing, mademoiselle Moscow." Chinoy was accompanied by the ruler of United Arab Emirates, Sheikh Zayed. "Sheikh Zayed, this is Louise Moscow."

The sheikh bowed with an air that conveyed his appreciation for her beauty but nothing more, much like her philosophy professor. "Sayeeda

Louise Moscow, I have heard much about your good work with BCCI."

"It is an honor to meet you." Louise had much respect for the sheikh who was probably the most honorable of all BCCI associates.

"It is reassuring to have such a competent and principled person in our ranks." His words were a subtle warning meant for Chinoy.

"Customer service is our number one priority," Louse said, echoing Chinoy's own words.

For the rest of the evening, Louise met as many high-ranking guests as she could and spoke as little as possible. All in preparation for her mission.

FORTY-FIVE

Jean-Philippe had been working with Interpol and the CIA to position Louise inside a rescue mission. By knowing as little as possible, Louise would be more convincing in the role she played with the Sultan of Brunei. Louise had no idea that the mission was a result of one of Abedi's exploits.

Abedi's road to profits had little to do with commercial banking. While in Karachi, Abedi established his most effective promotional tool, the *protocol department*, in 1975 at United Bank to look after the needs of his wealthy clients who came from the Middle East to visit Pakistan.

In 1978, when BCCI opened its doors in Karachi, the protocol department was in place with his confidant, Sani Ahmed, overseeing a staff of more than one hundred and an annual budget of $1.5 million. But by all accounts, Sani Ahmed had little technical banking skill or knowledge. The protocol department's purpose was to find out what clients wanted and to give it to them. And what clients wanted varied wildly. Ahmed's duties included anything from building and looking after the Pakistan palaces and homes of royal families to tour guide and factotum of major depositors who came to shop or to party. The protocol department kept more than one hundred limousines at the disposal of important guests.

For example, Zayed's passion, which he shared with many other Gulf princelings, was falconry. The sport consisted of setting trained peregrine falcons upon the relatively helpless houbara, a semi-rudimentary bird the size of a hen turkey that migrates from Iran and Iraq in the winters to the warmer Persian Gulf. After the houbara had been hunted out in the Gulf, Abedi invited Zayed to the province of Beluchistan, Pakistan, where the houbara was still plentiful. Zayed no longer squatted in the desert with his rifle. With Abu Dhabi's new money, Zayed's falconry trips now consisted of

Humvees and Land Rovers towing huge air-conditioned tents and scores of exotic birds.[39]

For other clients, the protocol department was responsible for sweeping the countryside in search of very young girls for the entertainment of the sheikhs and Middle Eastern businessmen. By 1988 the protocol department employed nearly five hundred people and was prepared to supply more than young beauties from Lahore. The Arabian Peninsula had long been known to be purchasers of sex slaves primarily from India and Africa. However, with the advent of oil wealth the Saudis became more selective. Furthermore, the Saudi Arabian government refused to sign the United Nation's treaty on slavery and extradition.

A company called Dyncorp was a large international defense contractor known to facilitate this trade. Instead of banning Dyncorp from further defense contracts, the United States granted Dyncorp major contracts for the Iraqi war, thus indirectly enabling the sex trade. Even more shameful was the wink and nod the U.S. State Department granted the Saudis. There had been several incidents where the media had reported a sex slave of a Saudi prince being brought into the United States and escaping. However, it had become customary for the State Department to intervene and return the escaped slave to the Saudi prince and the incident forgotten.

One unfortunate victim that became entangled in the Mid-East sex ring was the former Miss USA Shannon Marketic. She had been lured to Brunei by what she believed was legitimate modeling work. Because hers was a high-profile case, she was returned to the United States and filed a lawsuit against the ruling family of Brunei for $90 million. Marketic alleged that she and six other young women were paid $127,200 each for a modeling job in Brunei where they were supposed to provide "intellectual conversations" with visiting guests of the royal family. The women included future Miss USA Brandi Sherwood, invited by Marketic, as well as Miss United Kingdom runner up Paula Bradbury.

Marketic maintained that she and other girls were held as "sex slaves" at the sultan's palace and were "intimidated and coerced into performing physically and morally repulsive acts of prostitution." They were apparently ordered to dance for five or six hours every night at parties during which their bodies and private parts were groped and grabbed by men, one of whom was the sultan's son, Prince Azim. The women often were told to go with a man to "have tea" and then forced to have sex with him. After thirty-two days of being held against her will, Marketic managed to smuggle a letter out to the U.S. Embassy. Shortly afterward, she was allegedly paid $10,000 and flown back to the United States alone. The case was thrown out due to the immunity of the ruling family as heads of state. Paula Bradbury separately sued the sultan and won £500,000 in settlement.

Now another young American model had gone missing under similar circumstances. She was the daughter of a prominent U.S. senator, so the CIA had gotten involved. Louise's mission was to aid the CIA in locating the American model and bring her home. Her first task had been to get invited to the Sultan of Brunei's palace. Mission accomplished. Once at the sultan's palace, she would report back to Interpol and the CIA via Jean-Philippe all logistical information on the missing American.

The Rolls Royce whisked Louise from the Brunei International Airport to the palace of the Sultan of Brunei. As an Islamic country, Brunei Darussalam became a full member of the organization of the Islamic Conference in 1984 during the Fourth Islamic Summit, held in Morocco. However, unlike the desert climate of the Middle East and northern Africa, the State of Brunei Darussalam, or the *Abode of Peace*, is tropical. It is located on the north coast of the Southeast Asian island of Borneo, which it shares with Malaysia, in the South China Sea. The language, Standard Malay, was one of the three major learned languages of Islamic scholarship. European writers of the seventeenth and eighteenth centuries described Malay as the language of the learned in all the Indies, much like Latin was in Europe.

As Louise's car passed each village along the way, she looked for its mosque. It is customary for every town to build its own mosque as its center and unique place of worship for its citizens. When she arrived at the Palace Istana Nurul Iman, servants greeted her with cool towels, refreshing tea, and dates from the palace garden. She was taken to her suite, which was larger than her entire Paris apartment. The veranda overlooked the Brunei River that flowed to Brunei Bay. She looked out over the lush green gardens that extended throughout the kingdom. It felt about average 80°F and, having no dry season at all, the breeze provided little relief from the humidity.

Louise still wore her hijab of beige fine gauze linen over her head. She had embraced the custom of the hijab while living in Morocco.[40] Veiling herself had made life in Morocco easier. She found the anonymity liberating. It made her feel protected from the stern looks of men, especially being blonde. It also protected her from the sun and controlled perspiration.

Dressed in a long, beige linen skirt and lightweight white cotton blouse, she removed the veil and fluttered her shirt allowing the air between the fabric and her skin to cool her. She plunged into a down chair and drank some of the cool exotic fruit juice that was set out for her and tried to adjust to her surroundings.

She heard the call to prayer and looked at her watch. It was 6:00 p.m. and the sun was setting. A male voice rang out through a loudspeaker in a long, sustained tone that indicated it was time for the men to enter the mosque for prayer. The sound was spiritually soothing, so she decided to meditate on the veranda. A moment into her meditation, she felt herself rocking steadily back and forth slightly to her right in the rhythm of her heartbeat. It was a calming sensation that she synced with her mantra.

When she finished, she opened her eyes and took in the view of the river and the perfectly groomed grounds beneath the glow of the golden red sky. The surroundings evoked a magical feeling. Visiting such historic lands was like taking a transporter back in time.[41]

Louise imagined that the scents, sunlight, shadows and sea breezes were the same as they were thousands of years ago. She took pictures of the estate for the dossier using the spy camera Jean-Philippe had given her.

Back in her suite, she was struck by the lavish interior décor reflecting the elitist lifestyle of the Sultan Haji Hassan-al-Bolkiah, sumptuous and impeccable.[42] Louise looked in the mirror, took a deep breath, pulled herself together and freshened up. She also needed to be impeccable. There was a knock at the door.

"Come in," she said.

A servant girl entered and bowed. She was beautiful, very young. "The sultan welcomes you. Please follow me."

"Hello," Louise said. stalling for time. "What is your name?"

"Alimah."

"Oh, that means, *skilled in music and dance.*" Malay names are mostly taken from Arabic, so Louise knew the meaning. Alimah bowed her head. "My name is Louise. Could you give me a moment?"

Alimah bowed again and Louise went into the bedroom. She quickly changed into a floor-length designer caftan, traditional yet form-fitting, with a hidden pocket for her camera. She covered her head in a Hermes silk scarf, wrapping it turban style over her thick hair, which she stacked on the crown of her head, reserved yet enhancing her bone structure.

She returned and followed Alimah out. As they walked through the estate, Louise held the small spy camera down by her side and secretly took pictures of the corridors to get the layout. They arrived at an expansive courtyard encircled by a colonnade lined with arched doorways to guest quarters, in the style of a Kasbah. There was a lavish lounging area in the center of the courtyard with an inviting atmosphere, soft music, food, and beverage. A baby camel lay next to an ornate chaise longue where Bolkiah was seated. He stood to greet her.

"Sayeeda Louise, welcome to my humble domicile."

"Thank you. Your home is very beautiful."

"Adara, please serve our guest." Louise sat on the sumptuous antique daybed among the soft cushions and embroidered fabrics, the draping silk canopies fluttering gently in the breeze. Adara, a servant girl, brought a tray of fruits, dates, goat cheese, nuts, and more of the exotic juice. There was also a bottle of champagne on ice. Adara poured Louise a glass.

As an Islamic country, alcohol consumption was banned, and there was no sale of alcohol in Brunei. However, non-Muslims were allowed to purchase a limited amount of alcohol from their point of embarkation overseas for their own private consumption. Of course, Bolkiah was exempt from his own laws and offered endless libation. Louise enjoyed the expensive champagne but sipped slowly.

"Thank you, Adara." Louise knew the name meant *virgin*. She studied the girl's face. She appeared calm, almost tranquil but avoided Louise's eyes.

The sultan raised his glass of tea. "To our new association."

Louise toasted their relationship. "I'm looking forward to working with you. As you know, there is much BCCI can offer you…"

"No work. Tonight, we relax. Tomorrow we can discuss business." Then a man appeared. "This is my younger brother, Prince Jefri, the finance minister of Brunei."

Louise knew exactly who Prince Jefri was. His reputation as a sex-slaver preceded him. In the traditional show of respect, she lowered her eyes as Prince Jefri reverently bowed his head. What an act! Three other girls accompanied Prince Jefri. These girls were not locals. They appeared to be western, wearing expensive designer clothing and jewelry. They helped themselves to the champagne. Seductive rhythmic music played on a *qanum*, similar to an auto harp, along with an *oud, darbuka* and *ney*, lute, a drum, and a flute. The Arab music in the lively quarter-tone scale, along with the delicious refreshments, distracted Louise from her mission.

Prince Jefri signaled for the girls to dance. They rose and moved gently to the music. Louise glanced up and immediately recognized one of the girls to be Naomi McConnell, the senator's missing daughter. Louise hid her surprise and looked away. Although it was considered rude to stare, Louise felt Prince Jefri watching her.

"Do you like horses?" Sultan Bolkiah asked.

"Yes, very much. I grew up in the countryside of New York State. We had a stable, and my father bought me my first pony when I was five."

"Then I have something very special to show you tomorrow." Suddenly, Bolkiah rose to his feet. "Forgive me. You must be tired, and I have some business to attend to. We will leave you to relax."

Louise was startled by the abrupt ending to the evening. She stood as the sultan and the prince both bowed to leave. Bolkiah nodded for Alimah to accompany Louise back to her chambers and for the other girls to follow him and the prince. Louise wondered if Bolkiah had seen Prince Jefri staring at her and cut the evening short for her own protection.

The western girls also seemed confused but followed orders. The senator's daughter took her time, sitting down to take a final sip of champagne. She was the quintessential American beauty—long blonde hair, bronze skin, piercing blue eyes, full lips, and white teeth. However, she did not smile. Louise tried to assess the situation, looking for a sign from her. Naomi gave Louise a discrete look, signaling for her to remain silent. With cameras in every room, even the bathrooms, someone was watching every moment. Plus, the other girls were extremely competitive and vicious. The ultimate victory was for the prince to take you in. The girls had been forewarned not to speak to Louise, and they would not hesitate to warn the prince if Naomi spoke out of line. Louise watched them leave then Alimah escorted Louise back to her suite.

Louise lay on the bed and called Jean-Philippe on her mobile phone. "I miss you."

"I miss you too, my love. How are you doing?"

"Wonderfully well. I'll see you at the airport."

"Okay. Safe travels." The phone conversation was intentionally short on details in case of listening devices. Saying "I'll see you at the airport" was their code phrase confirming that the senator's daughter was on the premises. If she had said "I'll see you at the train station," it would have meant no senator's daughter. Louise suddenly felt exhausted, so she locked the bedroom door and went to sleep.

In the morning, Alimah came to escort her to breakfast out in the magnificent flower garden. Dramatic hedges created an enclosed private setting with a well-placed opening that framed a charming view of the river. They finished a breakfast of goat cheese, soft-boiled eggs, olives, tomatoes, and a Middle Eastern bagel with freshly made jam. They were also served a very strong hot tea that was as eye opening and comforting as Louise's beloved morning café au lait.

"Come see the view." The sultan led her to the opening in the hedges where she took in the full vista over green hills that dipped down to a vast valley with what seemed to be endless horse stables. The view of the *écuries* was so picturesque it seemed unreal. Several purebred Arabian horses roamed the green valley, and trainers were riding others on a full-sized racetrack. Bolkiah glowed with pride. This was his most prized accomplishment.

"I own two hundred of the most valuable award-winning horses."

"It is spectacular. Who rides the horses?"

"Anyone I allow. Would you like to ride?"

"I've never ridden an Arabian horse before."

"Piece of cake." The sultan enjoyed using American colloquialisms.

They took the Range Rover down to the stables. Prince Jefri was already there, dressed in riding gear. Bolkiah led her to a fully equipped guest quarters with men and women's riding boots and clothing of all sizes. She changed and came out as the stable hand brought her a breathtaking white Arabian horse. She greeted the horse like the experienced rider she was. She mounted her horse as the prince mounted his own black steed. Louise was puzzled that the sultan did not mount a horse.

"You're not joining us?"

"The prince is a better guide. I have much work to attend to. Enjoy the ride, and we will see you back at the palace."

They headed out to the trails. The horse seemed to glide as she rode, while the breeze provided some cool respite from the heat and humidity. The experience was an unexpected early fulfillment of one of her lifetime dreams to ride an Arabian horse in an Arab country.[43]

For centuries, the Arabian horse's beauty, grace, endurance, intelligence, courage, and affection for its owner have made it stand apart from all others. No breed of animal has enjoyed the universal admiration as that of the Arabian horse, nor has any breed of animal had a greater impact on the course of history. Saudi Arabia has even undertaken a national program to safeguard the breed and its unique characteristics. yet, the breed originated in North America, where it later became extinct.

The specimens Louise and her host were now riding were from a pure-bred source. As a lover of horses, this was the experience of a lifetime for her. The horse knew the way through the trails, so she let him take her, slowly at first then speeding up to a gallop. A fast-approaching fence gave her pause. But she closed her eyes and felt the weight of the animal rise up, glide forward, and land gently. She felt like a young girl again when she and her best friend used to ride horses bareback and barefoot, racing freestyle across the fields. She slowed, realizing that the prince had fallen behind. She hoped he hadn't been offended, but the prince strode up smiling calmly.

"You ride like Epona."

"I apologize. I got carried away, literally."

"Are you enjoying your stay here?"

"Yes, immensely. I wish I could stay longer."

"That could be arranged. I could make it worthwhile to you and to BCCI."

She weighed her response. An immediate denial would be an insult and cause for retaliation. "I would have to check with the protocol department. I believe BCCI offers live-in personal bankers for a mere $5 million bank deposit."

"Piece of cake, as you Americans say."

Louise laughed, keeping the interaction light. She subtly kicked the horse back into a trot and continued down the trail, letting the horse lead the way while allowing the prince to keep up. The horse knew every twist and turn, every jump, and every escape route. They came to a spectacular vista point, and Louise realized there was not another soul for miles.

They stopped and dismounted to take in the view. He awkwardly approached her, then brazenly forced her arms down to her sides and began biting at her breasts. His attitude of entitlement repulsed her. She could sense that he fully expected her succumb to his will, as he was accustomed to other women doing. The situation seemed comical. He continued to violate her, groping her, then letting go of her left arm not realizing she was left-handed, and reached between her legs. Although he knew letting go of her left arm freed her to defend herself, the last thing he expected was for Louise to overpower him. In one swift move, Louise reached her left arm over to his left shoulder and crossed her right foot over to his right leg then spun the prince to the ground.

"Brother!" She heard the sultan say in Arabic, as he approached on horseback. Louise quickly jumped back on her horse, turned away from the sultan, and let the horse lead her to her escape. Louise could hear the sultan yelling to his servants in the distance. They started their cars and mounted horses as she raced to the riverbed where Jean-Philippe was supposed to be waiting to take her to safety by boat. The horse seemed to know he was helping her to escape. Every time she pushed him onward not sure of the way, he seemed to show her by changing the direction of his head.

Soon the shouts of the others faded in the distance, and she could hear only the horse's gallop and both their heavy breathing. It felt like an eternity had passed riding to freedom when they emerge from the forest. On the docks far back upriver to the right, Louise could see the guards scrambling to get into boats, shouting orders through walkie-talkies. They hadn't noticed her emerging from the woods, so she veered left and raced as fast as she could to distance herself. She searched the riverbank for a boat that might be that of Jean-Philippe.

After five minutes, she came to a stilt village. It was near Brunei's capital city of Bandar Seri Begawan situated in the middle of the Brunei River. Thirty-nine thousand people lived in the Water Village, which was made up of small villages, consisting of over four thousand structures including homes, mosques, restaurants, shops, schools, and a hospital, all linked together by more than 29,140 meters of foot bridges.

She saw a forty-foot white speedboat that stood out from the traditional fishing boats and over-water huts. Louise kicked and the horse veered right toward the shore. Upriver, some of the guards in speedboats spotted her and rushed toward her. Just as she arrived at the riverbank, Jean-Philippe pulled up to the remains of an old dock. She dismounted, kissed the horse, and bade a grateful but brief good-bye. Then she turned him and smacked him on the rump, and he took off back toward the palace.

Louise quickly negotiated the planks of what was left of the dock and leapt into the boat. Just as deftly, Jean-Philippe spun the boat round and sped away, leaving the sultan's guards shouting after them in the distance.

FORTY-SIX

Louise awoke to the distinctly Parisian sunlight beaming through Jean-Philippe's bedroom window. An overall sense of order emanated throughout Paris. Perhaps because of its precise design around the Zero-kilometer marker at Notre Dame, with all the arched monuments built to straddle the line extending from that point to infinity, and the arrondissements spiraling out clockwise starting with the 1st at the center and ending with the 20th to the east. Her center of the universe lay next to her, and everything felt right again.

Jean-Philippe's mobile phone rang. "Oui?" Upon hearing the voice on the other end, he left the room to talk in private. The sense of harmony disrupted, she got up to brush her teeth and get dressed. They had slept until noon. Jean-Philippe was already dressed and at the breakfast table when she came down.

"Bonjour, mon amour. Vous avez bien dormi?"

"Don't *bonjour mon amour* me. Who called?"

"It was Direction Générale de la Sécurité Extérieure."

"French Intelligence? Oh, la la."

"Ce n'est pas une plaisanterie."

"I know it's no joke." She kissed him. "Is Naomi safe?"

"Yes, thanks to you, she was rescued from the palace right after we left. Your dramatic escape on horseback provided the distraction, allowing CIA agents to enter and escort her out of the country. The sultan cooperated fully. However, the whole incident has probably caused a permanent rift between the sultan and his brother, Prince Jefri."

"Oops."

"There is some suspicion that the prince is on a vengeful rampage. He may be out to get you."

"Do you think he would actually try to do something to me?"

"Apparently, someone is. There has been a lot of new activity over the wires. They're not sure who it is. But someone really wants you…"

"Wants me?" Louise asked.

"Dead or alive."

"What?"

"It's most likely Prince Jefri, who is pretty benign. But there are some conflicting signals…coming from the middle East," said Jean-Philippe.

"BCCI knows that I was involved with the CIA operation by now. Could it be the Black Network?"

"This doesn't appear to be BCCI related."

"Not BCCI related? Then who?" Louise asked.

"Some underground network. Perhaps it's the same ghost surveillance that was pursuing you in Seoul and then backed off. No one is sure yet."

Louise became quiet, thinking about the feelings of paranoia she had recently experience.

"What?" Jean-Philippe could see the wheels turning.

"Nothing. It's probably just that angry prince. I must have pissed him off when I tackled him. He will eventually calm down."

"To be on the safe side, I notified the Palais de L'Élysée that we would be arriving today to place you in protective custody."

"I have no desire to hole up at the French *White House*."

"It is the safest place for you, until we figure out exactly what's going on. Allez. Allons-y."

"Now?"

"Yes, we need to leave immediately. I have already packed your things." She followed him to the carriage house where Pierre was already placing her bag into the Ferrari. "Pierre, vous allez partir dans l'autre direction."

"You're sending Pierre as a decoy, and we're taking the Ferrari?" Pierre started up the Bentley, and Jean-Philippe started the Ferrari 348 TB. "You're driving?"

"I do have a valid driver's license."

"Of course, you do. I just mean, why?"

"It is just a precaution."

Louise got in and they waited as Pierre left, heading north toward Charles De Gaulle Airport.

"Isn't there somewhere else than the Palais de l'Elysée?"

"Don't worry. No one will think you're my whore." He drove heading east toward the Champs-Élysées.

"Normally, I would find your use of the word 'whore' adorable. But in this case, it isn't cute at all," Louise said.

"The Palais is the safest place for you." Although it was the official residence and place of business of the President of the French Republic, the Élysée Palace[44] has historically been known for being the place where French leaders kept their mistresses. It was therefore considered very secure.

Jean-Philippe turned right at rue du Faubourg Saint-Honoré and headed toward the Élysée Palace.

Louise became nervous. "Are you coming in with me?"

Jean-Philippe was eying his rearview mirror. "No. You're coming with me." He took a sudden right turn and headed the wrong way down Rue du Colisée.

"What are you doing? I thought you were taking me to the Élysée."

Jean-Philippe had been watching his rearview mirror for a while. "We are being followed." A honking car sped toward him, and Jean-Philippe jumped the curb and drove on the sidewalk, then veered back onto the street after the oncoming car passed. He took another quick right at Rue de Ponthieu when they heard the same car honking behind them at another car driving the wrong way.

"They're chasing us!" said Louise.

"We should have taken my horse."

"I prefer the horsepower of this car." The Ferrari tore through the streets, turning immediately left at Rue la Boétie and soaring through the intersection of the Champs-Élysées to Rue Pierre Charron, then taking a half-spin left onto Rue Francois Premier where Jean-Philippe sped up and merged onto La Voie Georges-Pompidou, the partially subterranean route along the right bank of the River Seine. A vicious chase ensued for several miles along the Voie, Jean-Philippe weaving expertly around cars, the driver behind him flashing his headlights and honking at other cars to get out of the way. They exited the Voie and turned right over Pont D'Austerlitz, across the river, up the Boulevard de l'Hopital, and then all the way down Boulevard Arago. By this time, they were all the way at the south end of Paris in the 14th arrondissement, approaching the Montparnasse Cemetery.

"I think you lost him," Louise said hopefully, looking around.

Jean-Philippe pulled into a narrow alley next to the Montparnasse Cemetery. "Listen to me, Louise. Do you trust me?"

"Yes."

"Get out."

"No!"

"Please. Go to the Catacombs. Hide in there, and I will come back for you. It is the only way."

"You can't leave me!" Louise said.

"Trust me. Get out of the car, go to the Catacombs like I told you before, and hide!"

Louise froze; her eyes locked on his, not sure what was going on. She didn't believe Jean-Philippe would betray her, but she was terrified of being left alone. She reluctantly opened the door and stepped into the alley. He didn't take his eyes off her until the door closed. Then he sped down the alley, and she heard the other car speeding up the street. She flattened herself against the wall, and the car went straight past the alley. She ran a few steps into Montparnasse Cemetery, *a gloomy city of the dead, dreary and bizarre,* of miniature temples marked with illustrious names, from Baudelaire to Beckett, Gainsbourg to Saint-Saëns. The joint grave of Jean-Paul Sartre and Simone de Beauvoir stands immediately right of the entrance on Boulevard Edgar-Quinet. Louise sometimes paid homage to the two bohemian philosophers by drinking at their favorite historic cafés, Le Dome and La Rotonde, just a few meters away on Boulevard Raspail where Sartre and de Beauvoir had lived. As she passed their graves, she kissed her palm and touched their tombstones. She crossed the street to Place Denfert-Rochereau and stepped onto the Avenue du Colonel-Henri-Rol-Tanguy, a street one block in length that hardly qualifies as an avenue.

The entrance to the Paris Catacombs is located on the odd-numbered side of the avenue, next to a stone building with three Romanesque arches across its facade. This building is directly across from an identical even-numbered building that houses the Directorate of Roads and Transport.

These two buildings, classified as historical monuments, were the pavilions of the old Barrière d'Enfer, (*Gates of Hell*), where tolls and taxes were collected on goods entering Paris. The pavilions were built in the elegant French neo-classical style of the nineteenth-century architect Claude Nicolas Ledoux, whose architecture pervades the city, providing its overall distinctly Parisian appearance. The Barrière d'Enfer, which sits directly above the Catacombs, is said to be one of the ten most haunted places in the city. The Catacombs are open to the public during the day only. However, there was a clandestine group that had ways of entering the Catacombs, and a whole subculture existed down there.

The days were getting shorter, and it was now dusk. Louise crossed the avenue to the Catacombs. But instead of going to the main entrance, which was closed, she continued up the street to the third double door on the right and entered the code 0 5 2 5. The door buzzed open, she walked to the back of the courtyard and down four cobblestone steps. She knocked on a door in code: knock-knock-knock; knock-knock; knock. She scrutinized her watch. Jean-Philippe had assured her it would be exactly 3.5 minutes before someone would come, and she was to knock only the one time. Like clockwork, after 210 seconds a man in his forties who said his name was "Henri, just Henri," opened the door.[45] Henri had spent many years of his youth in the *'combs*. He and his friends had been part of what they called the *Catophiles* and for a price of two thousand francs, he used to sneak people into the Catacombs and take them on a *tour*, a rather daring pastime.

Henri led Louise down the stone corridor of a seventeenth-century apartment building and into what seemed to be an old storage room converted to a tiny studio apartment. He handed Louise a flashlight and threw back a rug lying on the cheaply carpeted cement floor to reveal an ancient manhole cover. He lifted the cover and pushed it aside, revealing a deep dark abyss.

"Once you descend zee ladder, you will find steps you take all zee way down. Walk *doucement*, carefully. No one will hear you if you fall and hurt yourself."

"You're not taking me?" said Louise.

"I will do just about anysing for mon ami Jean-Philippe. You are not Jean-Philippe."

"But he said..."

"I never go down there...not anymore."

"Why not?" But Louise didn't really want to know.

"We don't deescuss eet. I know every secret entrance. But I don't go down."

"So, how do I know where to go?" Louise asked.

"Look for zee lotus."

"Lotus?"

"Allez, fonce."

She descended the 143 narrow steps into the infamous Paris Catacombs. During the end of the seventeenth century, the remains of three condemned cemeteries had been discreetly removed and relocated there, overseen and blessed by a priest, into what were abandoned quarries and mines underneath Paris. The result was a vast network of tunnels. Even today, no one knows all the tunnels; the plans had been lost long ago. Some of the tunnels are so small you'd have to crawl through them, and some so big you could walk ten men abreast and still not touch the sides.[46]

As she descended, the temperature changed markedly. At the bottom, she found the first signs of the bones of six million people that had been stacked up against the two thousand seven hundred feet of walls. Many were arranged painstakingly, often in the shape of a cross, with skulls on the walls above them. In some parts of the 'combs the bones were hastily stacked so that when you walked down the tunnel, you were actually walking on bones, crushing hundreds of them to dust.

The juxtaposition of the ancient bones and architecture with scattered graffiti of philosophical sayings and quotations on the walls was striking. The aura was sacred, somber, and spooky. There were bandits hiding out in corners, as well as people hosting parties in the "unofficial" sections. Louise hurried past them, trying to go unnoticed, keeping the flashlight beam low to the ground. The flashlight and the intermittent candles were all that lit her path. Her eyes adjusted, providing clearer focus on the walls and corridors. She searched for any sign of a lotus flower or any other symbolic meaning for *lotus*. She read graffiti and plaques but found no lotus. She seemed to walk for more than a mile, possibly in circles. As she hurried along, a rock jutting up from the dirt and stone floor sent her stumbling down to her hands and knees. Her flashlight escaped her grip, clanked, and rolled to a stop about ten feet in front of her. The beam was all she could see in the inky darkness.

Being on her hands and knees offered a new perspective. She crawled toward the light beam, which faced the bottom of the wall on her right and illuminated an engraving. Louise recognized it as the *Om Mani Padme Hum*, or Hail the Jewel in the Lotus, a twelfth-century Buddhist Sanskrit mantra, meaning the lotus of whose navel forms our universe. Taken symbolically, the Chinese believe it to mean the purity of the white lotus, born and grown in muddy water, remains unsoiled. But in practice, repeating the six syllables represents the purification of the six realms of existence.[47]

Louise held the flashlight as she searched the engraving for a button or a handle. She pressed and prodded, but it seemed to be solid stone. In frustration, she pounded the butt of the flashlight against the ground, triggering a latch in the floor and a narrow passage to open in the wall above the engraving. She peered into the opening with the flashlight then crawled halfway in. She stood and took a full step through the passage when the ground started to tremble. It was too late to step back out, so she lurched forward just as the passage slammed shut, trapping her inside an empty chamber. She called out, banging on the wall, hoping one of the Cataphiles would hear her, but the walls absorbed her cries for help.

She looked around and saw no bones, no other doors, and no latches in the floor or ceiling, just emptiness. After a few moments, she started to panic. She took a deep breath which helped her get into another state of mind: survival mode. She carefully scanned every corner of the chamber and felt the bumps in the walls where it looked like there might be a hidden latch. Determined to find an escape, she focused her mind. A trick she had taught herself when she had computer-programming problems was to close her eyes and let her thoughts fall away and focus her mind's eye on finding the solution. She sat leaning against the wall and concentrated. When that approach failed, she set the problem aside and tried thinking about something else. Neither method worked, and she was back in panic mode.

Her mind raced in search of a plan. Having been an avid reader of Russian literature, she recalled some of the survival methods used by prisoners of the Gulags that Aleksandr Solzhenitzyn had revealed. She initiated the method for counting the days, taking a key from her purse and scratching lines in the wall, forming three columns: Date, Time, Notes. She calculated how long it would take for various stages of captivity to kick in, phone and flashlight battery life, hunger, dehydration, and cold. She had her cell phone, but she had no cell coverage and without a battery charger, it wouldn't last long anyway. She decided to start conserving immediately and turned off her phone. Solzhenitzyn had written one of his books from memory while in the Gulag. She made mental notes of everything that had transpired that day and mentally noted any details she might need to remember. She filled in the first line of her wall chart. Under Notes, she wrote the make, model, and color of the car that had chased them: *black 1989 Renault 2L Turbo, driver French*. She assumed the driver must be French because, while chasing them in the tunnel, he had flashed his headlights at the driver ahead of him in the left lane, signaling for him to move to the right lane, as is commonly done in France.

She sat down and extinguished the flashlight. Her eyes adjusted, and the numbers on her Tiffany Grand Quartz Resonator watch began to fluoresce. The beating of her heart rose in her ears. She thought she might find a solution if she meditated. She checked the current time 18h02 and closed her eyes. She sank into the depths of meditation quickly, causing her head to bob. To someone watching her, it might seem like she was nodding off, only without the sudden jerking of the head. To her, it felt like her head was filled with helium or suspended on a string floating above her neck. The effect was a slight bobbing of the head with the rhythm of her heartbeat.

Her heart was beating harder than usual, causing her to rock slightly back and forth. She realized her heartbeat was gently thrusting her to the right. She knew that the right ventricle of the heart uses the pulmonary valve to help move blood into the pulmonary arteries from right to left. The left ventricle uses the aortic valve to do the same for the aorta, from left to right. But the left ventricle is much larger than the right, thus causing the rightward thrust. The double "DUB" is the sound of the aortic and pulmonary valves closing.[48]

While she sat meditating in the chamber of the Catacombs, she felt someone was watching her. She did not want to open her eyes, hoping that if she remained very quiet, she could make herself invisible. Opening her eyes would somehow reveal her presence. But after another minute, the presence seemed to be willing her to open her eyes. She was terrified.

She had researched the Catacombs and read many ghost stories. There were *Cataphiles* who went down in groups to explore the Catacombs only to become lost in a tunnel and eventually emerge having been traumatized by attacks from a demon. Others had lost friends who were separated from the group and never made it out. Her mind drifted, imagining the flustered tomb intruders coursing through underground tunnels. The "DUB" of her aortic and pulmonary valves seemed deafening.

She kept her eyes closed. She hated the dark. She had always feared her own imagination in the dark because it was so vivid. She feared that darkness could be a passage allowing spirits from the *world beyond* to sneak through to her vulnerably fertile imagination. Her dearly departed friend Diana had once confessed to Louise that she had a deep-rooted fear of darkness because she could see spirits. They never discussed it again. However, the fact that such a dignified and poised English woman confessed to such an ominous gift made it seem possible that her own fear of the dark came from her yet unrealized ability to see spirits that she did not wish to see. In reality, Louise had been using a nightlight to keep her from what lurked in the darkness. She had always felt it was inevitable that she would confront the beyond one day, but she had been putting it off as long as possible by closing her mind and keeping the lights on. Now, however, the inevitable seemed near. Knowing there was no exit from the darkness even with her flashlight, the feeling of panic and terror began to swell up in her. She thought: *This is it. The unknown is going to reveal itself to me now!*

Then a sense of warmth and comfort came over, calming her. She opened her eyes and turned on the flashlight. She saw a man dressed in a traditional orange kurta-pajama with red turban, indicating he was a guru. He wore a large gemstone at the center of his forehead, representing the *third eye*. The gemstone refers to the Light of Buddha that came out from Buddha's head. She recognized the man as Sri Sri Ravi Shankar, the spiritual leader and founder of the Art of Living Foundation, a Non-Government Organization that has consultative status with UNESCO. The foundation is aimed at relieving both individual stress and societal problems. Sri Sri had traveled with the Maharishi Mahesh Yogi. He teaches that every emotion has a corresponding rhythm in the breath, and therefore regulating breath could help relieve personal suffering. Sri Sri claimed his breathing exercise came to him in 1982, like a poem, an inspiration, after a ten-day period of silence on the banks of the Bhadra River.

According to Sri Sri, science and spirituality are linked and compatible, both springing from the urge to know. The question *who am I?* leads to spirituality. The question, *what is this?* leads to science. He sees breath as the link between body and mind, and a tool to relax the mind, emphasizing the importance of both meditation and spiritual practice and service to others. "Truth is spherical rather than linear, so it has to be contradictory."

Louise wasn't sure if she was hallucinating. Sri Sri appeared to be float-ing slightly above the floor. She had read about a certain form of transcendental meditation, TM-Sidhi, which could lead to the development of extraordinary abilities such as yogic flying, invisibility, walking through walls, mind-reading, colossal strength, extrasensory perception, omnisci-ence, the creation of world peace, perfect health, or immortality. The term *siddhi* means perfection and refers to the development of a perfected-mind-body coordination. She read that a person can disappear at a high state of consciousness because the body simply stops reflecting light.

Sri Sri spoke to her, "I have been sent to inform you of your elevated status among those within the order of the Rose Cross."

"The Rosicrucian order is real?"

"It is more than real. It is true."

The Rosicrucian order, or order of the Rose Cross, claims to have secret knowledge of the world. It was founded by Christian Rosenkreuz and is practiced through reading three manifestos published in the early seventeenth century. According to legend, Christian Rosenkreuz discovered and learned esoteric wisdom on a pilgrimage to the Middle East among Turkish, Arab, and Persian sages in the early fifteenth century. Christian Rosenkreuz is said to have died in 1484. The foundation of the Order is supposed to have occurred in the year 1407. The order is deeply rooted in math. Through the Manifestos, the Rosicrucians adopted the Pythagorean tradition of envisioning objects and ideas in terms of their numeric aspects. Pythagorean teachings profoundly influenced the greatest philosophic minds including Socrates, Plato and Aristotle. In his *Metaphysics*, Aristotle wrote, "With respect to the activity of these philosophers called Pythagorean, they began the study of mathematics and were the first to make progress in it. They arrived at the conclusion that the elements of numbers were the elements of all things, of all that exists on earth and that *heaven was harmony and numbers*."[49]

Sri Sri continued, "You have revealed *esoteric knowledge* and therefore are now *initiated*." He handed her a lotus flower. "This is your *marker*, much like a bookmark."

Louise opened her eyes from what seemed to have been a deep meditation. She must have dreamt the visit from Sri Sri after falling into a deep trance.

However, when she lowered her eyes and saw a lotus flower cupped in her hands. She raised it to her nose and found it to be fresh and pristine.

Something was happening to Louise; she could feel it. She was attaining some higher consciousness. She had always believed that there was some kind of metaphysical superhighway. When she read poetry, it fascinated her how someone could express abstract thoughts that she could comprehend on some super-conscious level. The only way for this to be possible was if there was some sort of higher knowledge that flowed between conscious beings.

The words *esoteric knowledge* echoed in her ears. She felt she must have created some kind of butterfly effect. Meaning, within the higher consciousness, or *The One*, we are each a unique thought, therefore any groundbreaking thought will affect the whole. In other words, the effect of a butterfly flapping its wings and causing a tidal wave on the other side of the world is a metaphor for an idea from one person within the whole collective mind can alter that collective mind. Had Louise conceived of some *esoteric knowledge*, which would change the course of history and human existence?

Suddenly, a concealed door opened, letting in light, and she was stunned to see her ex-fiancé.

"Michael?" She ran to him and he held her. Then she stood back. "Michael, what the hell is going on?"

"Jean-Philippe and I designated this as your hideout in case something happened."

"Jean-Philippe is with you?"

"No. He told us where to find you and that you would cooperate with us."

"Cooperate? I don't understand. I'm not telling you anything until you explain what's going on."

"Ever since your cryptic phone call, I have been having you followed, for your own protection," said Michael.

"Where is Jean-Philippe?"

"We don't know yet. But he told me you would have the photos and the list of names. You can save yourself a lot of pain and trouble if you just cooperate."

"Go fuck yourself."

"Louise, you still don't get it, do you? How do you think you got the job at BCCI? Your father set it up so BCCI could recruit you. He wanted you positioned to work from inside the company."

"You lie!"

"If I'm lying, how did I know where to find you?"

"How could you keep this from me?"

"If you had known, you wouldn't have been as convincing. This way, you were instrumental in bringing down the whole operation."

Louise was furious. "Let me out of here! I have to find Jean-Philippe!"

"That's not going to happen. This is how it's going to go. You give us the evidence, and we keep you safe. In case you didn't notice, the Black Network has been trying to kill you, and you won't be safe until the whole operation is shut down."

"But why are they trying to kill *me*?"

"Louise, I can't go into the details now, but you are in danger. We're sneaking you out of France and to safety in Switzerland. We can talk about it on the way." He put his arm around her shoulders. She pulled back.

"How could my father do this? Why did he make *you* do this?"

"You know why." The look in Michael's eyes was unmistakable. He still loved her. Their relationship was over, and she didn't want to go back. But she had no choice but to go with him now.

Two security guards escorted Michael and Louise through a secret door and a different tunnel than the one she had used to enter. There was no sign of Henri. They exited the Catacombs into an alley far from the main entrance. After twelve hours in the Catacombs, daylight seared her corneas. Michael handed her government-issued sunglasses, aviator style. They suited her. Considering she had just spent the night in a haunted dungeon, she looked good as she got into the back seat of one of three idling black sedans. They took off and turned onto Avenue Rene Coty.

The streets were animated with Parisians and tourists going about their business. The armored Mercedes made its way south to some private airport. The ride gave her time to think. She was still in survival mode and took a deep breath to relax, which only made her start to cry. She silently wept and looked down to catch the tears when she realized she still had the lotus flower in her hand. It was as perfect and fresh as ever.

"Will Jean-Philippe be in Switzerland too?"

"Doubtful. We have no word from him yet."

"I can't believe you and my father have been lying to me all this time."

"Your father took a chance and you accomplished much more than he could ever have hoped. At most, he wanted you to inadvertently give him information about what BCCI was doing through your movements. It was your trip to Panama that led us to the former head of BCCI's Panama office, Amjad Awan. He was the one who told us that BCCI secretly owned and controlled First American Bankshares."[50]

"Is that why they want to kill me?"

He held her hands and looked her in the eyes. "We will reveal more information later. Protecting you is now our top priority."

FORTY-SEVEN

They landed at a private airstrip in Geneva, Switzerland. Louise was led to lodging so she could rest and freshen up. She was impressed to find her quarters comfortable and adequate, the equivalent of about a three-star hotel. She opened the closet and found a set of clothing that had been purchased for her. She showered and changed into the new clothes, also comfortable and three-star.

There was a knock at the door, and she opened it to see Michael. He led her to a small dining room and closed the door for privacy. An attendant entered briefly and set an array of food and wines on the table, and then left, closing the door behind him.

"I need to find out what happened to Jean-Philippe," Louise insisted.

"We are doing everything we can," Michael said. "It is important to remain calm and stick with the plan."

"What's the plan?"

"I don't have a plan yet."

"Then I'm not waiting around for you to figure it out." Louise got up.

"Jean-Philippe wouldn't want you to do that." She knew he was right and sat down, her eyes filling with tears. "Look, I do have a plan, but it's risky."

"If it helps Jean-Philippe, I'll do whatever it takes."

"The plan is not to help Jean-Philippe. It is to help you."

"Help me?"

"If you cooperate with us you will be granted full immunity."

"Full immunity from what? I haven't done anything wrong!" Louise said.

"To start with, you delivered information to suspects in Panama, and we could go on from there. Full immunity will protect you from any possible charges against you."

"Fine. What's the plan?"

"The plan is to take BCCI down. Shutter the entire global operation."

"Take down the whole bank? How can we possibly do that?"

"You already have Jean-Philippe's photos and Abedi's secret client list somewhere safe in Paris, correct?"

"Yes."

"First, you must go to Paris to retrieve those items. Then, go to meet with Masihur Rahman in London."

"The BCCI London chief financial officer?"

"Yes. We convinced him to cooperate. He was certain someone was following him, so we were able to persuade him to help us in exchange for protection."

"How did you convince him?" Louise asked, truly curious. "As a rule, BCCI management is impenetrable."

"Your father got word that BCCI had just laid off about a thousand employees in London. The discharged BCCI employees started raising a public outcry over lost benefits. Mr. M was among them and therefore a perfect target: Disgruntled high-level management."

"You call him Mr. M?"

"You know how your father is. This is top secret. We have a source who has uncovered information about BCCI that only the tight inner circle of top management knows. As BCCI's chief financial officer, Mr. M is the highest level. Plus, his history goes way back. He was the son of a chief justice of the Supreme Court in Calcutta and was brought into United Bank by Abedi in 1966. He moved with Abedi when he created BCCI. Mr. M kept all the original handwritten ledgers of the bank's first year of operation in Abu Dhabi. When BCCI pleaded guilty to money-laundering charges last January 1990, it was a minor infraction for such a huge bank."

"Yes, I know," said Louise. "It was considered an isolated incident."

"It was the tip of the iceberg. BCCI is a huge money-laundering scheme."

"But it has passed all independent audits," Louise said.

"Not anymore. The money-laundering charges prompted Price Water-house to take another look after giving the bank a clean bill of health for years. The rise of global financial markets made money laundering easier than ever. Countries with bank-secrecy laws are directly connected to countries with bank-reporting laws. That makes it possible to deposit "dirty" money anonymously in one country and then have it transferred to another non-reporting country for use.[51] Therefore money laundering can be traced only if a prosecutor has the patience, manpower, and full disclosure and accurate bookkeeping from a bank. The cash trail may lead through a daunting number of transactions that would take many man-hours to reconcile. The only reason money laundering works is because no one is following the trail of the cash."

"But how could BCCI launder so much money?" Louise asked.

"Money laundering requires three steps that have to be perfectly coordinated in order to work. The first step is placement. The launderer inserts the dirty money into a legitimate financial institution. This is often in the form of cash deposits. This is the riskiest stage of the laundering process because large amounts of cash are very conspicuous, and banks are required to report high-value transactions. That's why Capone was indicted for tax evasion, because he couldn't explain large bank deposits, so they were deemed to be undeclared revenues.

"Next is layering, which involves sending the money through various financial transactions to change its form and make it difficult to follow. Layering may consist of several bank-to-bank transfers, wire transfers between different accounts in different names in different countries, making deposits and withdrawals to vary continually the amount of money in the accounts, changing the money's currency, and purchasing high-value items like boats, houses, cars, or diamonds to change the form of the money. This is the most complex step in any laundering scheme, and it's all about making the original dirty money as hard to trace as possible.

"Last is integration. The money re-enters the mainstream economy in legitimate-looking legal transactions. This may involve a final bank transfer into the bank account of a local business in which the launderer is "investing" in exchange for a percentage of the profits, or a company owned by the launderer who sold a yacht that was purchased during the layering stage. At this point, the criminal can use the money without fear of getting caught. Because of bank-secrecy laws, it's very difficult to catch a launderer during the integration stage if there is no documentation during the previous stages."

Michael paused and stretched then continued. "Anyway, Price Waterhouse performed a worldwide audit in March 1990 and discovered problems everywhere. Mr. M was placed in charge of an internal audit committee that was to substantiate any Price Waterhouse money trail questions. It only proved the books were in shambles. Hundreds of millions of dollars had been loaned or transferred from one account to another without paperwork, and hundreds of millions more had simply disappeared.

"Knowing the report could not be withheld from the Bank of England, which loosely monitored BCCI's operations in Britain, management quickly concocted a plan. First, Sheikh Zayed would contribute $700 million to cover the first gaping hole in the books. Then they would present to the Bank of England a plan to 'restructure' BCCI, place BCCI under Zayed's control, and move its headquarters back to Abu Dhabi. That is the move for which you were assigned to supervise the database migration in Seoul, Korea.

"Zayed is a shrewd old Bedouin and is well respected. But he's not getting any younger, and he thought the BCCI scandal might affect his succession. In addition to being the ruler of Abu Dhabi, Zayed was the president of the United Arab Emirates, and it had long been thought that his heir, probably Prince Khalifa, would automatically assume the presidency of the U.A.E. We knew Zayed would do anything to prevent a scandal, and we convinced Mr. M that Zayed wouldn't hesitate to use him as a fall guy. After hours of coaxing, Mr. M agreed to give us copies of all the audits in exchange for protection. The confidential audits are the smoking gun to bring the company down."

Louise now had the full picture. "Let me guess. You need me to go to meet with Mr. M in London and obtain the audit documents."

"First you go to Paris. We need you to go back to work to see Chinoy's reaction. If everything seems like business as usual, you will know they are trying to let the Brunei incident blow over, and they are going forward with the plan for Zayed to take over."

"But what about the Black Network?" Louise asked.

"We need to figure out if BCCI has made you a target of the Black Network. We have security following you, should anything happen. If you are treated like you are still a member of the team, you will still have access to the London office as well. Hell, Chinoy may apologize for the situation in Brunei. For all we know, he thinks you were attacked by the prince and were just trying to escape. They may not even realize you were working with us to rescue the senator's daughter."

"You're right. I might be considered another victim."

"But your Paris visit will be short-lived. You must inform Chinoy that you are needed in London. Get the photos and list and head to London, according to plan."

Michael walked her back to her quarters. "You need to get a good night's sleep. I'll make arrangements for your flight to Paris. Be ready to leave early in the morning."

FORTY-EIGHT

Louise returned to Paris the next morning by private jet; two bodyguards drove her to her apartment in a black Peugeot. Even with top-notch security protection, she felt scared and helpless, unable to reach Jean-Philippe and not knowing if he was even alive. She packed a small overnight bag for the London trip. Then she went into the secret chamber where she had hidden the incriminating list and photos. She carefully tucked them into her briefcase along with her passport. She looked out the window to make sure the black Peugeot was still there on surveillance and went to bed.

The Brunei drama had happened over the weekend, so on Monday morning, her usual driver had no idea she had even left the country. The Peugeot followed her car to work, and she went straight to Chinoy's office.

"Good morning, Mr. Chinoy."

"Louise! Are you all right? We've been so worried about you."

"Yes, I'm fine, thank you."

"The sultan contacted me about what happened and sends his apologies. He said the prince was not aware that you were a business associate, and his behavior was entirely inappropriate. If there is anything he can do, just ask."

"Thank you. I accept his apology and realize it was a misunderstanding."

"That is very gracious of you. Do you need some time off?"

"No, I would prefer to get back to work. Which reminds me, the migration of the wide area network and database to the Korean office is complete. The final stage requires that I go to the London office to check the network connections. Then we will be able to complete the move of the headquarters to Abu Dhabi. I should leave right away, today if possible."

"Yes, of course. Go ahead and book one of the BCCI flights and stay at the corporate suite."

"Thanks. It should be only for the day."

Louise knew that she would never return to BCCI, so she took some personal items from her office and had one last look around. It pained her to see Diana's empty office, so she bade good riddance, and her driver took her to the airport.

When she arrived in London, she went directly to the BCCI office. She really did need to review the network set-up. So, after a brief chat with the London branch officer, he led her to the IT department. The IT head was a brainy-looking Pakistani guy, tall and slender with glasses. He had the uncommunicative attitude she had grown accustomed to at BCCI and answered questions only with a "Yes" or a "No." Louise was counting on this dynamic to keep her visit as short as possible. He signed off on her status report and left the branch quickly to avoid any further interaction.

In order not to raise suspicions, she checked into the BCCI corporate suite and called Michael to give him the signal that everything was on schedule. She freshened up, took her briefcase, and left. The London security team was waiting for her in a black sedan. They drove her to meet Mr. M at a restaurant. The courtship of Mr. M was delicate and would last over five hours. Her security guards came with her to add pressure. They were both clean-cut and professional, but they assured Louise they could fight their way out of any dangerous situation. They were also very well informed about the case and helped keep the conversation moving forward.

Louise played the sympathetic BCCI ally. "Mr. Rahman, you are a good man. I was like you. I had no idea what was going on at the bank. You have been there from the beginning. Maybe you started to realize what was going on but couldn't stop it."

Mr. M was defensive about the bank's reputation. "BCCI's problems came only because Abedi began taking shortcuts. He sensed he was running out of time to realize his vision."

"Whatever the reason, now you know what has been going on at BCCI is criminal. We can help you."

"Please, excuse me. I must phone my wife."

"But you just called her."

"It is a signal, you see. If I do not call her, she will know something has happened to me. We have had many threats. There have been shots fired through our windows. Scotland yard has posted guards at our house."

Mr. M left the table, and Louise talked with the two men. "He's not going to help us. Clearly, he's too afraid. I'm afraid too."

"Don't let up on him. He's softening," one of the agents said. "How can you tell?"

"He wouldn't have stayed here for five hours if he didn't want to cooperate. We just have to motivate him. Let me handle it."

Mr. M took his seat again, and the FBI agent didn't waste any time. "Mr. Rahman, the bank is going down."

"There is a great deal of good in BCCI," said Mr. M. "You don't get to be a $28-billion bank by laundering drug money."

Louise stifled her surprise. She knew the bank had $20-billion public valuation, and Michael had told her about the alleged illegal acquisition of an American bank, First American Bankshares. The $28-billion figure Mr. M mentioned could be arrived at only by adding the assets of First American Bankshares and BCCI's stated worth.[52] She looked at the other two men. They had all picked up on Mr. M's gaffe.

"The FBI will grant you asylum," the FBI agent offered.

Mr. M realized his gaffe and knew that the jig was up. Louise and her colleagues were his best bet to get through the closing of BCCI.

"Let's get you out of here to somewhere safe," said Louise.

They left the restaurant and slipped down the dark street to Mr. M's gray Mercedes. Mr. M's stories of his life being threatened were too detailed not to be believed. It made Louise nervous, but the guards provided some reassurance, flanking them as they walked.

Mr. M opened the trunk and took out an armload of folders and papers, and they all climbed into the car. Louise and the agents looked through the documents. There were scores, hundreds, thousands of loans in staggering sums for which there had been no repayment for years. The Gokal brothers' shipping company held $404 million in loans against $62 million in collateral, and in the dry language of accountancy, the Price Waterhouse examiners cast doubt on the value of that collateral. Ghaith Pharaon and his brother, Wabel, had outstanding loans totaling $288 million.

Louise read out loud, "The auditors' notes state, 'There are no written loan agreements, promissory notes, or correspondence with the customers.'"

In the tone of reciting Miranda Rights, the FBI agent said, "Mr. Rahman, you will be contacted and instructed on what to do. In exchange for your cooperation, you will be granted asylum."

They gathered a short stack of the most incriminating documents and placed them in Louise's briefcase then got out of the car.

Before saying goodbye, Louise reassured Mr. M. "Thank you. Your assistance will not be forgotten."

Louise left London immediately, taking the audit reports, the photos, and the list on a private jet accompanied by her security to one of the most secure bunkers on the planet.

They arrived at Greenbrier Resort in West Virginia just before dawn. She was shown to private quarters where she got to work organizing the audit documents and the list for presentation. She then opened the package of Jean-Philippe's photos and flicked through them imagining Jean-Philippe taking the pictures, seeing the images through his eyes. It made her feel close to him. She was exhausted and lay down to sleep.

After about an hour she was startled awake by a knock at the door. "Jean-Philippe!" she said to herself. She got up and threw the door open. Hair disheveled, eyes puffy, she focused on the man standing before her.

"Louise, are you okay?"

His voice snapped her out of her stupor. "Oh, Michael. I must have dozed off."

"We're ready for you," Michael said.

"I'm ready." Louise straightened her hair and clothes and gathered up her presentation materials.

As they walked through the giant corridors of Greenbrier's underground facilities, Louise marveled at the 112,544-square-foot bunker built seven hundred and twenty feet into the hillside under the Greenbrier Resort's West Virginia Wing. A natural sulfur water spring is at the center of the Greenbrier Resort property that issues forth below the green dome of the white-columned springhouse, which has been the symbol of The Greenbrier for generations. But it was overwhelming to realize this would be the last place of refuge in a worst-case scenario for the highest-level officials in America.[53]

"Don't be intimidated," Michael assured her. "This meeting is with need-to-know level personnel. You will only get cursory introductions. But don't let that bother you. In many ways, you are higher up the food chain than most of the officials in the room."

FORTY-NINE

Michael escorted Louise to the secure conference room where the FBI team was waiting, along with several other official looking men. After brief introductions, Louise was ready to make her well-organized presentation of the ample evidence to take down BCCI.

Dispensing with formalities, Louise placed the first set of documents on the table before her. To make the greatest impact, she began with the most incriminating testimonial.

"These documents show that BCCI sold the American Navstar System to the Russians."

Navstar was a global positioning system operated by the U.S. Department of Defense that comprised approximately twenty satellites circling the globe, beaming down radio navigation information. It provided hair-splitting accuracy, giving three-dimensional positioning in latitude, longitude, and altitude anywhere in the world. Commercial ships and planes navigated by the signals. But because the military also used it to guide intercontinental missiles to their targets, or cruise missiles screaming down the streets of Baghdad, it was very sensitive technology.

The Defense Department system degraded the information beamed to commercial receivers by distorting the signals so that it would not provide positioning closer than one hundred feet from an actual location. At the flip of a switch, the Defense Department could, and often did, distort the commercial signals even further so that users couldn't position closer than one thousand feet from actual position. That was close enough for mariners.

Military receivers such as those in jet fighter planes, on the other hand, received another set of coded signals from the same satellites, called the *P-code*, which gave dead-bang accuracy.

"Jean-Philippe had made many connections working undercover in Russia," Louise explained. "I don't know how, but Jean-Philippe saw Navstar plans in a safe in the Kremlin at the offices of the Soviet space-agency,

Glavkosmos. Russia had been trying to upgrade their own Global Position-ing System, or GPS, which was less reliable, and they had many proprietary technical documents and secret manuals from the United States in their possession. One of the Glavkosmos directors bragged to Jean-Philippe that they had been procured for them by BCCI."

"It is crucial," Michael interjected, "for U.S. national security that CIA agents who work with BCCI know about this sale of Navstar to the Russians. CIA agents resist cooperating with the FBI because they believe it would break protocol, even if they think BCCI is committing criminal activity. However, if CIA agents knew that Abedi was working with the Soviets, they might be more open to cooperating with the FBI."

"How did Jean-Philippe get the pictures?" asked one of the men.

"Jean-Philippe was certain he could get into the safe at Glavkosmos where he saw the satellite manuals," Louise said. "Not the big Glavkosmos office on Krasnoproletarskaya next to Red Square, but the one near Space City, which from the outside appears to be just another office building." Louise was aware that she had just revealed information about Jean-Philippe that would convince her listeners that he was legitimate. Jean-Philippe was taking risks to infiltrate locations in Russia and bring these activities to light that could get him killed.

She continued, "If the Russians had caught him, he would have been accused of spying and hauled off to a Lubyanka Prison interrogation cell, or he would have been shot on the spot. But he went ahead with his plan to get in and photograph them."

Louise spread the enlarged photographs across the desk. They all stared in disbelief. The resolution wasn't very good, but there was little doubt they were looking at Rockwell International's technical manual for the Navstar Global Positioning System satellite inside the safe.

"Jean-Philippe even took establishing photos of the gray stone building with armed guards posted in front and two or three photos of Red Square," said Louise. One close-up photo of a newsstand showed the day's newspa-pers with the date.

An FBI agent picked up the last picture and laughed out loud. It showed a large canvas-topped army truck, a red star on the door, full of Russian soldiers all smiling and waving back at the camera.

"This guy has brass balls," he said. "He had a camera full of film that would have gotten him shot, and to get this picture he must have shouted something funny in Russian at these troops passing by."

Louise smiled to herself. She was comforted that the agent used the present tense when speaking about Jean-Philippe. Maybe this meant that he was still alive. Michael also picked up on the use of present tense, but he did not want Louise to get any false hopes.

"I don't know how confidential all this is anymore," commented Michael. "GPS technology is evolving rapidly. Our man says he thought the Soviets got this in 1989. But whatever the case, Ms. Moscow has just shown us the Soviets have a safe full of sensitive American technological documents, and the Russians bragged to Jean-Philippe that they got them from BCCI. We know Abedi himself had been traveling to Moscow in the late 1980s just before his heart attack, trying to persuade the Russians to let him open BCCI banks throughout the Soviet Union. Maybe this was *trade goods*, so to speak. Abedi was showing the Russians that what he knew about American politicians was more valuable to the Soviets than military or technical secrets."

Michael moved on to the next topic. "In the mid-1980s, Abedi and one of his top weapons merchants, Asaf Ali, were meeting secretly with Bill Casey, cooking up cooperative deals, probably having to do with the United States aid program to Pakistan. The Reagan administration was slipping them a lot of military and technological goodies in addition to what Congress had approved. We can assume that if Pakistan had it, Agha Hasan Abedi had it."

The men were startled on two levels by what Michael just said. First, that Abedi dealt with weapons merchants. Second, Abedi's relationship with Bill Casey, the director of Central Intelligence from 1981 to 1987. The more information was revealed, the more intense the energy in the room became. Louise took off her suit jacket.

"My source says Mr. Abedi was working directly with William Casey," Michael continued. "During the Afghanistan War, BCCI was working with the CIA. Abedi and BCCI are interwoven with Pakistan's intelligence agency Inter-Services Intelligence. The ISI was in charge of supplying the Afghan fighters. Pakistan's General Zia and Asaf Ali also were in meetings with Casey. They were all very chummy. Pakistan received a great amount of military technology from the United States under the table. My source says that Abedi is also working with the French, the Americans, the English, and the Israelis."

One of the gentlemen, who had been quietly listening, spoke up. "Abedi and William Casey were pals? If that's true, no wonder no one has busted BCCI."

This articulated what everyone was thinking: Abedi had the highest-ranked U.S. officials in his back pocket.

"I'll give you an example," Michael said. "I have been dealing with a U.S. deputy under secretary who was afraid to cooperate with the FBI. This guy was a state official who was right up at the top of the government, and he was worried that he was being tailed. When I met with him, he went through an elaborate exercise to make sure no one was following us. Once we finally stopped to talk in a noisy café, he spoke in a whisper and said, and I quote, 'you're onto something, and you're correct about there being no separation between Abedi and the ISI. A number of Pakistan's generals have been on Abedi's private payroll for years,' unquote. He said that several people in the State Department had resigned over the years in protest of our bias toward Pakistan. The United States gave Pakistan unauthorized satellite and communications technology. We even authorized giving them sophisticated technology like F-16 fighter planes. We also turn a blind eye to Pakistan's drug trade and nuclear bomb program. The deputy under secretary said that Abedi and BCCI were in the middle of all of it.

"I'll give you another example," Michael added. "We learned a couple of years ago that BCCI had three Colombine Heads, and they were selling them to Iraq. But I couldn't even find out what a Colombine Head *was*. The deputy under secretary told me that it was probably the trigger for the *fuel-air bomb*."

Everyone in the room was well aware that Iraq's bombardment of Israel during the Gulf war had created panic because it was feared Saddam Hussein possessed fuel-air bombs and that he might be able to deliver some of them with the Scud rockets. Fuel-air bombs were called the poor man's hydrogen bomb, and they worked by exploding a large cloud of vaporized gasoline. The resulting explosion rivaled atomic blasts. It was almost primitive technology, but it required an extremely sophisticated triggering system to ignite the gas cloud. That trigger may be the Colombine Head.

"Even the Scud missiles that Saddam Hussein was using were financed by BCCI," Michael said. "This all jibed with my other source who told me that BCCI had substantial business dealings over the years with one of the world's preeminent makers of military aircraft, Dassault Aviation, the

French producer of the Mirage jet fighter. Asaf Ali has always handled the Mirage sales; he's probably Dassault's biggest Third World broker, and he nearly always uses BCCI to finance the transactions. If Ghaith Pharaon is Abedi's front man to buy banks and businesses, Asaf Ali is his front man for major weapons transactions. My source detailed BCCI-backed Mirage sales to Pakistan, India, Peru, Iraq, Libya, and the Arab Gulf states. The French shot themselves in the foot when BCCI had brokered a batch of Mirage 2000s to Iraq for use in the Iran-Iraq war. The French Air Force was all but grounded during Desert Storm for fear that allied jets would mistake French mirages for the Iraqi Mirages over Kuwait and shoot them down."[54]

Everyone was silent for at least a minute. Then one of the men who appeared to be an FBI director said, "Why don't we take a break for lunch and pick this back up in an hour?"

After lunch, Louise guided them through the rest of the evidence, including her copy of the list of BCCI clients and the original photo Jean-Philippe had taken of Panama attorney general shaking hands with Noriega's attorney at the party in Cannes.

Finally, she revealed the smoking gun: the Price Waterhouse October 1990 and June 1991 audits. "After BCCI pleaded guilty to the minor money-laundering charges in January 1990, Price Waterhouse decided to conduct an audit of BCCI. They presented an audit report to BCCI's board on October 3, 1990. After seeing the October 1990 audit report, Chairman of the Board Sheikh Zayed bin Sultan al-Nahayan immediately fired Abedi and Naqvi and appointed Zafar Iqbal as the new BCCI president.

"One of the cornerstones of the fraud was Price Waterhouse. They wielded enormous influence. Up until the October 1990 audit, all audits of BCCI had presented a bank that, while growing very quickly, was otherwise unblemished. That, of course, was patently false. Anyone who would have looked critically at the bank's accounts would have known immediately something was wrong. Warning signs were manifest as far back as 1978, when the Office of the Comptroller of the Currency (OCC), the largest U.S. regulator of banks, ran its own audit of BCCI as part of a larger audit of Bank of America. At the time, Bank of America held 30 percent of BCCI's shares and remained BCCI's greatest ally, continuing to accept BCCI's letter-of-credit business after virtually no other western bank would touch it. Bank of America became the single most important financial institution helping BCCI stay afloat.

"The conclusions of the OCC audit showed that the bank's explosive growth had created strains on management. The bank had no lending limits, it often had no documentation at all supporting its loans, and it was whizzing money around the world from affiliate to affiliate and leaving no paper trail. Money was disappearing in "unsecured borrowings" into International Credit and Investment Company Holdings in the Cayman Islands. Worse than that, the bank's portfolio of bad loans was expanding at an unsettling rate. Bad or questionable loans constituted three and a half times BCCI's capital. Any of these conclusions would have been enough to shut down most banks in America and in Europe. Still, the OCC's alarming conclusions were made to disappear. That same year back in 1978, the bank got a clean bill of health from its two auditors: Ernest & Young, which handled the main European books, and Price Waterhouse, which looked after the Cayman Islands.

"This use of two firms to account for one company was highly unusual, but this was Abedi's way of ensuring that no one except for himself and Swaleh Naqvi would ever view the sprawling entity in its entirety. But then, in 1986 Ernst & Young resigned the account, believing correctly that it could not conduct a true audit without access to the growing number of accounts in the Cayman Islands. That left Price Waterhouse as BCCI's sole auditors, and, in the critical years 1987, 1988, and 1989, Price Waterhouse delivered unqualified audits of a bank with no capital, a bank whose accounts had become so devious, so grossly manipulated that even the auditors themselves would later admit that the bank's financial history could never be reconstructed.

"Yet as early as 1985, Price Waterhouse began giving BCCI an unqualified opinion even while noting that the bank had inadequate loan loss reserves, had no lending limits to individuals, kept little or no current financial information on any of its clients, and made loans without collateral. According to Price Waterhouse's own findings, not even BCCI's own staff knew the names behind thousands of numbered accounts. One reason Price Waterhouse continued to give unqualified opinions may have been because BCCI made $597,000 in loans to Price Waterhouse from its Barbados office.

"In spite of Price Waterhouse's egregious track record, in early 1991 the Bank of England hired them to run an 'independent' audit of BCCI. As though to atone for past sins, Price Waterhouse actually did an independent audit, one that revealed what the accounting firm itself called 'one of the most complex deceptions in banking history.'"

Louise passed out copies of the audit. "This is the audit delivered in June 1991, which contains the best analysis to date of how BCCI devised and executed the multibillion-dollar fraud. After eight full years of rendering bogus unqualified opinions, Price Waterhouse had finally delivered something akin to a real version of the bank. The June 1991 audit revealed with brutal clarity what had become Abedi's sweeping vision of the transnational Third World bank. However, still missing from the audit are accountings of BCCI's other businesses including weapons, drugs, mercenary armies, and a variety of commodities. Though immensely profitable and funded directly with depositors' money, these would never turn up on any audit."

Michael took over. "This brings us to why Abedi became so bold. It was out of desperation. BCCI had been built from oil, from the enormous wealth that flowed into the Middle East after the huge OPEC oil price increases of the 1970s. But that fantastic engine of growth that led Abedi to believe that BCCI could become the largest and most powerful bank in the world soon began to sputter. In 1979 during BCCI's growth, OPEC produced thirty-one million barrels of oil a day. By 1983 a collapse in demand dropped that production rate to a mere eighteen million barrels a day, a 43 percent decrease. What the auditors found in early 1991 was the wreckage left by the extensive and duplicitous efforts to cover up those losses and make BCCI appear to be something that it was not.

"At the core of the deception were some six thousand secret accounts kept personally by former Chief Executive Officer Swaleh Naqvi. So far as anyone knows, the only real reconciliation of BCCI's unreconstructable accounts took place in Naqvi's head. When Abedi needed new capital funds, he would create and sell stock, usually to one of his prominent Middle Eastern nominees like top-ranking men in Saudi intelligence Kamal Adham or A.R. Khalil, or to Ghaith Pharaon, who together had more than half a billion dollars in such loans. The money to buy that stock would be given to the nominees in the form of a loan from one of BCCI's secretive Caymanian affiliates. BCCI would then hold its own stock as collateral for the loan, which never had to be repaid. The result was a bank made to appear larger by the amount of the new capital from the sale of stock, out of thin air. The audit estimated that at least 55 percent of BCCI's stock had been sold in this way, and investigators have suggested a far higher amount.

"From fake capital, we move to fake deposits and fake loans. Buried in Naqvi's esoteric accounting were $600 million in "unrecorded deposits." That is, depositors had actually put real money into the bank, but the bank had not accounted for it. It could therefore be used as ready capital to plug holes or as instant cash, disguised as a transfer from a BCCI affiliate, run in through ICIC and out the other side again. These unbooked deposits helped fill the enormous hole created by BCCI's treasury losses. They could be anything Naqvi and Abedi wanted them to be.

"There was also BCCI's 'Islamic banking unit.' Islamic banking, as interpreted by BCCI, was a sham accounting trick that sidestepped the Koran's banning of usury. A strict Muslim is not allowed to pay or to earn interest. Instead, Islam allows only equity or ownership investments on which one can earn a fair return as the enterprise prospered. So instead of taking a 'deposit' and paying interest on it, though that is precisely what was done, BCCI's Islamic banking unit created a fictitious investment called a 'murabaha' transaction that would allow depositors to convince themselves that the money they earned came not from 'interest' but from the 'profits' of an enterprise. The transaction was the purchase of commodities, real, and tangible goods, as opposed to the abstractions of banking, and then selling them for a profit. To all appearances, the client was not 'depositing' money, he was 'investing' it.

"There were also billions of dollars in false loans, which were the most common method BCCI used to cover losses. For example, the Gokals were unable to pay even the interest on their $831 million in outstanding loans. This created a problem for BCCI because to write off those loans would have wiped out both its real and illusory capital. So, the illusion had to be created that the loans were performing, a slight of hand Abedi had begun practicing as early as 1978. BCCI would book a loan to Maktoum or Khalil without their knowledge or consent. The loan would then travel out of BCCI's main office to a branch or affiliate somewhere in the bank's global system. There the ingenious 'routing' system took over. Routing was the bank's internal money laundry, a method of concealing the true origin and nature of funds washing through its accounts. Naqvi's office was the source of all routing instructions, which would typically involve transferring the fake loan proceeds to one of the routing vehicles, which would then remit funds through the system, disguising them to look like interest payments on the performing loans to the Gokals. The 'special duties account' through which these funds ran held an average daily balance of $1.6 billion at its peak in 1986."

"Who actually performed the manipulations?" asked an FBI director.

"The Price Waterhouse audit suggests that they were almost all Pakistani employees in a bank in which Pakistanis were a small minority," said Michael. "Though Price Waterhouse blacked out the names of the individuals in the audits it released to investigators, their job descriptions remain, and they reveal much about what the core London executive staff did for a living. The actual stated duties of twenty-one people, variously, were the following: setting up nominee shareholdings, false confirmation of audit requests, false loan accounting, secret side agreements with shareholders, routing of funds to avoid detection of source and origin, creating fictitious loans to cover up misappropriated funds, rerouting deposits through ICIC, misappropriation of depositors' funds without depositors' knowledge, and creation of loans with 'no commercial substance' in the names of people without their knowledge. Together with what former BCCI employees have called a network of 'one hundred entrepreneurs' who worked smaller frauds at BCCI branches around the world and assisted in 'routing' actions, plus Abedi and Naqvi themselves, an estimate of how many were involved in significant criminal activity comes approximately one hundred and forty people.

"The most striking thing about the fraud is the utter chaos of it all. BCCI had no central computer system to keep track of its $20 billion-plus in assets. Its accounting system was ancient, and most of the ledgers that investigators have seen are handwritten. In the more corrupt branches, managers literally kept little black books of manipulations, falsified routings of funds, and off-books deposits and loans. Many of the books were kept in the Urdu language. One way that so much money disappeared was that it simply was not recorded."[55]

Every face around the table wore a stunned expression. "So...this bank has no capital at all?" one of the men asked. "It never had any capital, and it's not in the business of making loans?"

"That's the magic of BCCI," said Michael. "The bank got its start-up money when the ruler of Abu Dhabi, Sheikh Zayed bin Sultan al-Nahayan, let Abedi handle the remittances from expatriate Pakistanis working in the Gulf. There were millions of Pakistanis sending money home every month.

It was enough money to shore up Pakistan's entire economy, and Abedi got the float, which meant that he always had a few million dollars sitting in his bank."

"What about the shareholders, the people who bought stock in BCCI?" asked another agent. "What happened to that money?"

"That's the brilliant part," Michael said. "Apparently, the bank put loans to wealthy Arabs on the books for the purchase of stock in BCCI, but never actually loaned the money out. The bank would hold onto those shares as collateral for the loans, which, of course, were never repaid. At some point, they would liquidate the loans and seize the collateral. Nothing actually moved anywhere, but millions in assets have been created on paper. It's circular."

The room suddenly went up in a heated murmur of conversation. Louise was restless. "Excuse me," she said to Michael. "But I would like to go find Jean-Philippe." Michael glared at her. "You promised."

Louise stood to leave, but two FBI agents at the door obstructed her. Michael held her arm and whispered to her. "Louise, you are in danger and cannot leave here. Haven't you figured that out yet? I'm keeping my men on you until this is all over. It's for your own protection."

"Where were they when I was being chased through the streets of Paris, which was the last time I saw Jean-Philippe?"

Michael signaled for the men to back off.

"Can we discuss this later?" Michael picked up his attaché case. "Gentlemen, let's continue this meeting tomorrow morning." He put his arm around Louise and walked her to her room.

Once back in her room, Michael seated Louise on the bed.

"You need to get some rest," he said.

"You promised if I cooperated, you would help me find Jean-Philippe."

"Louise, Jean-Philippe is off the radar. He's gone."

"Bullshit! You know where he is. You know everything, don't you?"

"I swear I don't know where he is. You saw for yourself how elusive he is. How do you think he could have infiltrated that safe at Glavkosmos? Jean-Philippe can take care of himself. My only concern is with you."

Louise was steeped in self-doubt. Michael took some photos out of his attaché case and handed them to her. "You have been playing with fire, and you don't even realize it. Your dealings go beyond BCCI and Jean-Philippe." He then took out a compact tape recorder and pressed the "on" button. Louise immediately recognized the voice on the recording and looked at the photos. She recognized the man in the first photo that matched the voice on the recording. It was Greg Kessler, the widower that she had dated for a short time in Paris.

Greg's voice said, "We were representing a joint venture chasing a sale of military equipment to the Belgian government. We had gone pretty far down the line when suddenly BCCI showed up, representing the Italians. I was staying at the Hilton in Brussels, and I got a phone call from a BCCI guy asking me to come down to the lobby. When I went down, there was a BCCI guy, a Pakistani, and next to him is this two-hundred-and-twenty-pound French guy named André, the kind of guy who stuffs people in car trunks. They have business cards with a BCCI logo. Som André says, 'you're getting out of this thing. This is our deal.' Then the other BCCI guy says, 'you're out, and go and tell your client you're out.' They scared the hell out of me. BCCI has two functions: as bagmen, and as thugs. They pushed the competition out."

Michael tried to soften the shock. "I know you care about Greg. He's a respectable businessman. Only, his business is weapons. Over the past couple of decades in the weapons business, he has worked for two of America's largest defense contractors and participated in deals all over Europe and the Middle East."

Michael pointed to the Pakistani man in the photo who had ordered Greg to get out of the deal. "This guy, Mirza, he was Black Network. But he turned informant and testified to the grand jury. That testimony was suppressed, and Mirza hasn't been heard from since. Louise, you have no idea how deep you are into this. Jean-Philippe can't protect you now. You must trust me. It will all be over soon. Just be patient."

FIFTY

It was all over very quickly. Although the U.S. Federal Reserve does not have the power to subpoena or bring indictments under U.S. law, it is in many ways the most powerful of U.S. government agencies. It is politically independent and therefore can move swiftly, unilaterally, and with decisive force within its own domain. In March 1991, the Bank of Credit & Commerce International divested itself of First American Bankshares. At 1:00 p.m. on July 5, 1991, the worldwide financial scandal erupted with regulators in eight countries shutting down Bank of Credit and Commerce International, charging it with fraud, drug money laundering, and illegal infiltration into the U.S. banking system.

In an unprecedented sweep, regulators moved against BCCI, in Britain, the United States, Canada, the Cayman Islands, Spain, France, and Switzerland, overrunning BCCI's offices and informing startled bank officers that they were being shut down. The seizure covered more than 75 percent of the bank's estimated $20 billion in assets. The news exploded in the Third World where BCCI held large deposits, many from central banks. BCCI headquarters had recently been moved to Abu Dhabi, United Arab Emirates. The ruling family of Abu Dhabi, under the entity Abu Dhabi Investment Authority, was the major investor and faced huge liability claims from depositors around the world.

Hong Kong's financial markets were in full panic, as $1.4 billion of depositors' funds were frozen, including an estimated $200 million from the government of China. In Pakistan, the government posted armed guards at the gates to prevent a wholesale run. In neighboring Bangladesh, authorities declared that BCCI had "looted" the country, leaving it with huge losses. At least one third of Cameroon's national reserves was frozen and would eventually be lost. Nigeria lost $200 million. For BCCI's 1.4 million depositors, there would be less than $2 billion in real assets to pay them off.

The seizure was excruciatingly painful for the Bank of England, under whose nose Abedi and Naqvi had perpetrated their global deceit. But the most visibly angry of all of the victims was Sheikh Zayed and his chief lieutenant, the secretary general of the Abu Dhabi Investment Authority, Ghanim al-Mazrui. The Bank of England had abandoned them on July 5th. The shutdown had coincided with a meeting of BCCI's board in Luxembourg to discuss the bank's reorganization and new capital infusions from Zayed. The deal was to have been signed a mere ten days later. Zayed himself had been the principal mark in Abedi's con game. He had been coddled into pumping $1.5 billion in new capital and another $1.5 billion in deposits since mid-1990. That money was gone, never to be recovered.

The U.S. Justice Department, as usual, was nowhere to be found. But New York District Attorney Bob Morgan did something that only he could have pulled off: He put the U.S. Fed on his own grand jury, thus tightly binding together the New York District Attorney's investigation with the Fed's investigation. Morgan's July 29, 1992, indictment of BCCI's former heads—Agha Hasan Abedi, Swaleh Naqvi, Ghaith Pharaon, and Faisal Saud Al Fulaij—alleged in detail how BCCI systematically engaged in criminal activity with officials and prominent political figures from many countries to generate assets for BCCI's Ponzi scheme, both from the governments involved and from innocent, legitimate depositors.

One of the most shocking revelations to come out of the investigation was that, for a decade, BCCI had secretly controlled the largest bank chain in the D.C. area, First American Bankshares, Inc. Morgan's investigation is credited for the demise of BCCI's global operations. The Third World's first multi-national bank, which, in fact, never even took deposits, had been set up to handle the accounts of over three thousand high-net-worth criminals.

No amount of foot-dragging, lack of cooperation, or outright hindrance of the investigation by the Justice Department or any other U.S. government agency was going to forestall it. In the truest sense, Morgan stood alone on that day among world law enforcement as the only one who had dared to take on BCCI. On December 19, 1991, the failed BCCI agreed to settle federal racketeering charges by forfeiting all its U.S. assets. In 1994 thirteen former BCCI officials were tried, and twelve were convicted and sentenced to jail and civil damages of $9 billion. In 1996 the court acquitted two BCCI officials but upheld sentences against eight and ordered them to pay $8.3 million in addition to the original $9 billion in civil damages.

Graith Pharaon was an international fugitive due to the BCCI scandal.

However, he remained an active businessman and served as an important financier for terrorist organizations such as al-Qaeda. Pharaon was listed on Forbes's *The World's 10 Most Wanted* for his involvement in the BCCI scandal and the CenTrust savings and loan scandal, which cost U.S. taxpayers billions of dollars. He was wanted by the FBI and the IRS, yet he remained popular in U.S. military and intelligence circles. His Pakistani-based refinery, Attock Refinery Ltd, was awarded an $80 million U.S. Department of Defense contract to supply jet fuel to military bases in Afghanistan. Pakistani Interior Minister Shujaat Hussain, who had the authority to block extraditions, stated flatly that Pharaon was his friend, and he would give him citizenship, protection from extradition, and even immunity from local prosecution.[56]

While the west speculated on why it had taken so long for authorities to shut down BCCI, the reaction in Pakistan was one of angry disbelief. Though Abedi had been sick since his first heart attack and was living quietly in the affluent Defense Officers' Society in Karachi, he remained a towering figure to many Pakistanis, revered as a courageous Third World entrepreneur whose bank had been hounded by racist western financial interests. Abedi told the Pakistani press: "I am not responsible for the current crisis in the BCCI. I have not had anything to do with the bank since I was sidelined after my heart attack in Lahore in February 1988. I don't blame anyone, neither the west nor Sheikh Zayed. These things happen." He insisted that the bank was strong when he left it, and that its failure was the result of mismanagement.

The greatest mystery in all this was the size and location of Abedi's personal bank account. He had secretly controlled a large portion of the shares of BCCI, but those were now worthless. So, his wealth, whatever form it was in, lay somewhere else. He was almost certainly worth billions, but the very secrecy that allowed him to set up his untraceable international banking network also allowed him to hide whatever fortune he had amassed. He is undoubtedly a great man, although in the west he will be remembered more for his bad deeds than for his good ones. Like the bank he built, Abedi himself was ahistorical, existing in the margins and footnotes of the "official" history. Until BCCI self-destructed in 1991, due largely to Abedi's neglect, he was known to few outside the magic circle of the powerful elites he had drawn around him. He was also lucky, for that same destiny led him to the very axis of one of the great power shifts in history.

FIFTY-ONE

When Louise decided to stay in Paris, she negotiated with the landlords to take over the lease of her Paris apartment. She loved the apartment and preferred Paris to New York. Also, it would be easier for Jean-Philippe to find her there. She arrived at the apartment, dropped her bags, went to the bedroom and sat on the bed. After the closure of BCCI, she felt as though she was back at square one. No Jean-Philippe, no job, no friends. She was exhausted and overcome with heartache. She sobbed uncontrollably. Jean-Philippe had been the unifying force of her life. She felt lost without him. Tears rolled down her cheeks as she looked at the diamond ring Jean-Philippe had placed on her finger with the promise of grandchildren.

She got up and opened the secret bedroom chamber. She took off the ring, placed it on top of the manuscript in the hidden drawer, closed the door of the secret chamber, and sat back down on the bed, crying. She lay down and slept deeply.

The next morning, she awoke feeling famished and went down to the patisserie for a gâteau Napolitain and the newspaper. She came back upstairs, made a café au lait, and sat at the breakfast table. She leafed through the pages of *Le Monde*. On the third page, a small article caught her eye. The article speculated on the disappearance of Jean-Philippe de Villeneuve. She could feel he was alive, but the public speculation made her doubt herself. She went back to her bedroom and sat on the bed, sobbing.

Through the blur of tears, something caught her eye on the nightstand. She wiped her eyes and saw, there on the nightstand, the manuscript, on top of which sat the engagement ring. She shot to her feet. Blood rushed to her face and she looked around. Confused, she tried to remember if she had really placed the ring in the secret hiding place or not. She was sure she had. She reached down and picked up the ring with trembling fingers. Tears flowed but now they were hopeful tears. She placed the ring on her finger and raised her eyes upward. She took a deep cleansing breath and exhaled.

She lay down comforting herself and fell asleep for a long time. When she awoke, she was still holding the manuscript. She opened it and let the pages flip through her fingers. It looked to be about two hundred thousand words.

She groggily rolled out of bed and shuffled to the kitchen. On the way, she noticed a stack of mail that the postman had slipped under the front door, accumulating into a pile. She picked it up and continued to the kitchen. She sifted through the envelopes and set most aside to be thrown away, keeping mostly bills. Then she noticed a handwritten envelope addressed to her. She recognized the handwriting as Jean-Philippe's and tore it open. It was a fully executed legal document, detailing the chain of command for the corporation in the Grand Caymans that they had set up. It designated Louise as the treasurer and CEO, granting full signatory duties and proxy on the corporation. It also included an agreement detailing the sale of the violin that Roger Bing had sold to Philippe. Jean-Philippe had in turn resold the violin for a profit of $1 million. There was bank statement showing a Cayman Islands bank account with a $1 million balance. It was all under the control of Louise Moscow as managing member of the company.

Louise now knew what she had to do. She called her travel agent to book a flight to the Caymans for the next day. Then she went back to bed and began reading the manuscript.

END

AUTHOR'S NOTE

Dear Reader:

Did you enjoy FOLIAGE? If so, you can make an enormous difference. Reviews are the most powerful tool I have when it comes to attracting the attention of other readers. Reviews also increase a book's visibility on major book sales sites such as Amazon.

If you've enjoyed FOLIAGE and have five minutes to spare, I would be eternally grateful if you could leave an honest review, as short as you like.

Amazon
amazon.com/gp/product/B0186LATR8

Goodreads
goodreads.com/book/show/27510736-foliage

Bookbub
tinyurl.com/qog5cgj

Thank you, Lorraine Evanoff

ABOUT THE AUTHOR

Award-winning author Lorraine Evanoff's popular Louise Moscow Novels are high concept noir thrillers inspired by real-life banking scandals. Ms. Evanoff is a native of Chicago, where she received a BA in French from DePaul University then studied and worked for seven years in Paris. As a former finance exec, Ms. Evanoff held CFO positions in high tech companies during the Silicon Valley Dot-Com era, and more recently in Hollywood, notably as CFO of National Lampoon. She currently has a screenplay in development.

Lorraine's online home is lorraineevanoff.com
Facebook facebook.com/levanoff
Twitter twitter.com/levanoff
Email LorraineEvanoff@gmail.com

EXCERPT – PINOT NOIR

A LOUISE MOSCOW NOVEL BOOK II

BY LORRAINE EVANOFF

"There are way too many suspects with money at stake," Jean-Philippe said.

"And lots of it," Michael added.

"Whoever loves money never has enough – Ecclesiastes 5:10," Jean-Philippe quoted.

"Those in the sole pursuit of gold, money, and power will stop at nothing. I think I read that in Newsweek," Michael retorted. "So, you're thinking the Banker's Grave?"

"A banker who knows too much…"

"It's not a conspiracy theory if it's true." Michael leaned back and pondered. "I can think of three suspicious deaths of prominent bankers right off the bat. The chairman of Banco Ambrosiano, Roberto Calvi, hung by the neck beneath Blackfriar's Bridge in London in 1982. Then, there's the owner of Franklin National Bank, Michele Sindona, who died after drinking coffee laced with arsenic in an Italian prison in 1986…"

"And now the owner of New York Republic Bank, Ekram M. Almasi, who burned to death trapped in his heavily guarded penthouse in Monaco," Jean-Philippe said.

"Each of these dead bankers knew a lot of secrets. But, Calvi and Sindona were murdered after their banks collapsed."

"Exactly!" Jean-Philippe said. "Of those three, Almasi's death is the most curious. He died with his financial empire intact." Jean-Philippe spoke passionately, rising to his feet, pacing and emphasizing with his hands. In the setting of the dimly lit 14th century monastery anyone else would have thought Jean-Philippe had lost it. But Michael knew what it was like to have loved and then lost Louise Moscow. The heartbreak turned to wretchedness, which eventually evolved into tempered steel will…

ENDNOTES

Chapter 4

1. Jonathan Beaty and S.C. Gwynne, *The Outlaw Bank: A Wild Ride into the Secret Heart of BCCI*, (Random House, New York)

Chapter 5

2. Jonathan Beaty and S.C. Gwynne, *The Outlaw Bank: A Wild Ride into the Secret Heart of BCCI*, (Random House, New York)

3. Among Clark Clifford's breathtaking accomplishments was masterminding Harry S. Truman's come-from-behind victory over Thomas E. Dewey in 1948. He was also the principal architect of "Fair Deal" politics. He co-authored the National Security Act of 1947, which set up both the Central Intelligence Agency and the National Security Council. He was the prime mover in the creation of the Department of Defense. He participated in the formulation of the Truman Doctrine, the policy of Soviet containment that lasted into the first Bush administration. Clifford directed the transition from the Eisenhower administration to John F. Kennedy's New Frontier. He was Kennedy's personal lawyer and among other duties advised JFK in the dark days after the Bay of Pigs invasion. After JFK was assassinated, Clifford became one of Lyndon Johnson's most senior advisers, serving as secretary of defense, a job he took four days before the disastrous 1968 Tet Offensive in the Vietnam War. Before he left the Johnson administration, he led early efforts to extricate the United States from Vietnam. Later, he counseled President Jimmy Carter on the Panama Canal Treaty and acted as Carter's special envoy to Greece, Turkey, and India.

4. Jonathan Beaty and S.C. Gwynne, *The Outlaw Bank: A Wild Ride into the Secret Heart of BCCI*, (Random House, New York)

Chapter 7

5. Jonathan Beaty and S.C. Gwynne, *The Outlaw Bank: A Wild Ride into the Secret Heart of BCCI*, (Random House, New York)

Chapter 8

6. Jonathan Beaty and S.C. Gwynne, *The Outlaw Bank: A Wild Ride into the Secret Heart of BCCI*, (Random House, New York)

7. In those days, Abu Dhabi boasted fewer than two-dozen buildings, mostly unpaved streets, and dwellings that were barely more than shanties. Surmounting the town was the ancient stone palace of the emir, a Bedouin prince named Shakhbut bin Sultan al-Nahayan. This strange feudal kingdom stood poised on the brink of unimaginable wealth. Oil had been discovered in the Gulf waters just off the coast of Abu Dhabi in 1959. It had been a major strike reminiscent of the first finds in Kuwait and Saudi Arabia twenty years before.

Shakhbut bin Sultan al-Nahyan's ideas about money were primitive. He knew that banks existed, but he could not have described how one worked or why anyone would want to give a bank his money. Wealth, as he understood it, was measured in camels, weapons, tents, and rugs. Abedi would teach Shakhbut the benefits of banking and make him one of his biggest depositors. Shakhbut remained ruler of the emirate of Abu Dhabi until August 1966 when he was deposed in a bloodless coup by his brother Sheikh Zayed Bin Sultan Al Nahyan, who became the emir of Abu Dhabi, and eventually rose to become the undisputed leader of the United Arab Emirates. Sheikh Zayed Bin Sultan Al Nahyan's background as a tribal chieftain had more in common with the Arabia of the Middle Ages than with the western world of the Twentieth Century. When the explorer Wilfred Thesiger first discovered Zayed in the late 1940s, he described him as a *powerfully built man of about thirty with a brown beard sitting on the bare sand next to his rifle, wearing a Bedouin smock, a dagger and a cartridge belt.* He lived in a mud fort with walls ten feet high and, on behalf of his brother, supervised six small villages in the oasis of Buraimi, near what is today the border of Abu Dhabi and Saudi Arabia. Zayed's chief preoccupation was the *ghazzu*, or *Bedouin raid*, the object of which was to secure either territory or camels. According to Thesiger, Zayed could ride, shoot and fight and had a great reputation with the Bedouin.

In 1967 Zayed was now leader of the oil rich nation and had been wondering what he was going to do with all the new oil money. It was then that Abedi made the pilgrimage to the Persian Gulf, bearing gifts of Pahtan rugs, to introduce himself to Zayad. Abedi was a Muslim and a banker from the Third World who understood the ways of western money. Abedi traveled frequently to Abu Dhabi, cementing his relationship with the new emir Sheikh Zayed to ensure his continued patronage as one of United Bank's biggest depositors, and a close personal friend.

8. Jonathan Beaty and S.C. Gwynne, *The Outlaw Bank: A Wild Ride into the Secret Heart of BCCI*, (Random House, New York)

Chapter 9

9. Jonathan Beaty and S.C. Gwynne, *The Outlaw Bank: A Wild Ride into the Secret Heart of BCCI*, (Random House, New York)

Chapter 11

10. Jonathan Beaty and S.C. Gwynne, *The Outlaw Bank: A Wild Ride into the Secret Heart of BCCI*, (Random House, New York)

11. Jonathan Beaty and S.C. Gwynne, *The Outlaw Bank: A Wild Ride into the Secret Heart of BCCI*, (Random House, New York)

12. Jonathan Beaty and S.C. Gwynne, *The Outlaw Bank: A Wild Ride into the Secret Heart of BCCI*, (Random House, New York)

Chapter 12

13. Jonathan Beaty and S.C. Gwynne, *The Outlaw Bank: A Wild Ride into the Secret Heart of BCCI*, (Random House, New York)

14. Wikipedia
The hieroglyphic image of the beetle is thought to represent a tri-literal phonetic XPR or HPR translated as "to come into being." The ancients believed that the dung beetle was only male in gender and reproduced by depositing semen into a dung ball. The supposed self-creation of the beetle resembles that of Khepri, the god of the rising sun, who creates himself out of nothing.

Chapter 13

15. Louise believed language could be used to empirically solve metaphysical problems and articulate complicated thought processes. Deciphering feelings and thoughts using words required as much precision and discipline as the mathematical equations and scientific experiments used to arrive at empirical proofs. The effective articulation of an idea can *prove* the existence of extremely subjective philosophical concepts and even contribute to human evolution. Likewise, analytical mathematical thinking can help in learning to speak a language. For example, by breaking language down into syntax and vocabulary, one can learn to read and speak a new language fluently. Much the way breaking a word down phonetically is useful for accurate pronunciation. She suspected her dichotomy with math and language came naturally to her because she was left-handed.

Chapter 15

16. www.pbs.org/wgbh/pages/frontline/shows/wallstreet/weill/demise.html

In 1987 when stock values tanked and fortunes vaporized overnight, the Dow Jones Industrial Average dropped by 508 points to 1,738.74, or 22.61%. It is believed that the crash was caused by a combination of an inflated market due to recent deregulation, coupled with computerized trading. In 1986 the United States economy had begun shifting from a rapidly growing recovery to a slower growing expansion. In March 1987, the Federal Reserve Board approved an application by Chase Manhattan to engage in underwriting commercial paper, effectively voting to ease regulations under Glass-Steagall Act, and allow banks to handle several types of underwriting, including commercial paper, municipal revenue bonds, and mortgage-backed securities.

The Federal Reserve Board remained sensitive to concerns about mixing commercial banking and underwriting. However, the Board believed that the original Congressional intent of the term "principally engaged" in commercial banking allowed for some securities activities. The Board believed the new interpretation would increase competition and lead to greater convenience and increased efficiency. Then, in August 1987, the former director of J.P. Morgan, Alan Greenspan, a proponent of banking deregulation, became chairman of the Federal Reserve Board. One reason Greenspan favored greater deregulation was to help U.S. banks compete with big foreign institutions.

17. Stephen Zarlenga, Director, American monetary Institute

It boiled down to two different cultures, a culture of risk, which was the securities business, and a culture of protection of deposits, which was the banking business. The stock market advanced significantly, with the Dow peaking in August 1987 at 2,722 points, a 44 percent increase over the previous year's closing of 1,895 points.

Then, on October 14, 1987, the DJIA dropped 95.46 points, and fell another 58 points the next day. On Friday, October 16, when all the markets in London were unexpectedly closed due to the Great Storm of 1987, the DJIA closed down another 108.35 points. That weekend many investors worried over their stock investments. On the morning of October 19, the crash began in Far Eastern markets. Later that morning, two U.S. warships shelled an Iranian oil platform in the Persian Gulf in response to Iran's Silkworm missile attack on the U.S. flagged ship MV Sea Isle City. When the U.S. markets opened, virtually all the fund managers tried to do the same thing at the same time: sell short the stock index futures, in a futile attempt to hedge their stock positions. The sell-off created a huge discount in the futures market.

Some of the biggest wall Street firms found they could not stop their pre-programmed computers from automatically engaging in this derivatives trading. They had to unplug or cut the wiring to computers or find other ways to cut off the electricity to them. There were rumors about using fireman's axes taken from hallways. The New York Stock Exchange at one point on Monday and Tuesday seriously considered closing down entirely for a period of days or weeks.

One thing that the crash made very clear was that there was no real liquidity in the markets when it was needed. It was at this point that Alan Greenspan made an uncharacteristic announcement that the FED would make credit available to the brokerage community, as needed. Another outcome of the crash was to counter the deregulation with the implementation of maximum daily trading limits and the establishment of circuit breakers by the stock exchanges; a solution that the agricultural and other commodities markets had used successfully for decades.

Chapter 16

18. Jonathan Beaty and S.C. Gwynne, *The Outlaw Bank: A Wild Ride into the Secret Heart of BCCI*, (Random House, New York)

19. Jonathan Beaty and S.C. Gwynne, *The Outlaw Bank: A Wild Ride into the Secret Heart of BCCI*, (Random House, New York)

Chapter 19

20. www.tehelka.com/story_main28.asp?filename=hub140407Doctor_I_.asp

21. Autobiography of a Yogi by the great Paramhansa Yogananda written in 1946

Chapter 26

22. During the early sixteenth century, the area was a clay quarry for making tiles, or a *tuilerie*. In 1559 the Queen of France, Catherine de Médici, had the Palais de Tuileries built on that spot, which featured a large garden in the style of her native Tuscany, Italy. In later years, King Louis XIV commissioned the great landscape artist Andre Le Notre to extend the garden. Le Nôtre and his hundreds of masons, gardeners, and earthmovers worked on the garden from 1666 to 1672, creating the long tree-lined beginnings of the *Champs-Élysées*.

All road distances in France are calculated from the 'zero-kilometer point' located in the square facing Notre-Dame's west-end towers, which lie adjacent to the Tuileries Gardens. All the arches in Paris from Notre Dame to La Defense line up perfectly from the zero-kilometer marker. The *Champs-Élysées* was named after the mythical Elysian Fields, the place of the blessed dead in Greek mythology. The Champs-Élysées was originally fields and market gardens, until 1616, when Marie de Medici decided to extend the axis of the Tuileries Garden with an avenue of trees.

23. The Académie Française is the pre-eminent French learned body on matters pertaining to the French language. The Académie Française was officially established in 1635 by Cardinal Richelieu. It was modeled on the academy founded in Florence, Italy in 1582, devoted to winnowing out the "impurities" of the Italian language, formalizing the Tuscan dialect of

Florence as the model for spoken Italian. Members of the academy are known as *les immortels* (the immortals) because of the motto *À l'immortalité* (To Eternal Life), which appears on the official seal of the charter granted by Richelieu. *Immortels* are chosen by their counterparts and serve for life, or until resignation. Past Immortels include Alexandre Dumas, Eugène Ionesco, Marcel Prévost, Valéry Giscard d'Estaing, and Jean Cocteau. The Académie is France's official authority on the usages, vocabulary, and grammar of the French language. It publishes a dictionary of the French language, known as the *Dictionnaire de l'Académie Française*, which is regarded as official in France.

Chapter 27

24. Alix Kirsta

Peter and the two Chicago-based violin dealers Bing & Fushimi had made their fortunes together by carefully courting an elderly collector of rare violins. They began regularly visiting the man, Gerald Segelman, known for having spent his whole life acquiring his collection.

25. Nicholas Forrest, Art market Blog

He was the son of Austrian Jews who had fled the pogroms of Central Europe for the freedoms of the west. He and his three brothers had made their fortune building a chain of movie theatres in the 1920s. By the early 1940s, Segelman was wealthy enough to acquire the exquisite fiddles he had been denied in his youth, and he hardly could have picked a more advantageous moment. The war raging across Europe had driven down the price of rare instruments and other antiques, with owners unloading even their most valuable fiddles simply to obtain money for survival.

The purchases Segelman made after World War II were at rock-bottom prices: $3,360 for the "Mary Portman" Guarneri del Gesu in 1949; $18,941 for the "Sasserno" Stradivari in March 1946; $19,665 for the "Arditi" Stradivari in December 1947. In a few decades, these instruments would be worth millions. By 1962 Segelman had built an impressive inventory, including major Stradivaris, Guarneris, Amatis, Guadagninis, Stainers, practically every rare kind of fiddle ever made.

His living room overflowed with instrument cases and the cabinet in his bedroom was jammed with more than thirty violins at a time. The three dealers had ingeniously conspired to convert this very personal collection into the next fine art market boom of the 1980s. Published figures showed art and antiques to be one of the most lucrative investments with the values of high-grade collections having risen 785 percent over the previous twenty-five years. The instruments, handcrafted of maple and pine centuries ago in northern Italy, would become vehicles for quick profits, traded around the world as if they were pork bellies or cattle futures, in the way that paintings by Monet, Van Gogh, and other masterpieces had. Luck and perseverance eventually conspired to put Segelman's violins into the hands of the salesmen from Chicago and London.

In the early 1970s, Roger Bing and Jeff Fushimi (respectively a "bad cellist" and a "bad violinist," according to Bing) had been seduced by the mystique of rare stringed instruments, as well as the prestige and profits they could yield. Segelman's holdings never ceased to amaze them. Segelman's wife finally convinced him that it was time to sell some of his finest instruments. But he was out of touch with how radically the violin trade had changed. With prices having skyrocketed, a few world-class dealers now wielded enormous power over the marketplace, playing multiple conflicting roles as buyer, seller, investor, broker, appraiser, wholesaler, and retailer. They generally provided expert appraisals to a seller who had no other way to determine the true market value of an instrument. Once a dealer had told the seller how much an instrument was worth, nothing prevented the dealer from buying the instrument himself or investing in a portion of it, unbeknownst to the seller.

London-based Peter Edwards was tall, slender, and suave, and Bing and Fushimi's opposite in practically every way. His crisp enunciation sounded nothing like their flat midwestern speech. While Edwards entered the world of rare fiddles at its pinnacle, working for Sotheby's and London's pre-eminent dealer Charles Beare, Bing was self-taught and Fushimi merely another anonymous salesclerk. Linked by their ardor for rare fiddles, the three became fast friends.

When Edwards rang Segelman up in 1974, he gruffly challenged Peter, "Let's see how good you are. I'm going to show you my violins, and if you get one wrong, I won't show you anymore." Peter was very unnerved and asked Roger Bing to go to Gerald Segelman's with him. Bing had a superior eye. He had learned all these violins through books, and he had a photographic memory.

When the two dealers walked into Segelman's flat, they were appalled.

His cramped three-room apartment was fit for a pauper, not a collector of priceless violins. Segelman was eager to play name-that-fiddle. He went to the bedroom to get one of his violins, and as soon as he came into the living room, Roger would correctly identify it. Peter was in awe of Bing's uncanny talent for recognizing instruments in an instant. Roger would call out the names of the violins when Segelman came through the door, and he was always right. Gerald liked that.

Essentially, Edwards would sell an instrument at a wholesale price to Bing & Fushimi or to Chicago investor Howard Gottlieb, a Chicago Symphony orchestra board member. Gottlieb then would pay a fee to Edwards in the hundreds of thousands of dollars. After paying Edwards his cut, Bing & Fushimi or Gottlieb were clear to resell the instrument at steep mark-ups. Edwards allowed Bing & Fushimi and others to become wholesale middlemen, cutting large profits for themselves that otherwise would have gone to Segelman while he was still alive, and to his charitable trust after his death. According to Bing, these profits were wholly justified. They would buy at one price and sell at another, their overhead including payroll, rent, and restoration costs had to be covered as well. It was business.

For example, Segelman decided to sell one of his most valuable instru-ments, the 1735 Guarneri del Gesu, named the "Mary Portman." Because he had acquired the instrument in 1949 for £1,200 or approximately $3,360, Segelman probably believed that he turned the maximum profit when he sold the instrument, through Edwards in 1989, for £600,000, or $950,000. But Segelman achieved this profit by holding onto the instrument for more than forty years. Bing & Fushimi unloaded the fiddle in a little more than a year for $2 million, a mark-up of 105 percent, or $1.05 million. The middlemen divided the proceeds through an intricate process. Edwards sold the "Mary Portman" Guarneri for $950,000 to Gottlieb, an amateur violinist and successful Chicago entrepreneur.

He immediately handed over the instrument on consignment to Bing & Fushimi, who in turn sold the "Mary Portman" to a prime client for $2 million.

26. Wikipedia
Veuve Cliquot is both a champagne house in Reims, France, and a brand of premium champagne. In 1772 Philippe Clicquot-Muiron established the original enterprise, which at the time became the house of Veuve Clicquot.

Clicquot died in 1805, leaving his widow (*veuve* in French) in control of a company, which was involved in banking, wool trading, and champagne production. Under Madame Clicquot's guidance, the firm focused entirely on the latter.

The 1811 comet vintage of Veuve Clicquot is theorized to have been the first truly "modern" champagne due to the advancements in the méthode champenoise, which Veuve Clicquot pioneered through the technique of remuage. By the time of Madame Clicquot's death 1866, Veuve Clicquot had become both a substantial champagne house and a respected brand, easily recognized by its distinctive bright yellow labels.

Chapter 29

27. A Report to the Committee on Foreign Relations, United States Senate by Senator John Kerry and Senator Hank Brown, December 1992

Chapter 32

28. Jonathan Beaty and S.C. Gwynne, *The Outlaw Bank: A Wild Ride into the Secret Heart of BCCI*, (Random House, New York)

29. Jonathan Beaty and S.C. Gwynne, *The Outlaw Bank: A Wild Ride into the Secret Heart of BCCI*, (Random House, New York)

30. See endnote 3.

Chapter 33

31. The abbey was founded in the sixth century in the outskirts of early medieval Paris. At that time, the Left Bank of Paris was prone to flooding from the River Seine, so the Abbey stood in the middle of fields, or *prés* in French. Its bell tower is one of the oldest in France. After World War II, the area of St-Germain exploded into a hotspot for the arts. Picasso, Sartre, De Beauvoir, Beckett and Charles Gainsbourg frequented the famous restaurants Les Deux Magots and Café de Flore, adjacent to the Abbey.

Chapter 34

32. One of the most exclusive and beloved restaurants in the world, Taillevent was established in 1950 in the *hôtel particulier* built in 1852 by the

Duc de Morny. The name *Taillevent* was the nom de plume of Guillaume Tirel, the author of the oldest manuscript of recipes, written in French in 1379. Charles V ordered Taillevent to index all the recipes in use by La Cour de France, which basically consisted of anyone who lived in the direct entourage of the king. The result was an exact account of recipes of the Middle Ages.

Chapter 35

33. Jonathan Beaty and S.C. Gwynne, *The Outlaw Bank: A Wild Ride into the Secret Heart of BCCI*, (Random House, New York)

Chapter 37

34. Cayman Brac got its name from these cliffs, "brac" being the Gaelic word for bluff. It was this prominent bluff that made Cayman Brac the first of the Cayman Islands sighted by Christopher Columbus in 1503.

On Columbus's fourth and final voyage to the Americas, he stumbled across the islands. The ship's log stated that they were in sight of land surrounded by turtles, both on land and in the water, and for that reason the islands were first named "Las Tortugas" (The Turtles). For years afterward, the islands remained uninhabited, visited only by passing ships or pirates seeking to hide their treasure. Later, the mistaken identification of the large numbers of iguanas for alligators resulted in the islands being renamed the Cayman Islands, after the Caymanas alligator. Cayman Brac and Little Cayman grew in population, leaving their larger sister relatively undeveloped. In the twentieth century, Grand Cayman had grown up into a very popular hotel and banking center, while Little Cayman had fallen back into its sleepy way of life, and Cayman Brac had developed a nice mix of both worlds.

Chapter 41

35. adventure.howstuffworks.com/hang-gliding4.htm

The hang glider is actually a triangle-shaped airfoil, a modified parachute known as a flexible wing made of nylon or Dacron fabric. The triangular shape, using a rigid wing with stiff aluminum struts inside the fabric to give it shape, is designed to allow air to flow over the surface to make the wing rise. To launch, the pilot must run down a slope to get air moving across the wing at about fifteen to twenty-five miles per hour. This movement of air over the surface of the wing generates lift: the force that counters gravity and keeps the glider aloft. Once aloft, gravity from the weight of the hang glider and pilot pulls the glider back toward Earth and propels the glider forward, continually causing air to flow over the wing.

In addition to the horizontal movement of air, hang gliders can get lift from rising currents of air, such as columns of hot air called *thermal lift*, or air deflected upward by mountainous or ridge topography called *ridge lift*. As the hang glider and pilot move through the air they collide with air molecules. The frictional force caused by these collisions is known as *drag*, which slows the glider down. The amount of drag is proportional to the airspeed of the hang glider: the faster the glider moves the more drag it creates. As with soar-plane gliders, the balance of these three forces—lift, drag, and gravity—determines how high the hang glider can go, how far it can travel and how long it can stay aloft. The performance of a hang glider and the distance it can travel is determined by its glide ratio or lift/drag ratio, the ratio of the forward distance traveled to the vertical distance dropped. Unlike soar-plane gliders, hang gliders have neither movable surfaces on the wing nor a tail to deflect airflow and maneuver the craft. Instead, the pilot is suspended from the hang glider's center-of-mass, hence the term "hang" glider, by way of a harness, maneuvering the hang glider by shifting his or her weight, changing the center-of-mass, in the direction of the intended turn.

The pilot can also change the angle that the wing makes with the horizontal axis, called the *angle of attack*, which determines the airspeed and the glide ratio of the hang glider. If the pilot pulls back on the glider, tipping its nose down, the glider speeds up. If the pilot pushes forward on the glider, tipping its nose up, the glider slows down or even stalls. In stalling, no air flows over the wing so the glider can't fly.

Chapter 44

36. The history of the UAE dates back to 1400, about the time Dubai became a major crossing point on international trading routes in silk, pearls, spices and gold. In 1962 Abu Dhabi began exporting the oil it discovered off its shores. By 1965 Arab states signed the Charter of Arab Honor. In 1966

Sheikh Zayed bin Sultan Al Nahyan became the ruler of Abu Dhabi. In 1971 he founded the United Arab Emirates. The UAE is a federation of seven emirates, or territories, each governed by a hereditary emir, with a single national president. The constituent emirates are Abu Dhabi, Ajman, Dubai, Fujairah, Ras al-Khaimah, Sharjah, and Umm al-Quwain. The capital is Abu Dhabi.

By 1973 Abu Dhabi had a massive surge in revenue following an oil-price increase. By 1976 Sheikh Zayed of Abu Dhabi set up the Abu Dhabi Investment Authority (ADIA), which invested heavily in real estate abroad, while at the same time the government tightened control of property at home. On May 25, 1981, Sheikh Zayed urged five other Arab monarchies—Bahrain, Kuwait, Oman, Qatar, and Saudi Arabia—to join the UAE in forming the Gulf Cooperation Council in a unified economic agreement, often referred to as the GCC States.

37. www.resetdoc.org

Al-Jabri was one of the most important Moroccan intellectuals in the contemporary Arab world. He obtained a doctorate in philosophy from Mohammed V University in Rabat, Morocco, in 1970 and then took the position of professor of philosophy and Islamic Thought there. He authored more than thirty books and multiple essays on contemporary Arab-Islamic thought. His works have been translated into several languages. He was an expert in Arabic literature known for his academic project "The Critique of the Arab mind."

Al-Jabri's approach consisted of the exploration of the conflict between modernity and tradition in the Muslim and Arab world. In his writings, he focused on the rationalism of the medieval Muslim philosophers from the tenth to fifteenth centuries. Claiming that the modern Arab world needed a reason to survive in the contemporary world, Al-Jabri called for a "New Averroism" named after the twelfth-century philosopher Averroes. According to Al-Jabri, the conflicting situation that prevents Muslims and Arabs from reconciling contemporary events with the Islamic tradition of the *turath* had occurred during the Middle Ages. This recurring problem was the consequence of centuries of domination by powers such as the Omayyad Dynasty, who proclaimed to replace God on Earth, thereby sanctifying their own tyrannical and oppressive authority. This situation, made worse by Western colonialism and twentieth-century dictatorships, resulted in political stagnation of Arab-Islamic societies.

The only solution to this *impasse*, according to Al-Jabri, was democracy, claiming the principle foundations existed in the Qur'an itself. He believed the "endogenous" path to democracy in the Muslim world, as opposed to importing a democracy with Western characteristics, starts with the Koranic principle of the *shurà*, or "consultation." It offers Muslims a way of taking possession of democracy by referring to their cultural heritage and religious traditions.

38. Milken's financing tactics contributed to the growth a few major companies such as Ted Turner's CNN and Rupert Murdoch's News Corp. However, Milken and his cronies *destroyed* far more companies than they had built. Among the many corporations that they wiped out were a number of America's biggest savings and loans companies—massive financial operations whose collapse triggered the famous savings and loan crisis that inflicted serious damage on the economy and cost American taxpayers billions of dollars. The Federal Deposit Insurance Corporation (FDIC) asserted that Milken and his closest associates "willfully, deliberately, and systematically plundered certain S&Ls."

Milken's criminal enterprise used some of the same tactics, and some of the same people, who contributed to the financial collapse years later in 2008. A principal feature of the Milken operation was a variation on what mobsters refer to as a "bust out." As an analogy, mafia thugs would take over the corner bar, load it up with debt, siphon out the cash, and declare bankruptcy. Milken elaborated on the "bust out" and brought it to the world of high finance. The scheme worked as follows: To raise capital, Milken issued *junk bonds*, which have a higher risk of default, but which paid a higher yield to attract investors. The capital he raised from the sale of junk bond debt went to about a dozen of his closest associates, who used the funds to take over *good* companies. Under the direction of Milken's cronies, the *good* companies then took on more of Milken's junk bond debt. But rather than use the financing to grow the companies, the Milken cronies simply looted the companies of their cash.

They ingeniously create the illusion that there was a liquid market for the junk bonds. Milken cronies traded their bonds amongst each other at stair-stepping prices, in an illegal process known as "daisy-chaining." This junk bond merry-go-round was conducted with mafia-like secrecy – nobody other than Milken's closest associates knew that the only buyers for the junk bonds were Milken's other closest associates. When the Milken junk bond cronies were done looting their companies, Milken would cut off access to credit and other traders in his network would attack the companies with waves of short selling the stock. This sent the companies' stock prices spiraling downwards, so that even if the companies' boards were to remove the Milken cronies, the company would be unable to raise additional financing from more reputable sources.

By short selling the stock, when the companies went bankrupt, Milken and the other short sellers would make still more money by purchasing the companies' assets at fire-sale prices in the bankruptcy proceedings. And then they would repeat the process all over again, assured that junk bond merry-go-round would supply a constant stream of lootable financing.

In later years, the "bust out" concept was refined into such schemes as the "death spiral" through PIPE's financing. PIPE stands for Private Investments in Public Equity. As always, the basic idea is to finance a company, load it with debt, and then take it down. In the 1980s, Milken and his cronies orchestrated a number of *bust outs* in league with BCCI and its proprietors, including future Al Qaeda Golden Chain members Sheikh Mahfouz and Sheikh Yamani's Investcorp, who remained one of Milken's closest associates until Sheikh Mahfouz's death. Milken had thousands of associates and not all of them were bad. But the three dozen or so people who were his closest associates were criminals. These include the dozen or so people who benefited the most from his junk bond merry-go-round.

BCCI was one of the outfits that benefited the most from Milken's junk bond merry-go-round. For example, Milken's junk bonds financed the take-over of a savings and loan called Centrust, which became a BCCI subsidiary. Centrust was eventually looted and destroyed, but not before it played a role in the larger panoply of BCCI crimes. That all ended when, in early 1989, Milken was indicted on ninety-nine counts of securities fraud, market manipulation, and insider trading. He was scheduled to plead guilty to six securities and reporting violations but would never be convicted of racketeering or insider trading. Most people in America knew Milken as the greatest financial criminal ever to operate on Wall Street.

Chapter 45

39. See endnote 12.

40. *Hijab* is a generic term for "modest dress" worn by Muslim women. The only parts of the body to be exposed are the hands, feet, and face. But sometimes *hijab* is used to describe a scarf that wraps around the head. The hair is partly covered because it is regarded as erotic. Many women follow the age-old custom of veiling at least their hair, and it is not unusual to see women with full veils covering their faces. Women adjust their veils when men are present. Public affection between the sexes is unthinkable, and even spoken communication is rare. Muslims adopted the custom of veiling about three or four generations after Mohammed's death in 632 AD. It is believed Muslim tradition of veiling was copied from India, and therefore predates Islam. Veiling has been practiced for a long time by Hindus from India, where women seclude and veil themselves through a custom called Purdah, which was originally adopted by the upper classes as a status symbol.

Styles of veils vary by region. A red scarf with a black see-through chiffon cloth is worn around the face in Cairo; a vivid green veil with red and gold floral print is worn in Oman; Qatari women favor veils made from silk; Arabian women favor blue cashmere or *Saudi crepe*. There was also a new wrinkle-free chiffon material designed specifically for veiled women.

41. Indigenous people, called Bisaya, settled in Borneo thousands of years ago. The Bisaya were skilled in agriculture, hunting, and fishing. In the seventh century, when it was a subject state of the Srivijayan Empire under the name Po-ni, according to legend, an immigrant family of seven children, six boys and a girl, living in the north of the Borneo Island, took part in a boat race used to determine who was to become the rajah of the new southern region. Alak Betatar, the youngest brother, won the race. He became the first rajah of Brunei and later converted to Islam and became Sultan Mohammed, the first sultan of Brunei. The name *Brunei* came when Alak Betatar sailed the river estuary and landed on the shore and his first exclamation was "Baru nah!" In English, it loosely translates to "there it is!" and thus the name "Brunei" was derived from his words.

42. The palace was the official residence of the forty-five-year-old sultan and

Queen Pengiran Anak Hajah Saleh, whom he had married in 1965. With 1,888 rooms, two hundred and ninety bathrooms, totaling 2,152,782 square feet, it was undisputedly the world's second largest palace, only after Beijing's Forbidden City, which measured 7,749,504 square feet. But unlike the Forbidden City, the palace had modern amenities including five swimming pools, an air conditioned stable for the sultan's two hundred polo ponies, five aircraft hangars to house his five thousand cars, a banquet hall accommodating five thousand guests, and a mosque accommodating fifteen hundred people. The palace was built in 1984 at a cost of approximately $400 million.

It was estimated that Bolkiah paid his staff in cash, with annual wages alone of $13.9 million to housekeepers. His car collection consisted of 531 Mercedes, 367 Ferraris, 362 Bentleys, 185 BMWs, 177 Jaguars, 160 Porsches, 130 Rolls-Royces, and 20 Lamborghinis. Other transportation included two Boeings, a 747-400 Jumbo Jet, one Airbus, six smaller planes, and two helicopters. The family also had lavish homes in London, Los Angeles, New York, and Paris. Brunei was ruled by Britain before gaining independence in 1984. Bolkiah, a graduate of Sandhurst, rewrote his country's constitution to say: "His majesty the Sultan can do no wrong in his personal or any official capacity." It also warned against taking the sultan's name in vain in any court.

43. The horse has played an integral role in the development of human civilization. Traveling to Asia by the Bering land bridge, it was first domesticated in the steppes of Central Asia by nomadic tribes who used the animal to extend their reach, and later in their attacks on the settled peoples of the Middle East. It transformed life in the civilizations of the Fertile Crescent and Egypt. Up until the beginning of the twentieth century, the Arabian was the principal means of transport and an essential aspect of warfare.

The first traces of the breed that is now known as the Arabian appeared more than three thousand five hundred years ago. Rock paintings and inscriptions in the Arabian Peninsula depict horses that are extraordinarily similar to modern Arabians. To the Bedouin, goats and camels were necessities that made life possible in their arid land. But it was the number and quality of a man's horses that was considered the measure of his prestige and the extent of his power. Through scrupulous breeding, the Bedouin developed a horse that was smaller and more finely shaped than those that developed into the draft horses and warhorses of Europe and Asia. It was also endowed with extraordinary stamina and speed and was fearless in battle. And because the horse was tethered from birth in the shade of the Bedouin's tent in the heat of the day, the breed developed a loyalty and affection for man.

This fondness for the breed and its value to the Arabs ensured the survival of the Arabian horse over the centuries. It was with the advent of Islam that the Arabian horse began to have a major impact in other parts of the world. Mounted on fine Arabians, Muslims rode east and west, spreading Islam from China to Spain. In most of these lands, the Arabian was bred both as a separate breed and was also mixed with domestic horses to produce new strains. The Andalusian horses of Spain are one example of the latter. They also formed the original gene pool for royal stables established by European monarchs to breed Arabians. Several of these stables still exist today in Poland, Russia, and Germany and are sources of purebred Arabian horses.

Chapter 46

44. In the early 1700s, the city of Paris did not yet extend as far as the property where the Élysée Palace is located. The architect Armand-Claude Mollet possessed the property fronting on the road to the village of Roule, west of Paris, which is now the famed Rue du Faubourg Saint-Honoré. The property backed onto royal property on the Champs-Élysées. Mollet sold the plot of land in 1718 to the Count of Évreux, agreeing to construct a *hôtel particulier* for the Count, with an entrance court in front, and a garden in back. The resulting *Hôtel d'Évreux* was finished in 1722 and remains a fine example of the French Classical style. At the time of his death in 1753, Évreux's home was considered one of the most widely admired houses in Paris.

King Louis XV purchased it as a residence for his mistress, the Marquise de Pompadour. Opponents showed their distaste for the regime by hanging signs on the gates that read: "Home of the King's whore." After his mistress's death, the property reverted to the crown. In 1773 one of the richest men in France, Nicolas Beaujon, purchased it as a sumptuous "country house." Beaujon hired the architect Étienne-Louis Boullée to make substantial alterations to the buildings and design an English-style garden. He used it to house his fabulous collection of great masters' paintings. His architectural alterations and art galleries gave this residence international renown as "one of the premier houses of Paris."

The *Hôtel d'Évreux* was formally purchased for Louis XVIII in 1816. Under the provisional government of the Second Republic, it took the name of the *Élysée National* and was designated the official residence of the President of the Republic. Following his *coup d'état* ending the Second Republic in 1853, Napoléon III hired architect Joseph-Eugène Lacroix to do renovations. Napoléon III then moved to the nearby Tuileries Palace, but kept the Élysée as a discreet place to meet his mistresses, moving between the two palaces through a secret underground passage that has since been demolished. In 1873 during the Third Republic, the Élysée became the official presidential residence. Socialist President François Mitterrand in office since 1981 seldom used its private apartments, preferring the privacy of his own home on the more bohemian Left Bank. However, a discreet flat within the Élyséee was occupied by his mistress, Anne Pingeot, mother of his illegitimate daughter, Mazarine Pingeot.

45. secretcrypt.com/cryptz/stories/truestories113.htm

46. Jonathan Beaty and S.C. Gwynne, *The Outlaw Bank: A Wild Ride into the Secret Heart of BCCI*, (Random House, New York)

47. According to the fourteenth Dalai Lama, "It is very good to recite the mantra 'Om mani padme hum,' but while you are doing it, you should be thinking on its meaning, for the meaning of the six syllables is great and vast. The first, 'om' symbolizes the practitioner's impure body, speech, and mind; it also symbolizes the pure exalted body, speech, and mind of a Buddha. The path is indicated by the next four syllables. The first two, 'mani,' meaning jewel, symbolizes the factors of method: the altruistic intention to become enlightened, compassionate, and loving. The next two syllables, 'padme,' meaning lotus, symbolize wisdom. Purity must be achieved by an indivisible unity of method and wisdom, symbolized by the final syllable 'hum,' which indicates indivisibility. Thus the six syllables, 'om mani padme hum,' mean that, in dependence on the practice of a path which is an indivisible union of method and wisdom, you can transform your impure body, speech, and mind into the pure exalted body, speech, and mind of a Buddha."

48. www.nhlbi.nih.gov/health/dci/Diseases/hhw/hhw_pumping.html

49. www.rosicrucian.org/publications

50. Jonathan Beaty and S.C. Gwynne, *The Outlaw Bank: A Wild Ride into the Secret Heart of BCCI*, (Random House, New York)

Chapter 47

51. money.howstuffworks.com/money-laundering.htm

Chapter 48

52. Jonathan Beaty and S.C. Gwynne, *The Outlaw Bank: A Wild Ride into the Secret Heart of BCCI*, (Random House, New York)

53. Beginning in 1778, a local pioneer, Mrs. Anderson, came to follow the local Native American tradition of "taking the waters" to restore her chronic rheumatism. She built the residential area, which for the first one hundred and twenty-five years was known by the name white Sulphur Springs.

In 1858 a hotel was built on the property. During the Civil war, the property changed hands between the Confederate Army and the Union Army, almost burning the resort to the ground. Following the Civil War, the resort reopened and became a place for many Southerners and Northerners to vacation. By 1900 it fell into the hands of a prominent Baltimore family, the Calwells, under whom the resort would begin to take shape. They sold cottages—many of which still stand today—to prominent Southern individuals. In 1910 the Chesapeake & Ohio Railway purchased the resort property and built The Greenbrier Hotel in 1913. The original hotel, The Grand Central Hotel, known by the moniker "The White" and later "The Old White," was torn down several years after the completion of the construction of the current building in 1922. Its reopening was the social event of the season, attracting such luminaries as the Duke of Windsor with his wife, Wallis Simpson, Bing Crosby, and the Kennedys. The name officially changed to The Greenbrier and the neighboring town adopted the name White Sulphur Springs.

During World War II, the resort served both as an army hospital and as a relocation center for some of the Axis diplomats still within the United States. After the war ended, C&O Railway bought back the property from the government and reopened the resort, newly redecorated by Dorothy Draper. The resort has hosted dignitaries such as Jawaharlal Nehru, Indira Gandhi, Debbie Reynolds, and Prince Rainier and Princess Grace of Monaco.

During the Cold War, construction of the bunker began in 1958. Once the underground facility was complete in 1961, it was maintained in a constant state of readiness by a small group of government employees working undercover as a company hired by the resort for audio/visual support services called Forsythe Associates. The bunker boasts a 25-ton blast door that opens with only 50 pounds of pressure, decontamination chambers, eighteen dormitories designed to accommodate over 1,100 people, a power plant with purification equipment, three 25,000-gallon water storage tanks, and three 14,000-gallon diesel fuel storage tanks. A communications area includes a television show production area and audio recording booths. There is a twelve-bed hospital clinic, medical and dental operating rooms, laboratory, pharmacy, intensive care unit, cafeteria, meeting rooms for the House and Senate, the Governor's Hall, and the mountaineer room. Over the thirty years that it was an active facility, communications and other equipment were updated, keeping the bunker at full-operation status. The location of the facility had remained a secret for more than three decades.

Chapter 49

54. Jonathan Beaty and S.C. Gwynne, *The Outlaw Bank: A Wild Ride into the Secret Heart of BCCI*, (Random House, New York)

55. Jonathan Beaty and S.C. Gwynne, *The Outlaw Bank: A Wild Ride into the Secret Heart of BCCI*, (Random House, New York)

Chapter 50

56. articles.latimes.com/1991-08-12/news/mn-463_1_bcci-scandal – Pakistan Offers Sanctuary to Key BCCI Figure

Printed in Great Britain
by Amazon

48747139R00147